the BURNING TEARS *of* MORLAK

WAR OF THE TWELVE
BOOK THREE

· ALEX ROBINS ·

Copyright © 2021 by Alex Robins

Cover and Interior Design by Damonza
Maps by Alex Robins

ISBN 978-2-9576580-6-0 (paperback)
ISBN 978-2-9576580-5-3 (ebook)

Published by Bradypus Publishing
4 rue du vigneau, 49380 Bellevigne en Layon
Dépôt Légal : décembre 2021

www.warofthetwelve.com

For Juliana and Nolan

Your smiles will never stop bringing me joy

Laugh loud

Chase your dreams

And know that you are loved

TABLE OF CONTENTS

THE LAST DAYS
OF TALTH

"You sent riders to Morlak and Talth, did you not? Have they returned? They have not, and they will not. I am in contact with my brothers and sisters. Morlak is already under our control, and Talth? The Baron of Talth was stubborn and refused to comply. The greylings have taken the capital and burned their fields and villages. There is nothing left of Talth."

MINA, LAST OF THE TWELVE, 426 AT

⥀

BARON DAVAREL DEL Talth watched his city die. Flickering, incandescent fires spread as far as the distant horizon, their golden glow lighting up the night sky. Below him, hundreds of timber houses fuelled a colossal wall of flame half a mile wide, the uncaring wind pushing it inexorably towards the last remnants of the town guard lining the stone wall of the inner courtyard. Noxious plumes of grey smoke spiralled skywards, carrying the stench of burnt flesh up to the roof of the keep where he stood, his bony, blue-veined hands gripping the ancient parapet.

And ahead of the wall of flame came the greylings.

They were far too many to count, a boiling mass of grey-skinned bodies, scampering forwards on all fours, chittering and shrieking like bickering children. Threshers towered over their lesser brethren, some wearing rusty breastplates or crude iron helmets, others holding barbed whips that swished and cracked as they urged the smaller creatures onwards.

Davarel shook his head sadly. The heat from the distant blaze was not enough to warm his tired bones. Thirty years ago, he would have stood proudly on the walls with his men, but his fighting days were long gone. His coat of chainmail hung heavily on his skeletal frame. He could barely hold a sword. He looked down at his swollen, arthritic knuckles in disgust.

Old age had crept up on him, slowly leeching away his strength and resilience. He had lost his friends through disease or senility. His wife had died peacefully in her sleep. Yet still he endured, battling the merciless currents of time alone as they deepened the wrinkles in his face and fused the joints in his arms and legs. And now this, this final torture, the complete and utter destruction of his lands.

It had taken only two weeks for the greylings to lay waste to Talth. The Pit was first to fall, the small contingent of the Old Guard massacred within hours. The survivors had fled south to the temple of Guanna, Second of the Twelve, an ancient walled fortress high up in the northern hills.

The Knights of Guanna had quickly assessed the situation and split into two groups: one half riding south to the capital, the other half marching north to slow the greyling advance. One hundred men against thousands. A brave and selfless sacrifice. Davarel had not wasted this final gift, using the time bought in blood to organise the evacuation of Talth and the strengthening of the worn stone ramparts.

Days later, scouts posted along the northern outskirts had sighted the greyling horde. The enemy were advancing slowly, slaughtering sheep and cattle left unattended by their owners, burning the last of the crops, and polluting the wells and waterways with animal carcasses and faeces. Great swathes of woodland were put to the torch, leaving behind a monochrome wasteland.

There seemed to be no rhyme or reason to such wanton destruction, only the pure, unadulterated hatred of the greylings for all things made by man.

The walls of Talth had not stopped them, despite the valiant efforts of the Knights of Guanna. For a night and a day, they had held, as the massive armoured warriors accounted for hundreds of greyling deaths. But it had not been enough. For every greyling killed, two more had appeared to take its place. A crude battering ram made from a fallen tree trunk had shattered the main gate, allowing threshers to enter the city and assault the ramparts from the rear.

Surrounded and exhausted, the guardsmen would have been annihilated had it not been for Davarel's son and heir. The courageous noble had gathered the tattered remains of the heavy cavalry and led a desperate countercharge down the main street, clearing an avenue of retreat for the beleaguered defenders. A brief respite, as now the last few survivors manned the inner wall surrounding the keep itself. The final line of defence, with no means of escape.

And his son had not returned.

An inhuman screech, strident and piercing, came from somewhere down below. An enormous wooden litter came into view, supported by eight sweating threshers. On it sat a hideous, malformed creature, over twenty feet long, grimy grey and slug-like. It had no legs, only a long, slimy tail spattered with a dark red substance that could only be human blood. Small, stick-like arms gestured wildly towards the wall. Its porcine nose sniffed the air, searching for something.

The creature opened its distended mouth and screeched again, loud enough to make Davarel's ears ring. The cry was answered by a cacophony of discordant sounds and the greyling horde surged forwards. A deadly rain of steel-tipped arrows pattered down among them, killing dozens, their bodies trampled into the dirt. The first of the greylings reached the base of the wall and began to climb. Sharp claws punched easily into crumbling mortar.

"I must go down to meet them," muttered Davarel to himself, one wasted hand straying to the pommel of his gilded longsword. He would not die up here all alone.

"My Lord," came a voice from behind him and he turned to see that one of the Knights of Guanna had joined him on the roof; a well-built, fair-skinned man with short, spiky black hair and indigo eyes. The knight was wearing a suit of heavy plate armour, complete with a steel gorget that covered his neck and lower jaw. A metal buckler was strapped tightly to his left forearm, leaving both hands free to wield the well-worn longsword sheathed at his side.

Davarel tried to recall the man's name and failed. "Ah, what is it, Sir …?"

"Gaelin, my Lord."

"Of course. My apologies. My mind is not what it once was, Sir Knight."

"No need to apologise, my Lord. I came to discuss what should be done about your heir. I fear the walls will not resist the greylings for long."

"My heir? My son has been found?" Davarel felt his heart beating insistently in his chest. *Maybe there is still a reason to hope!*

Gaelin gave an embarrassed cough. "No, my Lord. I fear that your son did not survive the night. Although his bold efforts saved the lives of many. I was talking about your grandson, Kayal."

At the sound of his name, a young sandy-haired boy, no more than nine, peered cautiously out from behind the big knight's legs where he had been hiding, lost in the shadows. "Grandfather," he said in a squeaky voice, barely audible above the sounds of battle echoing up from below.

Davarel stared at the child's tear-streaked face as conflicting emotions flooded his mind. The boy looked so much like his father; the same light-coloured hair, the same sky-blue eyes. Love and grief intertwined. For a moment, they threatened to overwhelm him, but he resisted, drawing on the last of his fading strength.

"Kayal, of course." Here was something worth fighting for. He felt as if a veil had been lifted from his eyes. Davarel stood straighter.

"Approach, boy. Down on one knee. Sir Gaelin, if you would bear witness?" The knight nodded.

Baron del Talth drew his ornate sword, ignoring the pain that burned through his hand as his fingers wrapped around the grip. Kayal was kneeling before him, trembling with fear. The old man touched the boy's shoulders lightly with the tip of his blade.

"Kayal. As is my right as Lord of Talth, and as witnessed by this Knight of Guanna, I hereby declare you heir to the Barony of Talth, with all the titles and honours that such a rank entails. May the Twelve guide you, Lord Kayal."

The boy rose on shaking legs. "I thank you, Grandfather," he said formally, bowing at the waist.

"Excellent," Davarel replied, sheathing his weapon. "Sir Gaelin, how long do we have?"

The knight surveyed the carnage below. "A few minutes, my Lord. At most."

The greylings had gained a foothold on the ramparts despite the heroic endeavours of the defenders. Several of their number were tying coarse ropes around the merlons, ropes strong enough to support the weight of a thresher.

A large clawed hand appeared, then another. With a snarl, an eight-foot-tall hulking beast pulled itself over the battlements and landed heavily among the defenders. A reverse swipe of its cudgel brained one of the guards and sent another reeling back into his fellows.

"Very well," said Davarel, nodding curtly. "Then there is no time to waste. Follow me."

They left the roof and descended the twisting stairs to the Great Hall where two more armoured knights awaited them. The green banner of Talth hung proudly on the wall at the far end above an elevated dais. Davarel took a moment to gaze upon his coat of arms. A prancing stag, its antlers raised defiantly.

"This way. Below the dais," he said, breathing heavily. He forced his aching body forwards and pointed to one of the large slabs that paved the floor of the hall.

"My Lord?" asked Gaelin.

"It's hollow, Sir Knight."

The Knight of Guanna nodded and drew his longsword, cutting through the joints surrounding the slab with a series of precise strikes. With a grunt of effort, he pulled on the stone square, lifting it from its bedding and revealing a locked trapdoor beneath.

Davarel reached under his chainmail and produced a rusty iron key. "This should still fit. It works both ways, so lock the door behind you once you are through. The passageway leads to a cellar below one of the farmhouses on the southern road. We will just have to hope the exit has not been blocked … half of those old timber structures have already been burnt to the ground."

A scratching sound came from the far side of the hall, beyond the barred double doors. Claws on wood. The two Knights of Guanna silently unsheathed their swords.

"Once you are out of the tunnel, I suggest you aim for the coastal village of Haeden. They have ships leaving for Kessrin almost every day. Find the Baron, Derello. Tell him what has happened here."

"My Lord, would it not be better for you to accompany us? I fear that reaching the Baron may be difficult without your support."

The Baron gave a tired laugh. "I barely made it down five flights of stairs, Sir Knight, I would only slow you down.

If the Baron refuses to see you, remind him of the time I saved his father from drowning in the River Trent. It was a closely guarded secret that the previous Baron, the so-called Lord of the Western Coasts, could not swim."

The scratching became more insistent. Davarel sighed and once more tugged his own sword laboriously from its sheath.

"I thank you for all your Order has done for us, Sir Gaelin," he said. "It is a debt I fear I will not live to repay, but my heir will do his best, won't you Kayal?"

The young boy nodded, eyeing the wooden trapdoor warily. Gaelin unlocked it and threw the door open. The first few rungs of a metal ladder disappeared into the darkness. "Time for us to leave, young Lord," he said, beckoning with one gauntleted hand.

Davarel looked on fondly as his grandson lowered himself carefully onto the ladder and descended into the tunnel. Gaelin followed close behind, his massive frame barely squeezing through the hole. He nodded one final time to the Baron before closing the door with a loud thud. Davarel heard the click of the key turning in the lock.

With a satisfied smile, he turned his attention back to the doors at the end of the Great Hall. The two Knights of Guanna were standing a few feet from the entrance, helms on and bucklers raised. Cracks began to appear along the wooden plank barring the doors as it buckled under the pressure. It would not be long now. Davarel felt adrenaline course through his body, numbing his fear and filling him with vigour. He strode down the length of the hall and positioned himself between the two knights.

"Gentlemen. It is an honour to stand beside you," he said, watching the cracks spread across the surface.

Suddenly, without warning, the scratching ceased. An uneasy silence filled the hall. Davarel frowned and glanced at his stoic companions, their faces hidden behind their helms.

"Maybe they've decided to give up?" he said tentatively. Then the doors exploded in a hailstorm of rivets and splintered wood. The largest thresher that Davarel had ever seen emerged from the wreckage, its bare, muscular torso a mass of sores and badly-healed scars. A crude necklace of what appeared to be severed human hands hung around the thing's neck, and it carried an enormous saw-toothed blade of corroded metal spattered with blood. It fixed Davarel with two dirty-yellow eyes.

"Uuuu-mann," the creature grunted, the word barely intelligible as it twisted its jaw in an effort to mimic human speech. From somewhere behind it came the cackling of greylings.

"You do not belong here," Davarel replied, fighting to keep the tremor from his voice.

The thresher bared its teeth. "Ourrr laaaand. Ourrr time."

The Knights of Guanna attacked, charging forwards far faster than Davarel had thought possible for two men in heavy plate. The thresher blocked one swing with its blade and took the second on its left shoulder. The sword drew blood, but the wound did not seem deep enough to bother it. It retaliated. A vicious kick to the chest sent one knight reeling backwards, his breastplate cracked and dented. A quick forward jab knocked the weapon from the other knight's hand. The saw-toothed blade came down again. The knight raised his buckler to parry the blow, only for the rusty sword to cleave straight through his upraised arm and cut deep into his neck.

The thresher ripped its blade free in a shower of crimson and bellowed a series of animalistic snarls. Greylings scampered out of the shadows behind it and set upon the fallen knights with tooth and claw. One of the men managed a hoarse cry before his throat was torn out.

Davarel tried to move but found himself rooted to the spot, his body refusing to respond. His sword fell from arthritic fingers. The colossal thresher loomed over him, its eyes burning with a deep hatred. The Baron felt a powerful hand clamp down on his skull.

"Ourrr time," the thing repeated, and squeezed.

CHAPTER 1

HIDING IN PLAIN SIGHT

"Ah, Morlak. My favourite town in all the nine Baronies. Remote, but full of lucrative opportunities. The people there are so … corruptible. I've yet to find a place that's easier to get into, and even easier to get out of. I just need to make sure I have the necessary funds to grease all those palms along the way."

NISSUS, UNKNOWN

❦

A THICK BLANKET OF glimmering whiteness covered the trees of Dirkvale Forest, the evergreen pines bowing under the weight of the snow on their branches. Winter had arrived, bringing with it cold, icy days and even colder nights. The larger forest animals had already begun to hibernate, tucked away in their sheltered dens and caves. Only the smaller rodents and other mammals still ventured outside, driven by the need to seek sustenance.

A rabbit emerged slowly from its underground warren, supple nose twitching as it searched for signs of danger. After a moment's hesitation, it hopped forwards into the clearing, leaving the safety of its lair behind. Most of the forest floor was buried under a layer of frost, but the centre of the clearing was open to the sky and a few weak rays of afternoon sunlight had melted enough of the hard surface to reveal a single withered shrub, a splash of dark green against the pristine white.

The rabbit sprang closer, drawn to what would be its first meal in days. Then it happened. A glitter of grey on white. Something cold and metallic around its neck. Panicking, it tried to escape, pulling the noose even tighter as it fought to break free but to no avail. With a final shudder, the rabbit kicked and lay still.

Jeffson stepped calmly from behind a large pine tree on the far side of the clearing. The balding manservant was tightly wrapped up in a motley array of fur, including a sheepskin cap to protect the top of his head. He stamped his feet in an effort to return some warmth to his stiff limbs and made his way over to the snare, pulling off a mitten to check the rabbit's pulse. He had spotted the warren the night before and set up the wire trap in the hope of supplementing the dwindling winter stores hoarded by the Knights of Kriari.

He liked it out here alone in the cold. People bothered him. Well, most people. Lord Reed was held slightly higher in his esteem than many others. The man had a good *core*, as his mother used to say, and nothing was more important than that. An internal moral compass that always seemed to guide him towards the most honourable choice; be it defending a town under siege from a horde of greylings or leading an expedition down into the depths of one of the Pits to rescue a group of prisoners.

Honourable, but not always very perceptive. For example, the last time Jeffson had seen Reed, he had been holding his own against an unknown number of assailants firing arrows at him from higher ground. Far from the most logical choice of action, despite it enabling Jeffson and Baroness Syrella del Morlak to escape.

Nevertheless ... a good core. The manservant wasn't sure what sort of core he himself had, but it was definitely *not* good.

He sighed and brushed a sheet of snow off a nearby fallen log. Leaving the unfortunate rabbit to its fate, he sat down wearily, taking the weight off his tired legs. He removed his other mitten and dug around inside his furs until his grasping fingers caught hold of a slim book bound in red leather. The words '*Morlak, a political conundrum*' were stamped in gold across the cover. Jeffson leafed through the well-worn pages until he found what he was looking for, and began to read.

The crack of a breaking twig somewhere in the undergrowth behind him made him spin around, eyes searching. A lithe female figure appeared on the edge of the clearing, her thin body bundled up in animal furs. Long, braided black hair hung down her back almost as far as her hips. The paleness of her skin was offset by two startling mismatched eyes: one green, one blue.

"Baroness," said Jeffson, snapping the book shut and rising to his feet. He bowed smoothly.

Syrella del Morlak inclined her head in recognition and

gave a small smile. Her lips had a slight blueish tinge from the cold.

"Jeffson. Why is it that every time I go in search of you, I find you further and further from the temple of Kriari? It's almost as if you are trying to run away!"

"Not quite, my Lady. Just looking for a bit of solitude. I am not used to all this … mingling."

Syrella caught sight of the dead rabbit and her nose wrinkled in disgust. "I find that quite hard to believe. What of your years working for Listus del Arelium? If memory serves, the keep is home to a great host of servants and their families, not counting the dozens of guests the Baron received every month."

Jeffson gave a thin smile of his own. "Ah, yes, the servant's paradox. Present, yet invisible. Privy to a hundred conversations a day without ever uttering a word. Do you remember the face of the man who served you wine every evening, my Lady?"

"Well, no, but it has been many weeks since—"

"Perhaps, yet I would surmise this man has been serving you for years and years. And his features remain a blur. We have probably exchanged more words in the last few minutes than you have spoken to him during your entire tenure as Baroness."

Jeffson took a deep lungful of crisp, wintry air. "Solitude and society are not incompatible, my Lady," he said. "It was one of the many things that led me to this line of work in the first place. Hiding in plain sight." He bent over the snare and removed the metal wire from around the animal's neck.

Syrella coughed uncomfortably. "Well, let us hope you

will not need to *mingle* for much longer. I came to tell you that Vohanen has returned. He may have found Reed."

∽

The temple of Kriari was hidden deep in the heart of Dirkvale, a fortified network of buildings constructed on a raised area of land that gave it a commanding view of the surrounding terrain. Two concentric palisades ringed the temple; one at the bottom of the hill, dotted with watchtowers, and a second, smaller one surrounding the summit. The foundations had been laid by Kriari himself several hundred years ago, some time before his unexplained disappearance.

Jeffson and Syrella arrived at the base of the first stockade, their fur boots glistening with melted snow. A huge wooden gate blocked the way forwards, its tightly roped logs coated with pine tar and covered with tanned animal pelts. Two square towers bordered the gate, topped with burning braziers.

A Knight of Kriari glowered down at them from one of the towers. He was wearing half-plate armour and a black fur mantle stippled with frost. Two silver rings pierced each eyebrow and across his back hung a rectangular metal-banded shield.

"Krelbe!" shouted Syrella, her breath turning to mist in the cold air. "Were you not already on watch yesterday? Lose at cards again?"

The dour-faced knight muttered something unintelligible and disappeared from sight. They heard boots clumping on the rungs of a ladder and, moments later, the big gate trundled open.

"Hurry up," Krelbe growled, giving Syrella a dark look. "He's waiting for you."

"Vohanen?"

The knight nodded. "Aye. First time he's been back in weeks. Rode his horse half to death coming here." He gestured up the hill towards the temple. "You'll find him in the Conclave Hall with the others."

"Thank you, Sir Knight," Jeffson replied. "If you would be so kind as to deal with this?" He pressed the dead rabbit into Krelbe's hands and turned away, oblivious to the angry retort forming on the other man's lips.

The path wound up a steep incline and through another barred gate into the inner compound. A cluster of outbuildings encircled a larger, rectangular stone structure with a thatched roof and a reinforced door. Two fur-clad guards waved them inside.

A crackling fire filled a circular pit in the centre of the hall, banishing the cold. Jeffson was immediately hit by a wave of warm air. He removed his close-fitting fur cap and mittens as he moved closer to the fire. A set of benches had been placed in a rough semi-circle around the pit, and these were occupied by a dozen Knights of Kriari. Opposite them stood Vohanen, his hands stretched out, palms facing the flames.

The older knight had aged ten years in the last few weeks. His braided corn-coloured beard was scraggly and unwashed. Dark patches ringed hollow, bloodshot eyes. He had lost weight, the skin of his cheeks and jaw sagging slightly, giving him a drawn, cadaveric look. Jeffson met the man's gaze and saw something hard and bitter buried there. Anger. Anger and hatred caused by insufferable grief.

Vohanen had lost his eldest son, Avor, less than a month ago, cut down by a greyling claw as they had fought to rescue a group of prisoners from the depths of the Morlakian Pit. Avor had died so that others could escape, holding off their pursuers long enough to allow them to flee the underground tunnels, which were about to be flooded by the icy-cold waters of Terris Lake. It was a good death; a warrior's death. And yet, Vohanen still believed it was all his fault.

Jeffson was well aware of the stages of grief. The denial, the anger, the bargaining, the depression …. There was no miraculous cure for such a terrible thing. Only the passage of time would eventually blunt the pain and, even then, it would never go away. Jeffson knew this because he was still recovering from his own gut-wrenching loss, an aching scar on his soul that haunted him despite the passing years, a horrendous memory from another life. With a shudder, he pushed the dark thoughts from his mind and focused his attention on Vohanen.

"We found the bodies," the knight was saying. "Still lying where they fell, over a week later. It looked like Reed and the others had tried to take the fight to the enemy. They failed."

Jeffson glanced across at Syrella. The Baroness was chewing her lower lip nervously.

"I'm still not sure who fired those black-feathered arrows," Vohanen continued. "But they were extremely competent fighters. Over a dozen of our own men dead, and we couldn't find any trace of their attackers. The corpses bore wounds consistent with a long, sharp-edged blade, probably a sword of some sort, albeit wielded with considerable force: one of the bodies had been cut nearly in half." He sighed and rubbed his tired eyes with his thumbs. "I must also regretfully inform you, my Lady, that we found the body of Quinne, your guard captain."

Syrella nodded as if expecting this. "And Merad ... I mean, Sir Reed?"

Vohanen shook his head. "No, thank the Twelve. We spent a few hours searching. No more bodies, only tracks leading south, barely hidden. A group of horses, most likely. It was as if the enemy didn't think they would be followed, or didn't care. We gave the dead a decent burial and pursued."

One of the knights listening proffered a tankard of ale, and Vohanen accepted wordlessly.

"The path south was difficult. The cold was beginning to set in and with it the first of the winter snow. Not much, but enough to obscure the tracks. We strayed off-course a couple of times. In fact, if it hadn't been for wily old Taleck over there, we might have lost them altogether." He raised his tankard in salute to a grey-bearded knight sitting close to the fire, his right ear a mass of scar tissue. Taleck returned the gesture with his own ale.

"On the third day, we found the remains of a campsite. A burnt-out fire and some old animal skins. Proof that we were going the right way. Oh, and we also found this."

He dug deep into his padded tunic and drew out something small and metallic that glinted in the firelight. Jeffson leant forwards and saw it was a clasp shaped like a snarling wolf's head.

"We kept on heading south, and it soon became clear what their final destination would be. They were going to Morlak."

Syrella flinched visibly at hearing the name of her capital. Vohanen caught her eye.

"I'm sorry to say that nothing had changed there, my Lady," he said. "The doors to the inner keep were still shut tight. We managed to make it into the outer town, but the place was half-deserted; it appears that visitors are being turned away or forced to leave. And those that remain ... a bunch of brigands and cutthroats for the most part. There's no one to keep the peace, you see? The knights we had garrisoned there were thrown out, and the town guard are holed up beyond the inner wall, close to the keep."

He paused and took a long drink of ale, wiping the froth from his unkempt beard.

"We did see something, though. Taleck and I bribed one of the few remaining guards on duty, who got us up onto the lower ramparts. From there, we had a good view of the inner keep and our former garrison. There was a new flag flying from the roof of the old barracks. A black motif on a field of white. The silhouettes of two identical faces. Twins."

This last revelation was greeted with angry murmurs from the assembled Knights of Kriari. Jeffson and Syrella looked at each other in confusion.

"Sir Knight," said the Baroness loudly. "I am afraid you must enlighten us. This motif of which you speak means nothing to us."

"Aye, and well it shouldn't, my Lady, as we had thought never to see it again. It is the sign of the Order of Mithuna, Third of the Twelve."

"Another of the Knightly Orders? I still don't understand. Why would they side with the imposter now residing in Morlak keep? Have they not sworn to protect the nine Baronies and the will of the Council?"

Vohanen's gaze flickered to a hunched, elderly figure sitting apart from the others, his weathered face covered in scars. The man nodded almost imperceptibly.

"You are right, my Lady," Vohanen continued. "All of our Orders swore such an oath. And then, sixty years ago, some of us broke that oath. It was a dark time; many were lost on both sides. We call it the Schism. The dissident factions were all but eliminated, the Order of Mithuna among them. But we were apparently not thorough enough. Somehow they have survived and managed to rebuild."

"I see," said Syrella icily, her eyes flashing dangerously. "And when exactly were you going to make your Baroness privy to this information?" She turned to the old, scarred knight. "I know you, Sir Bjornvor, you have been first master of this temple since before I was born. I saw you renew your oath to my father by cutting open your palm and swearing on your own blood. Did it not cross your mind to tell him then?"

The temple master cleared his throat. "My apologies, my Lady, but I *did* tell him," he said in a low, scratchy voice. "We discussed the Schism many times. I confess I thought he would have told you all of this himself. I do not know why he chose not to."

"I do," Syrella muttered angrily to herself. Her relationship with her father had always been strained at best and had only grown worse in his twilight years. She was his greatest disappointment: born a girl when he had hoped for a boy, refusing to marry when he had yearned for a son-in-law, uninterested in producing an heir when he had argued time and again the importance of continuing the bloodline of del Morlak. They had still spoken often, right up until the day he died, but he had never managed to hide the regret in his eyes.

"I think that is a discussion for another day," she said curtly. "Let us concentrate instead on what to do with this new-found knowledge. I think we can all agree that there is only one logical conclusion here: the Knights of Mithuna are responsible for the attempts on my life, the murder of my subjects, and the capture of Merad Reed. Even worse, they appear to be in league with the greylings."

"Aye, that sounds like the sum of it," said Vohanen. He found an empty spot on one of the benches. "Though doesn't it seem a bit too easy? Why leave the bodies for us to find? Why not cover their tracks? Why fly their flag over our old garrison? It seems strange to be so careless after years of skulking in the shadows."

Syrella frowned. "Either they are taunting us, or—"

"Or it's a trap," Jeffson interjected. "That is what I would do. Take something my opponent wanted, make sure they knew I'd taken it, and show them how to get it back. Easy."

"And then?"

"Then all I'd have to do is wait, my Lady."

"So, you're telling me the only reason Reed is still alive is so that he can be used as bait?" said Vohanen, swirling the last few drops of ale around the bottom of his tankard before downing them with a flourish. "It matters not. There are close to one hundred knights here. We can ride to Morlak in force and lay siege to the keep. Restore the Baroness to her rightful place. Rescue Reed. Destroy the Knights of

Mithuna. Finish what we started sixty years ago. Who is with me?"

Silence. Bjornvor rose slowly to his feet.

"Attack the keep head-on?" he rasped. "Our losses would be high. How many of your brothers are you prepared to sacrifice to save one man?"

Vohanen's face clouded with anger. "I gave my oath, Master. I held his arm and promised him I would either save him from his fate or punish those responsible. It is an oath I intend to keep."

"That is your choice. And all of us here respect that. But your fellow initiates have taken no such oaths. I will not tell them to throw their lives away on a whim."

"And what of the Knights of Mithuna? Our greatest shame. Are they to be left to their machinations, free from reprisal? To go unpunished after all they have done? Where is your honour? Why I—"

"*Enough*, boy!" thundered Bjornvor. He moved closer to the fire, the shadows from the flames cutting deep lines in his scarred visage. "Do not presume to talk about things you cannot understand. You describe the Schism like it is a fairy tale. I was *there* when the others betrayed us. I *saw* them stab us in the back; kill my brothers, my sisters, my friends. I remember how one of them cut into the flesh of my cheeks with a knife, laughing as the blood ran down my face. Do not lecture me on vengeance. I am sorry for your loss, Vohanen, sorrier than you can know, but that does not give you the right to question my honour or integrity. And if you do so again, I will have you flogged."

Vohanen looked as if he had been slapped in the face. He stared wide-eyed at the temple master, his lips forming words he could not speak. "I ... I am sorry," he said finally. "That was not my intention. And you are right, attacking the keep would be a costly endeavour. But the Knights of Mithuna are plotting something, I am sure of it. What if they are massing to attack Dirkvale? Or Lostthorn? If a frontal assault is not possible, maybe there is some other way into the keep. My Lady, can you help us?"

"I ... I wish I could," Syrella said regretfully. "But my father always told me that the inner keep was impregnable."

Jeffson felt an ice-cold chill run through his body. The familiar pain that he worked constantly to push aside fought its way back to the surface, smothering him. He gritted his teeth as memories of a past life assaulted him in waves, terrible flashes of events he had tried so hard to forget. Blood, death, and broken promises. And something else, something he had almost overlooked. His hand went to the leather-bound book secreted inside his coat pocket, the tips of his fingers touching the spine. His breathing slowed.

He could help them. But that would mean going back to Morlak. Back to the place that had caused him so much grief. Was he ready to re-open those old wounds?

A good core.

"My Lords," he said, his voice calm and composed. "I know a way. I know how to get us into Morlak keep."

CHAPTER 2

LADY OF THE
WHITE WOLF

"Have you ever smelt the stench of a hundred burning bodies?
Charred flesh has a particular odour: nauseating but sweet,
putrid but meaty. Fat and muscle sizzle like a side of pork. You
can try and wear a mask although, to be honest, it doesn't really
help. The worst is the way it clings to your skin like tar. I spent
an hour scrubbing myself in the salty waters of the Bay of Doves
and I still reek of death."

HIRKUIN, CAPTAIN OF THE KESSRIN GUARD, 426 AT

⤴

T HE PROBLEM WITH skipping stones across the
surface of the sea is that you have to account for
the waves. Jelaïa had been practising for weeks now,
but she had yet to manage more than ten or eleven ricochets
before losing her pebble to the murky depths.

A gull squawked mockingly, swooping low to alight on one of the barnacle-studded rocks poking out of the shallows like a giant's tooth.

"I don't know what you find so funny," Jelaïa muttered, searching around for another flat stone on the shingle beach of the isolated creek. Coming here had become part of her daily routine ever since she had found the old half-hidden dirt path at the end of the Kessrin docks. The perfect way to exercise, release some stress, and breathe in some fresh air. Oh, and above all, enjoy some well-earned peace and quiet.

Her hand closed on a good candidate: flat, round, not too thick. She weighed it thoughtfully in the palm of her hand for a moment, then sent it arcing out over the water with a flick of her wrist. It bounced off towards the horizon with a series of plops.

A cool wind whistled down the natural corridor formed by the walls of the creek, tickling the soft hair on the back of her neck and making her shiver. She pulled the ocean-blue shawl closer to her body. Another gift from Derello.

The stone hit the crest of a small wave and disappeared from sight. Jelaïa sighed. If Praedora were here, she would probably make some shrewd comment about how the pebble represented Jelaïa, leaping along towards her destiny, trying to avoid the treacherous waves as she set a course for the distant horizon.

But Praedora was not here. The First Priestess had left with Brachyura, Aldarin, and a small contingent of knights the day after the collapse of Kessrin keep. The day they had recovered Sir Manfeld's crushed, headless body from the Great Hall.

Manfeld had been the first master of their temple, and a

tomb had already been reserved for him deep in the bowels of the fortress monastery he had called home. Preparations for the last rites would take several days, and they were to be followed by a ceremony of investiture officialising Aldarin's ascension to the rank of first master.

She had barely spoken to her friend before his departure. Aldarin had spent all his waking hours working tirelessly with the rescue crews; shifting rubble, shovelling dirt, looking for survivors. And, against all odds, they had found some. A servant who had managed to reach a cellar. A baker and his family who had avoided being crushed by hiding in a massive oven. Others were just plain lucky, saved by a table, a bed, a fallen pillar.

But the dead still far, far outnumbered the living. For every Kessrin who had survived, a dozen more had been dragged lifeless from the debris and carted away to the morgue. For every miracle praised, a dead child mourned. The morgue was not big enough to hold them, so Derello had the bodies burned and their remains buried in a communal grave.

Jelaïa had been to the rescue site once and come away numb, her fingernails chipped and grimy, her clothes and hair permeated with smoke from the funeral pyres. Now, at last, the search was over and the mass grave filled. The Baron had finished the job himself before ordering the headless statue of the writhing sea-serpent — the one decapitated by Mina during her duel with Brachyura — to be placed on top.

Jelaïa sent another stone skipping out from the shore, wondering what Aldarin was doing now. Some important *temple mastery* stuff, probably. As far as she knew, it was the first time a scrier would occupy such an important position. Caddox would be livid when he found out, but his disapproval would not be enough to overrule Manfeld's dying wish.

The sun was in her eyes, bright and blinding as it descended slowly towards the western horizon. She would have to go back soon, back to Derello, Praxis, Lady Arkile, and the endless mounds of paperwork. For she was no longer Lady Jelaïa, Heiress. She was Baroness Jelaïa del Arelium, Lady of the White Wolf; a title she both hated and loved depending on the time of day … and who was asking.

Once the wreckage had been cleared and the dead buried, it was Derello who had suggested she stay a bit longer before returning to Arelium, ostensibly to further strengthen the relations between the two Baronies. For Jelaïa, the proposition had been the perfect excuse to postpone her departure. She would never openly admit it, but she was dreading the trip home for two major reasons. The first was her secret fear that she would not be up to the challenge of ruling her Barony. The second was that Loré del Conte would be waiting for her. Loré del Conte, her father.

No matter how many times she rolled those words round and round in her head they didn't sound right. In fact, if anyone other than Praedora had said such a thing, she would have laughed and waved them away with a smile. But there had been an undeniable sincerity in the First Priestess's voice, and no conceivable reason her … *aunt* would lie to her. No, Loré was her father, and she would have to confront him.

Another flick of the wrist, another stone sent to its inevitable end at the bottom of the sea. The gull had returned to its rock, a wriggling fish in its beak. It dropped its meal and tore into it with gusto, ripping through the scales to sample morsels of white flesh.

Jelaïa had soon found out that most of the 'alliance strengthening' involved debating the finer details of trade agreements, road maintenance costs, border disputes, and other equally complicated documents for hours on end. Derello was generally the first to lose interest, his gaze wandering from the dusty piles of parchment to the window and the Bay of Doves beyond. Jelaïa lasted longer, but it always ended the same way, with Lady Arkile and Steward Praxis monopolising the conversation, snapping back and forth at each other like a pair of duelling crabs. Both were highly intelligent. Both had been gifted with a dry, acerbic wit. And both, Jelaïa learnt, were insufferably arrogant.

It was a side of Praxis that had surprised her. Before her father's — Listus's — death, she had seen Praxis as a benevolent teacher, selflessly helping her to understand the intricacies of running a Barony. Now, that sheltered life was long behind her, the naive girl burnt away by the fires of Brachyura. She had learnt many hard lessons over the last few months, but the most important one was simple: nothing is as it seems.

As the daily interminable meetings wore on, she began to see the cracks in Praxis's facade. She could now hear the slight tone of condescension in his words when he gave his advice, see the way his brow creased in frustration when she questioned his affirmations, or how he drummed his fingers on the table when he grew impatient. Even his half-smile, which she had once thought so charming, was perhaps not quite so sincere.

None of this meant that he was a *bad* man, of course, just not quite the man Jelaïa had believed him to be. She used to feel flustered in his presence and unhappy when she didn't see him for a few days whereas now … well, he was just *there*. She enjoyed his company, and he had been extremely gracious in stepping down from his temporary Regency, allowing her to return unimpeded, but she was also quite happy to leave him to his own devices as often as possible and spend time alone.

Aldarin was a different matter entirely. She wasn't quite sure what he was to her yet: a friend, a brother, or something else, but they *needed* to talk. It had been weeks now since, in a fit of uncontrolled emotion, she had professed her love to him. *That* was certainly a subject that merited discussion. Then there was their unfinished conversation in the temple smithy. He had sworn to accompany her to Arelium, to serve and protect her. Was that still what he wanted? Or was that even possible, now that he was a temple master? Questions that begot more questions like an unravelling ball of yarn. Human relationships were hard.

She found another suitable, featureless stone. *Right, this will be the last one,* she thought.

"You need to flatten your aim, Jelaïa," came a voice from close by. She let out a small squeak of surprise and dropped her pebble.

"Praxis?"

"Yes, Jelaïa?"

"Please stop sneaking up on me like that." What had once been endearing was now becoming slightly annoying … and more than a little creepy.

"Apologies. I did not wish to alarm you. I worry about

you, Jelaïa, slipping away all the time. So, I had you followed. You shouldn't be out here on your own. There are plenty of unsavoury characters hanging around the Kessrin wharves looking for easy pickings."

Jelaïa took a deep breath and fought to control the anger simmering in her stomach. "Firstly, Praxis, I would prefer you to address me as 'My Lady'. I do not remember you calling my father 'Listus', I hope I am deserving of the same courtesy. Secondly," — she lifted the silver axe medallion hanging around her neck — "I am definitely *not* easy pickings. You have seen first-hand what the fires of Brachyura can do, and I have used mine against Brachyura himself. I don't think a few dock thugs would pose much of a challenge."

Praxis gave her a winning half-smile that distorted the deep scar on his cheek. "Of course, my Lady. I forget myself. It will not happen again. And it is true you are far from defenceless. You never did explain to me just how these *fires* work … I take it the medallion is the source of your power, is that correct? What would happen if someone managed to steal it from you? Dextrous fingers would have no trouble removing it from your neck. Then you would have no means to protect yourself, would you?"

His tone of voice was strange, as if he was speaking rhetorically rather than to Jelaïa directly. She took a step backwards. Her hand was still firmly wrapped around the necklace.

"What's that?" said Praxis suddenly, looking past Jelaïa towards something on the horizon. She followed his gaze. A silhouette of a ship. An enormous ship, too big to be a caravel. A carrack, approaching at speed. Even at a distance, she could see the sails had been dyed a bright shade of purple. "Pit!" she heard Praxis say.

"What is it?"

"I'd recognise that eyesore of a craft anywhere. It's the *Summer Dream*. Bansworth is the captain, one of Derello's vassals."

"An official visit, then?"

"No, you don't understand. Bansworth was at the battle of the Bay of Doves. Not just *at* the battle, *leading* the battle. Once things turned sour, he fled like a coward, leaving his own fleet to be torn apart by the krakens. The Baron told me he'd flay the man alive if he ever returned."

"So why is he here?"

"I don't know. He must be either very brave or very stupid. And having met the man, I'd go with the latter. Come, my Lady, Derello must be told."

Jelaïa took one last look at her precious haven of tranquillity, then turned to follow Praxis out of the creek. The seagull croaked at the two departing figures before returning to the fish, finally able to finish its meal in peace.

∾

They found Derello pacing back and forth across the meeting hall, hands gesturing in all directions as he cursed and blustered. Lady Arkile looked on impassively, her back ramrod straight, her thin hands clasped in front of her.

"Looks like he's already heard the news, then," said Praxis wryly.

With the collapse of Kessrin keep, the Baron had lost his Great Hall, his living quarters, his guest rooms, his barracks, a great number of storerooms, his kitchens, and his stables. The central tower would be rebuilt, but these things take time and, in the interim, the Baron needed a place to conduct his affairs.

It was Aldarin and Praedora who had come up with the best solution. Kessrin, like many other provincial capitals, had a garrison; a multi-levelled, fortified building situated near the keep and reserved for a contingent of Knights of the Twelve. The Kessrin garrison had stood unused for years, ever since the Knights of Brachyura had no longer had the means (or the desire) to occupy it.

"I'm going to cut his toes off one by one and feed them to him," the Baron was saying to Lady Arkile. "I'll have them cooked first, of course, so they're nice and crispy. Then I'll move on to his groin and — Oh, Praxis. My Lady. I was just going to send for you. That grunting piglet Bansworth has returned. His carrack is pulling into the Bay as we speak. I would appreciate it if you could stay here while I welcome him home."

Derello had lost most of his extensive wardrobe when the towers fell, but it didn't seem to matter. Since the battle of the Bay of Doves, he had always dressed the same: a knee-length coat of chainmail, belted at the waist, soft leather boots, and a pair of intricately crafted vambraces covering a set of throwing daggers. Today, however, there was a very slight change in his attire. The belt had been replaced by a pink sash, adding a touch of colour to his typical drab military outfit. Perhaps some small indication that Derello was starting to heal.

"Wine, anyone?" the Baron offered, striding over to a crystal decanter and pouring himself a generous glass.

"I do not think any of us would like a drink at the moment, my Lord," said Lady Arkile reprovingly, taking great care to emphasise the word 'any'.

"Any of us?"

"Yes, my Lord. I believe we have already discussed this several times."

"Well, you can't expect me to remember everything, Lady Arkile, it has been a difficult week—"

"Today, my Lord. Several times *today*."

Derello set his glass down in a huff and crossed his arms, one foot tapping rhythmically on the floor in frustration. He reminded Jelaïa of a pan of water that was about to boil over.

Luckily, they did not have long to wait. The door to the meeting hall was pulled open by a pair of town guard and three weary figures shuffled into the room, their cloaks soaked with brine.

Lord Bansworth had lost a lot of weight since fleeing Kessrin. His once tight-fitting, gaudy silk shirt now billowed down from his shoulders like a ship's sail. He wore a wide-brimmed hat too large for his head, only prevented from slipping down over his eyes by being balanced on his prodigious ears. He was trembling, although it was impossible to tell if this was due to the cold of the sea or the fear of seeing the Baron again.

Behind him came two more travellers, as different as night and day. The first was tall and muscular, his black hair sprouting out of his head in all directions as if not sure in which way to grow. He was fully armoured under his cloak, his left vambrace fitted with a round buckler. He stood protectively in front of his charge, a child of nine or ten with dripping hair, his eyes round like saucers.

"*Lord* Bansworth," said Derello, his smile as sweet and sickly as a pot of Morlakian honey. "I was hoping we would meet again one day. So many things were left unsaid ... and undone. It gives me great pleasure to see you. What brings you to Kessrin?"

The disgraced vassal didn't reply, only stepped aside to allow the child to come forwards and go down on one knee.

"Lord Baron," the boy began. He was concentrating hard, trying to recite something he had learnt by heart. "Greetings to you. My name is Baron Kayal del Talth, last of my line. I come to beseech your aid in ridding my lands of the greylings and aveng ... aveng ... avenging my predecessor."

A tear escaped his left eye and trickled down his cheek. "My grandfather is dead, Baron. My father is dead. My people are losing their homes and their lives. I do not know what to do. Please help me. Please."

And bowing his head, he began to weep.

CHAPTER 3

SEEDS AND SNOWBALLS

"Must we really talk of this again? I am getting tired of your continual refusal to accept my methods. Subterfuge is not always pretty, but it is an essential part of any viable strategy. In fact, I would argue that it has saved numerous lives. Take Kadex, for example, the wily old bandit leader who was plaguing northern Morlak. I slipped into his tent one night, slit his throat, and took his place. Then, the next day, I led his men into an ambush. They were slaughtered. And guess how many Morlakians I lost? None."

MITHUNA, THIRD OF THE TWELVE, 46 AT

✦

"**A**WAY INTO THE keep?" said Vohanen sceptically, and Jeffson could see that the haggard knight did not believe him. And why would he? What could a simple manservant know that they did not? Such insufferable hubris. It was this constant pontification that kept the Knightly Orders from greatness. They were undoubtedly brave, selfless, and righteous, but they never thought to question their own values. A pity.

"Yes, Sir Knight. I have worked in Morlak before, I still have some old contacts there."

"As a thief and a cutpurse, you mean," said Vohanen unpleasantly.

"You are correct, Sir Vohanen," Jeffson said, unperturbed. "I congratulate you on your excellent memory. If I may go on?"

Vohanen scowled and gestured for him to continue.

"Thank you. One of them in particular had some knowledge of the inner workings of Morlak keep. I could maybe persuade him to help us get inside."

"Us?"

"Yes, you will need me to make the introductions. I fear he will not be as welcoming to a Knight of Kriari."

"I will be coming too, of course," added Syrella del Morlak in a voice that left no room for discussion. "I have waited here patiently for weeks, pulling my hair out, biting my nails, and walking in circles while someone wearing my face is sleeping in my bed and ruling my subjects. My Barony has been taken from me and I will be among those who take it back."

"That sounds … fair," Bjornvor agreed. "And I have not forgotten the oath made to your father. I will send a company of knights to escort you, as many as I can spare. If you set up camp away from the town walls, you should not draw too much attention. Taleck will lead them."

"What?" sputtered Vohanen.

"You are not ready, Sir Knight. Can you, in all good conscience, tell me that you are in control of your emotions? Taleck will lead, and you will follow his orders to the letter. If you do not, he will send you back to the temple. And you will have to explain to me how you failed your brothers and your Order. Now, that is enough for this evening. We will reassemble here tomorrow at first light."

"Yes, Master," said Vohanen sullenly. He heaved himself up off his seat and wandered away from the fire in search of more ale.

Bjornvor watched him go. "He was always rash and impetuous," he said in his rough, brittle voice. "But since the death of Avor, I fear he has lost all sense of self-preservation. A dangerous combination. I thought he would be the one to take my place, but now I am not so sure."

"Music!" shouted one of the knights, clapping his neighbour on the shoulder. A fiddle was produced from somewhere and soon the fast-paced rhythmic sound of a traditional Morlakian folk song echoed around the Great Hall. Benches were pushed aside and some of the younger initiates attempted to dance and sing along, with varying degrees of success. One of their number tentatively approached Syrella who hadn't moved from her spot by the fire. The Baroness, not unkindly, shooed him away.

Tankards were refilled from a newly-tapped barrel of ale. Pipes were lit. In one corner, an enterprising group of knights started up an impromptu card game.

Jeffson felt the subtle shift in ambience as the tension drained from the room. The door banged open and two figures entered, accompanied by a swirl of fresh snow. Krelbe, his long watch finally over, struggled out of his layers of fur pelts and made for the group of gamblers at the far end of the hall.

As the second figure removed its winter clothing, Jeffson recognised Evie, Priestess of Kriari and wife to Vohanen. Her roving gaze soon found her husband and she went cautiously to greet him, laying a comforting hand on his arm. He flinched as if stung and jerked away. The couple exchanged a few terse words until he turned his back on her. Evie raised her hand again, then thought better of it and went to sit by Lady Syrella.

"She reminds him of his son," said Bjornvor softly from close by. Jeffson almost jumped out of his skin. How had the old man managed to sneak up on him like that? "It is a terrible sight to see, the way he pushes his friends and family away. They would be so much stronger confronting grief together than apart."

"Some things are better faced alone," Jeffson replied. He heard the faint sound of a child laughing, no louder than a whisper, before it was drowned out by the frenetic sounds of the fiddle. His head began to ache. "If you would excuse me, Sir Knight, I think I will retire to my room and start packing for tomorrow."

Bjornvor looked at him strangely. "As you wish. Would you accompany an old man to his chambers first? I am not as young as I once was and the icy snow can be treacherous underfoot."

Jeffson tied on his fur cap and held out his arm for the temple master. Bjornvor's grip was strong and firm. The two men pushed out into the twilight, leaving the warmth and noise behind. Thousands of tiny crystal-clear snowflakes spiralled down around them. They crossed the inner courtyard in the direction of the living quarters a few minutes' walk away, crunching through the thick layer of snow.

"I've been meaning to ask you something," Bjornvor said as they navigated around a group of rowdy children engaged in a merciless snowball fight. "You told them you knew of a way to get us into Morlak keep. That wasn't entirely correct, was it?"

By the Pit, thought Jeffson. *I have underestimated this frail old man.*

"No," he answered. "Not entirely. I do have a way inside but not for twenty Knights of Kriari. Not even for *one* Knight of Kriari. I will have to bring Sir Reed out on my own."

A snowball spun through the air, hitting one of the children full in the face. He roared indignantly and jumped on his attacker, tackling him to the ground and shovelling cold snow down his neck.

"I see," mused Bjornvor. "Well, I suppose Taleck will understand. Vohanen will be another kettle of fish, of course, he will not appreciate having been lied to." They walked on in silence for several minutes. "I have another question," the temple master finally continued.

"I'm sure you do," Jeffson replied wryly, brushing half-melted snowflakes from his face. The building housing his guest quarters was only yards away now. He would soon be alone again.

"Morlak is a dangerous place. The Baroness, for all her courage, is not a soldier. She will need someone to watch her back. I would think that someone with your ... history is the right man for the job."

"Hmmm," Jeffson agreed absently. His headache was getting worse.

"Sir Merad Reed, if you manage to find him, will be likewise at risk. My question is this: where does your allegiance lie? With the man or the woman? The guardsman or the Baroness? Reed is your friend but without Syrella, Morlak may crumble. If, when the time comes, you can only save one of them, who will you choose?"

Jeffson felt the man's grip tighten on his arm like a vice. He stopped abruptly and turned to look the temple master in the eye.

"I do not know, Sir Knight," he said truthfully.

Bjornvor grunted as if expecting such an answer. "Something to think about on the trip south, Friend Jeffson," he croaked hoarsely. The temple master released the bemused manservant and shuffled slowly away, humming softly under his breath.

∽

Merad Reed was sure the rat was mocking him.

It sat a couple of feet away from his rickety wooden bed, staring up at him with its black beady eyes, its tail swishing back and forth across the sodden straw that covered the floor of the prison cell.

It edged forwards a few inches, whiskers twitching.

"Come on, come on," Reed whispered. His right hand gripped a broken shard of pottery, the tip sharp enough to cut through skin and bone. He forced himself to remain absolutely motionless.

The rat took another tentative step in the direction of the bed and Reed sprang into action, leaping off the hard planks with his arms outstretched. The rodent darted backwards at the last moment with a terrified squeak, squeezing through the rusty bars of the cell and out of reach. Reed hit the ground hard, his makeshift weapon spinning from his hand.

"Damn you, rat," he cursed, rubbing a bruised elbow. "Damn you to the Pit."

The rat looked at him from its safe spot and began grooming itself calmly.

"You'll be back," continued Reed conversationally, pulling himself up into a sitting position and eyeing the creature through the bars. "All it takes is one small moment of hesitation and it'll be over. I've had rat before, you know. Hode brought me some up on the walls above the Southern Pit. Poor old Hode. Rat stew was the last meal he ever had."

A clanking sound echoed down the tunnel outside his cell, a key turning in a lock. The rat cocked its head, then scuttered away into the darkness. A slender, indistinct figure appeared, clothed in a dark blue cloak and carrying a tray of food. The only light in the cell came from a window barely larger than an arrow-slit set high up on one wall but, despite the gloom, Reed recognised his visitor immediately. It was the only person he had seen in weeks.

"Nidore!"

"Talking to yourself again, Reed?" asked the young noble. He set down the tray and brushed a strand of blond hair from his face. Nidore del Conte had once been exceedingly handsome — a perfect picture of Arelian aristocracy — from the long locks of his golden hair to the perfectly-manicured nails of his soft, uncalloused hands. Handsome and well-liked by all save the Baron himself, who saw in him the heir to his greatest rival, Loré del Conte.

But time changes all things.

The man now standing before Reed was a thin shadow of his former self. The blond hair was still there, but knotted and patchy, as if it had been pulled or torn. The beautiful nails had been bitten and gnawed; the cuticles stained with fresh blood. And the eyes. The eyes were the worst. Glazed and devoid of all emotion, like a porcelain doll. For that is what Nidore had become, transformed by his own feelings of misguided love and devotion into a malleable puppet.

It almost made Reed feel sorry for him. Then he remembered the hum of black-fletched arrows. The sound they made as they punctured the flesh of the Old Guard rescued from the Morlakian Pit. The bodies filling the ravine. There would be no forgiveness.

He took a deep breath and forced himself to smile. "Not much else to do down here, is there?"

Nidore shrugged and pushed the tray closer to the cell then stood back, arms crossed. Reed inspected what would be his only food for the next few days: half a loaf of bread, two carrots, a dark wrinkly shape that he hoped was a potato, and a bowl of water.

"Still no meat?" he grumbled, reaching through the bars to grab what food he could. The bowl wouldn't fit without being inclined slightly, spilling some of the water onto the floor.

"Sorry, this is all I could manage to steal," confessed Nidore with a shrug. "I think Verona is still angry with you. In fact, I don't think she even knows I'm coming down here to see you at all."

"She knows," Reed replied, lifting the bowl to his mouth. He took the smallest mouthfuls of water, just enough to wet his lips. "That woman knows everything."

"*Mithuna* knows everything. Verona knows ... most things."

Reed grunted. Maybe if he had a carrot now, he could keep the potato for dinner and the bread for tomorrow?

"How are you faring?" Nidore asked, looking around the cell. It had been cut directly into the rock under Morlak keep and the walls had become coated in moss. When Reed was first brought there, the ceiling had been covered in stalactites from which water dripped, but now, with the early days of winter fast approaching, the droplets were gone.

"As long as my friends are still alive, I'll be fine," said Reed, rising to his feet. "And I am sure they *are* still alive, or I would be speaking to Verona or Mithuna instead of you, wouldn't I? They would be falling over each other to come down here and tell me in person."

Nidore said nothing, one hand rising to his head to scratch at his scalp. His hand came away bloody.

Reed bit into a carrot. "It's been what, two weeks now? Three? I've been trying to keep track, but it's surprisingly difficult."

"That makes two of us. I thought I'd be in the keep with Verona, but they've given me quarters in the garrison, with the Knights of Mithuna. They have not been particularly ... welcoming. Especially the one called Yonis. He's always looking at me like he wants to cut me open with a fileting knife."

"He looked at me like that, too. Maybe that's just his face."

"Maybe." A ghost of a smile flitted across the young man's features, faster than a heartbeat. "In any case, I am to be tested soon, to see if I am worthy to join them. As an initiate, I mean."

"Is that what you want?"

"I ... It's what Verona wants."

"That's not what I asked."

Nidore looked at the older man, his eyes filled with anguish. "You cannot understand. You have never known love, Merad. You do not know the things it makes us do."

Reed sighed. "You are right. But I *have* let my emotions make my decisions for me. Running away from my responsibilities. Leaving my mother to die alone. Decisions I now regret. It is one thing to let our feelings guide us; it is another to let them define us."

Nidore did not reply. His lower lip began to tremble.

"I have often heard it said that between two people 'love is enough'," continued Reed. "I do not think it is. It cannot stand alone for long, it must be supported with trust and understanding or it will start to be washed away, like grains of sand on a beach. Do you trust the one you love?"

"I ..."

"Do you understand her?"

Nidore tore his gaze away and turned his back on Reed, walking back up the corridor. After a few steps he stopped, shrugged off his cloak and threw it back towards the cell.

"You'll need this. It will only get colder."

Reed listened as the footsteps faded away and the key turned once more in the lock.

A seed of doubt, he thought to himself, sitting down on the wooden bed. *It's a start.*

He took another bite of carrot.

And a seed of doubt, carefully nurtured, can grow into something much, much greater.

Time to plan my next move.

CHAPTER 4

More Complications

"Trust is a difficult thing to gain, and an even more difficult thing to maintain. Nevertheless, it remains an essential tool of our Order, as a trusting target is one that can be easily manipulated and controlled. There are three effective ways to appear trustworthy. The first is to listen to others and keep secret what was said in confidence. The second is to accept criticism and admit to your own weaknesses. And the third is to place the other person's life above your own."

ZYGOS, SEVENTH OF THE TWELVE, 120 AT

⤸

*J*UST WHAT WE *need*, thought Praxis, as Jelaïa rushed forwards to console the orphaned Baron of Talth. *More refugees, more diversions, and more unforeseen hurdles to my plan.*

The last few weeks had been a disastrous series of

setbacks. Brachyura had arrived minutes before he could escape with Derello, and ever since the return of Lady Arkile (who had been found safe and sound, hiding in the Treasury of all places), he could feel his hold on the young man slipping away.

Then there was Jelaïa. He watched her now, her eyes glistening with tears as she listened to Kayal recount the last days of the battle for Talth. Such intelligence, so quick to learn and understand, but so much wasted empathy. He'd felt a minuscule spark of hope when he had seen her on the wall of Kessrin, bedecked in the dress and necklace of a priestess of Brachyura. He had thought that maybe she would stay at the temple and leave him to guide Arelium with a stern — but fair — hand.

Unfortunately, that was not to be the case. Jelaïa had made her decision and declared that her heart lay with Arelium. He had had no other choice but to relinquish the Regency. This had always been a possibility, of course, and one he had accounted for. He still had a few contacts in Kessrin. Another assassination attempt would have been easy enough, or he could have done the deed himself, just to be sure. The road to Arelium was long and fraught with danger …

But something terrible had happened that would make such attempts nigh on impossible. Jelaïa was no longer defenceless. She had awakened and now wielded the fires of that Pit-spawned Brachyura. He had not seen her do so himself, but he had seen first-hand what such a gift could achieve. Praedora, the First Priestess, fuelled by grief and anger, had used it to annihilate Mina, Last of the Twelve. Praxis remembered watching the flesh slough from her bones, the fat popping and crackling as it burned. He was not quite ready to risk such an agonising death, no matter how much he wanted Jelaïa gone.

No, there was another, safer way for him to regain control of Arelium. If he could not be Regent, he would have to settle for Baron. He had already spent several years laying the foundations for this: rallying with her against her father, lending a consoling ear when needed, an appreciative glance when she was well-dressed, a hand that stayed a moment too long on her shoulder, or accidentally brushed against her hair. It was easy really, seduction, especially when there was no competition.

So why wasn't it working? Since arriving in Kessrin, he had continued to apply the same tricks, the same half-smile, the same consolatory gestures, but something was different. The reciprocity he had felt before was gone. Surely there couldn't be someone else? Derello? No. Who then? Maybe it was just that she was still grieving for her father and that she was far from home. When they returned to Arelium, he would have her undivided attention.

"Of course, we will help," he heard Jelaïa say, drying the young Baron's eyes with a handkerchief.

Pit! What's happening now? More dallying! More complications!

"We already owe much to your vassal, Sir Bansworth, my Lord," Gaelin, the Knight of Guanna, said to Derello. "We had made it as far as Haeden, but the greylings were never far behind, snapping at our heels. We found Sir Bansworth in a tavern there, and on hearing our sorry story he immediately offered us his services."

"In a tavern, eh? Fitting, I suppose. Did they still have any wine left to serve you, or had Bansworth drunk it all?"

"Er, I do not know, my Lord, there were more pressing issues. Sir Bansworth helped evacuate the women and children onto his carrack. Then, he sent some guards to bolster the village militia so we could get away. He saved not only our own lives but dozens of others. We would be rotting in the middle of Haeden square instead of speaking to you now if he had not come to our aid."

"I see. Fleeing another battle, then. And did he tell you he was a wanted man, here in Kessrin?"

"No, he did not, my Lord. Otherwise, we would not have let him come ashore."

Lady Arkile coughed politely. Derello shot her a sideways glance and threw up his hands.

"Fine. Fine. Get over here, Bansworth, on your knees." The man scuttled forwards and sank down before his liege lord, removing his hat and holding it in shaking hands.

"I despise cowardice, Bansworth. I do not think the presence of the *Summer Dream* would have turned the tide of battle, but you should not have left the others, whether it was a tactical withdrawal or a coward's flight." He looked at Kayal, who was still clinging to the hem of Jelaïa's dress as if it was a lifeline.

"How many did you save, Bansworth?"

"Forty-three."

"What? Don't mumble! How many?"

"Forty-three, my Lord."

"Hmmm. You are a lucky man, Bansworth. If I had sworn an oath to kill you, I would have no choice but to do so, despite what you have done. A del Kessrin does not break his oath." He sighed, his countenance softening. "But I did not, and I am forced to admit that you have done a good thing, here. Not enough to balance the scales, but enough to save your life."

He beckoned to one of the guards. "This is what I have decided. Your lands and titles are forfeit, to be passed down to your next of kin — if you have any — or to me if you do not. The *Summer Dream* will be signed over to me, as a replacement for the *Emerald Queen*. Is that acceptable to you?"

"Y ... yes, my Lord," burbled the relieved noble.

"Oh, and one more thing, Bansworth. You are aware of the penalty for desertion, I am sure. No man is exempt from this, no matter the reason or his past actions." He turned to the guard. "Take him to Captain Hirkuin, please. Ten lashes, then two days without food or water. Tell me when it is done."

The guard nodded and accompanied the snivelling Bansworth to meet his punishment.

"Was that really necessary?" scolded Lady Arkile as the door clanged shut.

"I believe so. I must not be seen to be too weak. My vassals rallied around me when we had a common cause, but they have lost much: ships, men, supplies ... it only takes a series of small events to turn adoration into sedition. Traitors and deserters must be dealt with — no leniency."

"A good answer," admitted Arkile with a twitch of her nose. "You'll amount to something yet."

"Why, Lady Arkile, that was nearly a compliment!"

"Nearly," she replied, the corners of her lips rising a

tiny fraction in what could possibly be considered a smile. "Nearly."

"So, you will help me?" asked Kayal, disengaging himself from Jelaïa and wiping his eyes with the sleeve of his tunic. "When do we leave for Talth?"

"It's not that easy, little Lord," said Praxis. "We are still licking our wounds from two major engagements in Kessrin and Arelium. Both our Baronies have been sorely tested and need time to regroup."

"Yes, my Lord," Gaelin intervened. "But the enemy will be doing the same. They too have suffered. My brother knights led a diversion when the greylings first appeared. They killed many before being overwhelmed. The defenders on the wall of Talth fought long and hard, further adding to the dead. And the boy's father led a cavalry charge straight into their midst. He took a slew of greylings with him on the way to meet his ancestors."

A servant appeared from a side door and bent to whisper something in Lady Arkile's ear before retreating, brushing against Praxis as he left.

"We will help you," Derello said. "But it must be done right, or we could lose everything we have gained. I will send a fast ship down the coast to the temple of Brachyura, asking for aid. If it leaves now and the winds are favourable, we will have their answer in a day at most."

"There is something else," Lady Arkile said. "Loré del Conte. He is on his way to Kessrin with important news. He claims to have found another of the Twelve."

Jelaïa's face grew deathly pale. "Lor ... Loré?" she stammered. "I thought he was badly wounded. How can he travel? He could barely walk the last time I saw him."

"I don't know, but he must be feeling better. They are arriving tomorrow."

"Tomorrow?"

"Yes, is that a problem?"

"No, no, not at all. It is just that I must … prepare. If you would excuse me?" Jelaïa gave a quick curtsy and exited the room faster than Praxis thought was really necessary. He frowned, then felt something crinkle in the palm of his hand; a tiny scrap of paper, left there by the servant as he passed by.

There were only two words inscribed hurriedly on the parchment, but they were enough to send a chill down his spine.

Loré knows.

&

Praxis buttoned up his high-necked leather coat and checked his travel pack one last time. A change of clothes, ink and parchment, a couple of stubby candles, a tinder box, soap, a canteen, a loaf of dry bread, and some salted meat. Enough for a few days on the road. Enough to get out of Kessrin.

He would be leaving on foot. Taking a horse would raise too many questions, and there were no outbound ships before midday tomorrow. The main gates into Kessrin were closed at this late hour, but Praxis knew of another way, a tiny postern gate hidden in the shadows of a back alley on the far eastern side of town. Perfect for entering and leaving unseen.

Three Baronies shared their borders with Kessrin. It had not taken Praxis long to pick a destination. Talth was crawling

with greylings. Arelium was full of people who knew his face
and might ask the wrong questions. That left Morlak. What
was it Mina had said to Derello? *Morlak is already under our
control.* Ominous, but not very helpful. Under the control
of whom? Another member of the Twelve? The greylings?
Maybe Syrella del Morlak had been persuaded to switch
sides? There was only one way to find out.

And after that? A small part of his brain reminded him
that he was still a Knight of Zygos and technically still on
the mission given to him over ten years ago. The temple
masters would be waiting for his report; which would mean
explaining why he had attacked Mina and killed several of
her knights. Not a conversation he was looking forward to.

He emerged from his guest house, a square, flat-roofed
structure a stone's throw from Kessrin keep. The street outside was empty save for a one-armed beggar sitting on the
porch steps of one of the larger buildings. He rattled his tin
cup hopefully at Praxis, who pointedly ignored him, walking
briskly eastwards towards his salvation.

It took him a good half-hour to find the postern gate.
In the end, he only discovered it by retracing his steps and
rechecking all the back alleys one by one. The gate had been
painted to look like part of the wall, the work so detailed
and realistic that he had missed it. There was no lock, no key,
and no handle. Praxis drew one of his stilettos and inserted
it into what looked like a crack in the mortar. He heard a
satisfying click, and the gate swung open.

Freedom, at last! he thought.

A fist whooshed out of the darkness beyond the door
and crunched into his cheek. He yelped in surprise as pain
flared across the left side of his face. The fist came at him

again, and he scrambled backwards, tripping over a mound
of detritus and landing on his rear. His knife came up, the
tip pointing at the figure emerging from the other side of
the gate.

Captain Hirkuin, his carefully waxed ginger foxtail shining in the torchlight, stepped through the opening, curling
and uncurling the fingers of his right hand. Behind him came
Derello and three burly guardsmen armed with crossbows.
The young Baron looked devastated, close to tears even.

"Praxis ... I prayed so hard to the Twelve not to find you
here. I couldn't believe it. Not you. After all you have done
for Kessrin."

"What are you talking about?" retorted Praxis from his
spot down on the cobbles.

"The *note*, Praxis. The note the servant passed you. It
was all a test. The messenger from Arelium told us that Loré
was coming, but that wasn't all. He also has in his possession
a warrant for your arrest."

"On what charge?" Five against one. He'd faced worse
odds before and won. But three crossbows ... at this range
... even one lucky shot would be enough to drill a hole right
through his coat and armour. He hadn't done all this hard
work to wind up butchered in a back alley.

"Treachery. Treachery and murder." Derello shook his
head sadly. "Pit, Praxis, I thought it was some sort of joke!
You saved my life on Kingfisher Isle. That was not the act
of a traitor. So, I consulted with Lady Arkile and we devised
this simple trick: a forged note, a faked accusation. If you
were innocent, you would have said something or stayed in
Kessrin. Instead, I find you here, running like a dog with
your tail between your legs. You were so quick to leave, you

didn't even wonder what that one-armed beggar was doing outside your house. Or who had paid him to be there."

Cogs and gears clicked and whirred in Praxis's mind, rifling through every ounce of information he had amassed over the last ten years, every favour he was owed, every deal he had made, every person he had blackmailed. Faster and faster, growing more and more desperate, looking for a way out.

There was none.

One tiny sliver of hope remained. Derello was teetering on the edge of condemnation but was not *quite* convinced. It would take time, but if he could sway the Baron onto his side, he might make it out of this sticky predicament with his head still attached to his shoulders.

"You are right, Derello," he said, catching the man's eye and holding his gaze. "I *was* trying to flee. Loré del Conte is a hot-blooded, stubborn man; quick to judge, and even quicker to anger. Someone has planted this ridiculous idea in his head and he has let it overwhelm him."

Praxis held out his hands in submission. "I ran because I was afraid for my life. Because I was afraid of what he might do to me. But, if you can guarantee my safety and a chance to defend myself against these heinous accusations, then I will gladly stay here in Kessrin."

Hirkuin snorted. "Yeah, right, as if you have any choice."

The Baron studied Praxis, then grasped his forearm and pulled him to his feet.

"You saved my life," he repeated. "No matter what else you have done before or since, the least I can do is offer you the chance to tell your side of the story. Hirkuin! Escort the steward back to his quarters. A guard on the door at all times, just in case, although I don't think we need to worry about that, do we, Praxis?"

"No, my Lord," Praxis replied softly. "No need to worry. No need to worry at all."

CHAPTER 5

THE JEWELLED NECKLACE

"Look, Syrella, it's just not that simple. I don't see how you think you can govern the entire Barony by yourself. You'll need to keep the vassals in line, protect our borders, balance the books, negotiate trade deals with our neighbours, and, if it comes to it, take up arms to defend Morlak from its enemies. It is not for a woman to carry such a heavy burden. I've sent riders to the neighbouring Baronies. We will find you a husband, and you can return to your sewing, or whatever else you do to pass the time."

BARON DEL MORLAK, 410 AT

❧

J EFFSON DID NOT remember much of the long journey south from Dirkvale to Morlak apart from that it was cold, wet, and uneventful.

Bjornvor had finally decided on a contingent of twenty-eight Knights of Kriari to escort Lady Syrella back to her capital: far too few to attempt a frontal assault on the keep, but more than enough to repel any ambushes — greyling or human — that may lie in wait along the way.

Taleck rode at the head of the convoy with Vohanen to his left and Krelbe to his right. Jeffson had been surprised to see the taciturn gambler among those chosen to accompany the Baroness. Either the knight really was unbelievably bad at cards, or there was some other reason for him following Vohanen around like a faithful hound.

Behind the leading trio came the remaining knights, surrounding a covered wagon not unlike the one Jeffson and Reed had used to travel all the way from Arelium to the Morlakian Pit. This one was slightly larger, with extra storage worked into the wooden bows, and enough space for Lady Syrella to travel comfortably amid the tents, food, and other supplies needed for the journey. Its spoked wheels left deep furrows in the powdered snow as it rumbled ponderously southwards.

Jeffson had volunteered to drive the cart and spent his days with his feet dangling down from the box seat while his left hand gripped the reins of the enormous war horse harnessed to the wagon tongue. He had a complicated relationship with horses, which basically boiled down to the fact that he didn't like them, and they didn't like him. He could ride well enough but only chose to do so if there was no other option, as there was always the added danger of being thrown into a ditch by an irate mount.

In any case, nothing beat the slow, methodical movement of a horse and cart. Much more relaxing, and plenty of time to dive back into his book. Or try, at least. For the first couple of days, it was so cold that he could only remove his fur mittens for a few minutes before his hands started to tremble.

The Knights of Kriari did not seem in the least troubled by the onset of winter. Jeffson was forced to admit that the thick fur mantles he had always thought looked rather ridiculous were well-suited to the recent change in weather, as were the padded armour and gloves they always wore. The war horses were similarly equipped, with decorated blankets covering their long-haired winter coats.

They made good time, stopping only briefly during the day and pushing on into the early evening until the fading light made further progress difficult. Krelbe put his cooking skills to good use, conjuring up various mouth-watering concoctions night after night using only a few vegetables and whatever meat the hunting parties had managed to find.

On the third evening, Jeffson found himself sharing a spot by the fire with Syrella. The Baroness was picking listlessly at a morsel of fish caught hours earlier in the small stream running along the edge of the campsite. The Knights of Kriari were spread out in groups of three or four, drinking or playing cards. Luckily, no one appeared to have brought a fiddle.

"How do you know so much about Morlak?" Syrella asked suddenly, catching Jeffson off guard. He licked his lips and thought for a moment. How much could he reveal without getting into trouble?

"I ... worked there for a time, my Lady," he said carefully. "Before moving on to other things."

"Vohanen called you a thief. Is that right?" She was

looking at him intently, the light from the fire reflected in her heterochromatic eyes.

"Yes, my Lady."

"Interesting." A smile tugged at the corners of her mouth. "I'm sure you have plenty of fascinating stories to tell."

"There are certainly stories, my Lady, although, to be honest, I would rather forget most of them."

"Fair enough, we are all entitled to our secrets. Would you at least tell me how you found yourself in such a situation?"

Jeffson shrugged. "The same way most orphans do, my Lady. Begging and stealing was the only way to survive. There was a sort of natural selection there, too. Those who were not proficient at either grew weak and died. The older boys preyed on the younger ones. Street gangs recruited promising orphans into their ranks, mostly by force. As we grew older, it became necessary not only to steal but also to stop others from taking our ill-gotten gains away from us."

"Hence the knuckle knives."

"Yes. That was one of our many means of dissuasion."

"And so, you were part of one of these gangs?"

Jeffson nodded, his face expressionless. "Part of, and eventually leader of, my Lady."

Syrella looked down at her plate and set it aside. "What were you called?"

"The Red Sparrows. Terrible name, although we were quite proud of it at the time."

"Hmmm. That rings a very distant bell. Something about a necklace." The Baroness stared into the fire, one finger tapping her knee. "Ah yes, I remember now! Lady

Canderdash, I believe her name was. Nasty specimen. She wasn't at court long but, by the Pit, was she insufferable! Her husband owned a vast expanse of land south of Lostthorn, acres and acres of wheat fields. From what I could gather, he made large amounts of money from agricultural tithes, then let his wife spend it all."

A string of expletives came from the other side of the campfire. It was Krelbe, losing once again. The impromptu chef threw his hand of cards down in disgust and stamped off angrily into the night. His fellow players chuckled amiably as if this was a common occurrence and returned to their game.

"I'm sure she was a dutiful housewife in return, my Lady," said Jeffson dryly. "Although I believe there is a less *polite* name for a woman who performs such services in exchange for money."

"Yes, well, in any case, this Lady Canderdash had more jewellery than she knew what to do with, enough to wear a different piece every other week or so. Her favourite was a silver necklace studded with amethysts. A remarkable work of art. It must have cost hundreds. I think she knew I was insanely jealous as she began to wear it more and more frequently, then suddenly, one day, she stopped."

Jeffson was silent, remembering. Remembering the approach across the rooftops, jumping from house to house, one death-defying leap after another. Scaling the walls of the private estate with nothing more than a length of rope and a couple of metal spikes, pressed tight against the rough stone as the town guard patrolled mere feet below.

"The necklace had been stolen," Syrella continued with a mischievous glint in her eyes. "Someone had broken into her bedroom and taken it from her dressing table. Right next to her bed! Quinne, my guard captain, led the investigation himself. Do you know what they found had been left there in its place?"

"Something over-the-top and unnecessarily theatrical, my Lady?"

"A dead sparrow."

"Wonderful," said Jeffson, his voice neutral.

"Quite. My vassals talked about nothing else for weeks. The culprits were never found, much to Lady Canderdash's disappointment. We didn't see her so much at court after that."

"Sounds like you owe whoever stole that necklace your thanks then, my Lady."

Syrella let out a burst of laughter, drawing some strange looks from the nearby Knights of Kriari.

"I think I like you, Jeffson. And I can see why Reed likes you too."

"Sir Reed? I think you must be mistaken, my Lady."

"Perhaps, but I rarely am. Call it a woman's intuition. Now, if you would excuse me, I must retire to my chambers." She gestured at the wagon. "I do hope we will be able to talk again some time, it has been quite entertaining."

Jeffson watched her go. *What a strange woman,* he thought, and turned back to his book.

❧

Morlak had been built on the lower slopes of the Redenfell Mountains. Behind it, jagged snow-capped peaks stretched thousands of feet into the sky, casting their long, triangular shadows over the small cluster of humanity clinging to their base, like a family of giants looming over an ant's nest.

Whoever had designed Morlak had eschewed all sense of decoration or fantasy, focussing instead on bleak functionality. The town was split into two levels. The lower level housed most of the town's residents, merchants, shops, and inns. Harsh, angular structures of basalt or granite that the nearby quarries provided in abundance. The lack of space meant that the buildings were piled almost on top of one another, linked by a web of meandering alleyways barely wide enough for two horses. These enclosed streets and passageways received little light, the overhanging roofs of the shops and houses blocking out the sun.

Above the lower level stood Morlak keep itself, surrounded by an impressive defensive wall as high and thick as the curtain wall of Arelium. The wall was topped by crenellated ramparts, patrolled day and night by the shieldmen and archers of the Morlak town guard, who had a near-perfect view of the outer town and the flat terrain beyond.

The keep resembled a smooth, rectangular block of featureless dark grey stone. No towers, no flags, no exterior sign of decoration save for a single metal-plated door on the ground floor and several rows of thin arrow slits dotted along its sides like pockmarks. It could almost be thought uninhabited if not for the flickering candlelight emanating from the upper windows at night.

Close to the keep stood another, smaller, fortified structure built in the same simple style. The barracks. For years, a ram's head flag had been proudly flown from the centre of its flat roof, now replaced by the two identical silhouettes of the Order of Mithuna.

"Those half-dozen peaks behind Morlak are known as The Demon's Smile," said Taleck to Jeffson conversationally. They were about a mile from the town gates, far enough away to be a couple of black specks to the guards up on the walls. Thick clouds hung heavily over the mountains, the air dank and cold.

"Spent a fair bit of time at the garrison here as a young-ster. Most of the temple initiates pass through Morlak at one time or another. Must have been thirty years ago, when the Baron was still alive. The garrison master was a right piece of work, I can tell you that. Used to send groups of us up into the mountain passes on patrol with nothing more than our armour and weapons."

Taleck rubbed at the scarred stub of his ear, remember-ing. "It can get cold up there, real cold. If you couldn't find enough wood to get a fire going, you were in trouble. Plenty of wild animals, too, just as starved as you were. Wolves, lynx, and the like. Nasty creatures." He gestured at the high-est peak, its white dome just visible above the low-hanging clouds.

"That's the most treacherous one. Don't know if it has any sort of official name, but us knights call it the Spike. Great view of Morlak keep from the top, if you can get there without freezing your member off."

"No risk of an attack from behind, then?" wondered Jeffson.

"Pit, no. We barely scraped by out there and we're Knights of the Twelve. You'd have to be completely mad to try and send an army through those mountain passes."

"So, unassailable from behind and well-defended from the front. Has Morlak ever been taken?"

"No, never." Taleck glanced back down the road where the wagon and its escort were trundling along to meet them. "Until now, of course."

The knights made camp a few yards from the main road, hidden from prying eyes by a copse of fir trees. The snow from further north had not yet reached the town and environs, and Jeffson was relieved to finally remove his fur cap, replacing it with his wide-brimmed black preacher hat.

"So, where are we going to find this contact of yours?" asked Vohanen as soon as they were settled. His cheeks were flushed an unhealthy shade of red; Jeffson wasn't sure whether it was from the cold or the leather skin of wine that never left the knight's side.

"Hopefully, he's still in the same place I left him, running a tavern on the north-western edge of the lower town. If memory serves, he called it *The Crimson Wing*."

"Interesting name," said Syrella del Morlak from her seat by the fire. "The wing of a bird, I presume? A sparrow, perhaps?"

"I couldn't say, my Lady," said Jeffson, his expression carefully blank. "In any case, he is, I am sure, quite loyal to the Baroness of Morlak."

"Yes, well that's the problem, isn't it? For all intents and purposes, the Baroness of Morlak is holed up somewhere in the keep. Do you think this ... innkeeper will be able to get us inside?"

Images of burning timber and bright red blood came unbidden into Jeffson's mind. He swallowed and pushed the memories away. "He will. He owes me," he said firmly.

"Then there is no time to waste," said Vohanen. "We

should set off immediately. Slip into the town before night-
fall. Once we get the location—"

"Enough," interrupted Taleck. "You will not be going
anywhere, Vohanen."

"What? Why not?"

"Your face is far too well known."

"Nonsense, I—"

"Think, man! Last time you were here, you marched up
to the inner gatehouse and stood there blowing your ram's
horn until the Baroness, or rather her imposter, came to talk
to you herself. We cannot risk the entire rescue attempt on
you being recognised. I know you are angry. As am I. But
this must be done right, or not at all. I will be accompanying
Jeffson while you help Krelbe manage the camp."

Vohanen said nothing, only stared daggers at the older,
grey-haired knight. Taleck held his gaze without flinching
and, after a moment, Vohanen snorted and stalked off, muttering under his breath.

"Right, let's get going, then," said Syrella, standing up
briskly. "There can't be more than a few hours of daylight
left."

"Surely you jest, my Lady?" said Taleck incredulously.
"Did you not hear what I just said? The guards at the gate are
lazy, not stupid. Why, you'd be snatched up as soon as you
got within ten paces of the gatehouse, especially with your
… particular, um, facial, um—"

"By the Twelve, Taleck, I know my eyes aren't the same
colour. No need to tiptoe around the subject like a Da'arran
pole-dancer."

"I don't quite know—"

"What a Da'arran pole-dancer is? I suspect you do,

Taleck, especially if you spent time with my father. But let's leave that story for another time, shall we? You are quite right, of course, I stand corrected. I would be recognised instantly. I will stay here, suitably chastised." She gave a mock half-curtsy and retreated to her wagon, pulling the tarpaulin closed behind her.

Taleck stared after her with a puzzled expression on his face. "She doesn't act much like a Baroness, does she?" he said to Jeffson.

The manservant shrugged. "Not really, but that's not necessarily a bad thing. Shall we head out, Sir Knight? The horses should stay here, the alleys near *The Crimson Wing* will be too narrow for them. I would suggest leaving your shield behind too; a cloak will hide your armour, but no one is going to mistake that great big rectangular piece of wood for anything other than what it is."

Taleck reluctantly shrugged the embossed tower shield from his back and set it down near the fire. "Krelbe!" he shouted, spying the man unloading one of the packhorses near the rear of the camp. "I'm leaving this with you. If there is so much as a scratch on it when I get back, I'll rip those rings from your eyebrows!"

The dour-faced knight made an obscene gesture in reply and returned to the horses.

Jeffson slipped his knuckle knives into one of his many hidden pockets. The two men left the campsite and walked unhurriedly down the last mile or so of road to the town entrance. A queue of people had formed outside the main gate, waiting patiently as a red-faced farmhand wrestled with an uncompromising ox blocking the entire width of the gatehouse. One of the purple-uniformed town guard had left his post and was trying to lead the beast forwards with a handful of hay but to no avail.

"Pit!" swore Taleck. He tapped the woman in front of him and she swung round, her long straggly hair framing a slightly crooked nose dotted with large red spots.

"What?" she spat, revealing a row of tobacco-stained teeth.

Taleck recoiled slightly. "Pardon me for bothering you, um, Madam. I was wondering how long this ... spectacle has been going on for?"

"Dunno. 'Alf-hour. Hour maybe. What's it to you?"

"Well, we have business inside."

"Don't we all, pretty boy. Now shuddup and wait, like the rest of us."

Taleck shook his head ruefully and returned to Jeffson. It took the irate farmer another ten minutes to move the stubborn animal and for them to be finally allowed into the lower town, waved through by the tired guardsman. On the other side of the gatehouse, they stopped to get their bearings. They were in a dirt square, bordered by near-identical plain stone buildings. Numerous side-streets led out of the square in all directions.

"We need to head westwards, I think, my Lord," said Jeffson. "Then cut north. We still have plenty of time."

"'Ow 'bout a little company, boys?" cackled the crooked-nosed woman from a few feet away. "I can show you all the best whorehouses for a couple of copper Barons, what d'ya' say?"

Jeffson looked at her sternly. "Thank you, but no, Lady Baroness, I do not think that will be necessary. Although now that you have proved yourself to Taleck, I am sure he will not object to you coming with us to the tavern."

Taleck's eyes widened in shock, realisation dawning across his wrinkled features. His jaw dropped open with a small popping sound. "By the Pit! My Lady! But your nose! Your hair!"

"No need to shout it to the rooftops, Sir Knight," Syrella replied smugly, tapping her spotty nose with one dirty hand. "Makeup and a bit of rubber. Been perfecting it for years. Very useful when I need to go somewhere unnoticed."

"But your eyes ..."

"Yes, I can't change them, only draw attention away from them. You didn't even look at the eyes, did you? Too busy gawking at my nose and teeth."

"It is very well done, my Lady," Jeffson said. "I'm not sure I would have seen through it so quickly if I did not have some experience in the matter."

"Why, thank you, Jeffson," Syrella replied with a smile. She pointed at one of the side-streets "Onwards?"

"To *The Crimson Wing*," agreed Jeffson. A flash of movement caught his eye and he turned with a frown, his eyes searching. Nothing. Maybe he had imagined it. *More unwanted memories,* he thought, increasing his pace to catch up with the others.

As his footsteps faded away, a cloaked figure detached itself from the shadows on the far side of the square. It had been observing the gatehouse for days, scrutinising all those entering and leaving Morlak, and it seemed like its patience was finally paying off.

"A knight, an Arelian, and a Baroness," it said in a deep, gravelly voice. "A mystery worth following."

And drawing its hood up around its face, it set off in pursuit.

CHAPTER 6

BROTHER AND SISTER

"There is no need for further payment, Listus. I am already a rich man. In any case, I am not doing this for the money. I am doing it so that one day in the future the bloodline of del Conte will rule Arelium. My progeny will never know it. The people will never know it. But I will. And that is all I have ever wanted."

LORÉ DEL CONTE, VASSAL TO THE BARON OF ARELIUM, 405 AT

꧅

A TARNISHED AXE. *A wounded stag. A splintered helm.* Jelaïa moaned in her sleep, tossing and turning. *A crushed sparrow. A bloody hand. A rusty chain.*

She spasmed, arching her back as the final vision exploded into her mind like a roaring furnace.

Burning tears. Burning tears. BURNING TEARS.

"NO!" she screamed, sitting bolt upright. Her nightdress

was soaked with sweat, her chestnut hair damp and clammy. The vision was already fading, the images becoming transparent and monochromatic before disappearing altogether.

She hauled her tired body over to the nightstand and poured herself a large cup of water to wet her parched mouth. Hirkuin had brought word late last night of Praxis's arrest — something she was still trying to wrap her head around — and now, on top of that, the Twelve were sending her more visions? Perfect. Just perfect.

"Everything all right, M'Lady?" came a muffled voice from the other side of the bedroom door. One of the many Arelians who had volunteered to guard her quarters. What was his name? Pogdon?

"Yes, Pogdon, everything's fine, thank you."

"It's Prigdon, M'Lady."

Pit!

"Of course, Prigdon. Sorry. Just a bad dream."

"Yes, M'Lady. Shall I send for the handmaiden?"

"Um. I suppose so." Jelaïa never thought she'd regret not having Mava around, but the servant Derello had assigned to her was doing a marvellous job at being even more insufferable than the big-boned matron who had been serving her since she was old enough to walk.

She set down her half-finished cup of water and drifted over to the window, pushing open the shutters to let in the morning sunshine. The guest house that Lady Arkile had found for her was perfectly situated, its small balcony offering a panoramic view of the Kessrin docks, the Bay of Doves, and the Sea of Sorrow beyond.

The fishermen of Kessrin had been awake and working for hours, and Jelaïa could just make out a small fleet of boats on the horizon: distant black smudges circling the most profitable spots, with flocks of gulls hovering overhead. Closer to shore, oyster farmers with their comical thigh-high waders checked and emptied wire baskets filled with shellfish, loading mature oysters into backpacks or flat-bottomed dinghies.

Jelaïa inhaled a healthy lungful of maritime air, relishing the tangy taste of salt on her lips. With the defeat of Mina and her krakens, the merchants and traders had returned, setting their crews to work rebuilding the broken wharves and boardwalks so that they could once again ply their wares. The ebb and flow of human traffic reminded her of her arrival in Kessrin with Aldarin, what seemed like a lifetime ago. She had knocked over a barrel of fish and had had to deal with an irate captain. Or rather, Aldarin had dealt with him.

Her gaze fell on the ships moving in and out of the Bay. A trio of caravels flying Derello's colours. An enormous barge, weighed down with what looked like stone slabs from the quarries in Morlak. And a smaller skiff with a blue lateen sail. The skiff swung to port, slowing as it approached the docks. There was a motif stitched into the sail, an axe over a silver tower. The boat came to a halt, and a figure leapt over the prow to tie off the mooring line. Jelaïa caught a flash of burnished argent and her heart skipped a beat as she recognised the pronged helm. Aldarin!

Once the line was secured, Aldarin turned to help a second figure ashore, her fiery-red hair tinged with grey. Praedora, Jelaïa's aunt. The last of the travellers needed no such assistance. He stepped confidently onto the dock, his movement rocking the skiff. He towered over the others, close to ten feet of metal and muscle, his dark-skinned, hair-less scalp gleaming. A colossal battle-axe, the double blades curved like the wings of a butterfly, protruded over his shoulder. Power radiated from him in waves, his commanding presence drawing the attention of all present. Brachyura, Fourth of the Twelve, a giant among men. A demi-god.

Jelaïa had learnt that this near-indestructible being had been badly wounded during the battle of the Bay of Doves by Mina herself. Looking at him now, she found it hard to believe such a thing had happened. Brachyura was striding up the boardwalk towards one of the main gates, exuding strength with every step. Aldarin followed more slowly, guiding the First Priestess.

Jelaïa stood watching them for a moment, idly chewing on a stray strand of hair that had surreptitiously found its way into her mouth. Then, realisation hit her through her sleep-addled brain. Aldarin was here! Well, Brachyura and Praedora too, but *Aldarin* was here! Already! She became aware of her sweat-stained nightdress and unruly hair.

"Prigdon!" she yelled, louder than she had intended. "Please tell the handmaiden to hurry!" Such auspicious guests deserved to see the Baroness of Arelium at her very best.

⚓

Two hours later, Jelaïa paused for a moment in front of the meeting hall doors, trying to calm her frazzled nerves. She was breathing fast, and the suffocating corset that she was wearing was not the only culprit. *They're just friends,* she thought to herself, adjusting her axe-shaped amulet for the hundredth time. *I'm just meeting up with some old friends I haven't seen in a while. No need to be nervous.*

She took one last deep, calming breath and pushed open the doors.

"Baroness Lady Jelaïa del Arelium," a strident voice rang out. "Lady of the White Wolf."

The soft background burble of conversation stopped abruptly as heads swivelled round to see her. Derello, Arkile, Gaelin, and Kayal were standing over a map of Talth with Hirkuin and Orkam nearby. Brachyura, unarmoured, his back to the others, was looking out over the Bay of Doves. And finally, Praedora was sitting in one of the chairs, with Aldarin hovering protectively over her, one hand on her shoulder. The olive-skinned knight was staring at Jelaïa in amazement, his pugilist jaw hanging open.

Well, I guess all that preparation was worth it.

Jelaïa had picked out a low-cut crimson-red dress trimmed with white, the colours of Arelium. Her hair had been washed and perfumed, then swirled into a raised chignon that left her neck and shoulders bare. Five diamond-studded hairpins held the chignon in place, complementing two oval-shaped jewelled earrings.

A smattering of powder had been used to soften her features, a hint of mauve mascara to brighten her eyes, a touch of red lipstick to bring out the fullness of her lips. Hours of work, vindicated by the look on Aldarin's face.

He approached her now, still wearing his silver plate. "Jelaï … I mean my Lady … Lady Baroness," he said, flustered. "Allow me to be the first to compliment you on—"

He stopped, half-caught between a kneel and a bow. Jelaïa had brought her hand to her mouth to hide her smile.

"My Lady, is everything—"

She skipped forwards and threw her arms around his neck, kissing the startled knight on the cheek. "Aldarin! I've missed you! Don't you dare go back to calling me 'My Lady' again. I had just about managed to relieve you of that bad habit before you left!"

Aldarin shook his head ruefully, visibly relieved. "I have missed you too, my Lady. *Jelaïa*. It brings me great joy to see you again. Great joy."

"I should hope so," she replied teasingly, wiping a smudge of lipstick from his cheek.

"I would love to come and greet you too," called Praedora from across the room. "But I seem to have lost my chaperone."

"Allow me, my Lady," said Hirkuin, offering his arm. The First Priestess consented to be guided over to Jelaïa. Her questing hands found the Baroness's face, her fingers tracing the lines of her eyes and nose.

"There you are," Praedora said, half to herself. The hands descended lower and brushed the silver necklace. "You clean up nicely, it seems. I cannot see for myself, but I'm sure Aldarin will describe you to me in great detail later on."

The knight's face turned as red as Jelaïa's dress. "Now, I—"

"Quiet, Aldarin. I'm talking. Show some respect for your elders. So, Jelaïa, you have gained two titles in under a month? Priestess and Baroness? That's quite an accomplishment."

"I suppose so … though neither has been officially rati-fied yet."

"Pfff, details. You have mastered the fires of Brachyura.

You are a priestess. We shall have the official ceremony when you next come to see us. It will give you an excuse to visit."

"I'd like that."

"Me too. Seeing you, I mean. The ceremony is incredibly long and boring. Now, let's finish here so that you can take me to lunch."

"I ... I have been having more visions, Praedora."

The priestess studied her with her creamy-white eyes. "You have? Strange. Neither I nor my fellow priestesses have been afflicted since the battle of the Bay of Doves. Interesting. What did you see?"

"I—"

"Lord Loré del Conte," the servant next to the door bellowed. "Xandris, Ambassador to Kessrin. Lady Kumbha, Eleventh of the Twelve."

"WHAT?" thundered Brachyura, wheeling round.

A golden-haired woman stepped into the room, tall and slim, dressed in a simple white dress and sandals. Her hair seemed to flow and reshape itself around her face despite there being little breeze. Pitch-black obsidian eyes alighted on Brachyura and she smiled, a radiant smile of pure joy that sent ripples of warmth and vibrancy throughout all those present.

"Brother," she murmured happily, her melodious voice ringing like the peal of wedding bells.

"Sister," Brachyura replied.

"Is it true what I hear? You have renounced the Pact?"

"I have, Sister. It took some very brave men and women to make me see the error of my ways, but this time I decided to listen."

"Nevertheless," came an intrusive voice. "You doomed humanity by your selfish choice."

Kumbha had such a magnetic presence that Jelaïa had almost ignored the other two figures behind her. Xandris looked much better than when she had seen him last, his ample cheeks glowing, his goatee carefully combed. Next to him stood the man who had spoken, his hair shorn down to a fine layer of stubble, his handsome face contorted in anger.

Loré! Her ... father ... But that couldn't be right. She had left him a faceless abomination, one eye ripped from its socket by a greyling claw, his leg shattered, his cheek mauled, his throat ravaged. It was a miracle he had survived. No one could recover from such horrendous wounds. How was this possible?

"My Lord ..." said Orkam, his habitually gruff voice tinged with wonder. "You ... you are healed! A miracle!"

Loré's anger vanished as quickly as it had appeared. He smiled broadly at Orkam, revealing two rows of perfect white teeth. "You are right, it *is* a miracle. A miracle carried out by a goddess made flesh." He gazed upon Kumbha with rapt adoration. "I have been made whole again. Whole in body and spirit. And that is not all. The infirmary has been emptied. Close to fifty injured men healed in ten days! I cannot explain it, Orkam. Tissue reforming over flesh! Broken bones made as new! There is no end to what she can do. Pure, unconstrained power! The greylings do not stand a chance against us now!"

Kumbha smiled down at him benevolently and touched him lightly on the arm. "I admire your fervour, my Lord, but your zeal lacks pragmatism. I have tried to explain this many times already. Nothing is limitless and certainly not the use of my gift. I am governed by the same laws as any who have such skills." She shot a glance at Praedora. "Everything has a cost. Each time I draw upon my gift, it takes something in return. It drains me. It saps my strength. And the greater the injury, the greater the cost."

"Nevertheless," continued Loré, unperturbed. "Arelium has never been stronger. We now have a sizeable reserve of men manning the walls and, thanks to the valiant efforts of the Knights of Brachyura, the gatehouse is nearly rebuilt. Once we bolster our defences with the Arelians still here in Kessrin, we will be well-equipped to deal with any further incursions from the south. Especially with Kumbha by our side."

"But ... what about Talth?" asked Kayal in a small voice.

Loré glanced at him in annoyance. "Who let this child in here? We are to discuss serious matters pertaining—"

"This child is Baron Kayal del Talth," interrupted Sir Gaelin forcibly, his hand on the pommel of his sword. "I would have you speak to him with respect."

"Baron? What happened to Davarel? Or his son, for that matter?"

"Talth has fallen," intoned Brachyura. "The greylings have laid waste to the Barony and its capital. The Knights of Guanna have been decimated. The northern forests burn."

"I ... I see," said Loré. He rubbed at his cheek, his fingers probing the skin as if remembering an old wound. "I am sorry. All the more reason to consolidate our defences in Kessrin and Arelium. I am sure we can grant you asylum, Lord Kayal. Our best chance now is to batten down the hatches and weather the storm."

"That is not for you to decide," said Jelaïa, more sharply

than she intended. "Unless, perhaps, things have changed and you do not wish me to take my place as Baroness?"

"No ... no, my Lady," Loré replied, inclining his head. "I have always wanted what's best for Arelium."

Liar! A voice screamed in Jelaïa's head. She wanted to run over to him and slap that perfect smile he was wearing right off his face. Later. Once things were finished here, she and her father were going to have a very long talk.

"That is good to hear, Sir Loré," she said. "Let us take our seats."

All were soon seated, save for Brachyura, his muscular bulk being too big for the chairs.

"So. Here is what we know," said Derello, his finger stabbing down at the map as he talked. "The attack from the Southern Pit was stopped at Arelium. Talth is overrun. Kessrin has survived Mina. But what of the other Baronies? Morlak? Da'arra? Talth? Klief? I have sent messengers north and east. None has returned. I fear we will need to decide our next course of action without them. In my opinion, there are but two possibilities: attack or defend. We know where the brunt of the enemy will appear; it is more a question of whether to take the fight to them or not."

Brachyura let out a long sigh. "Your actions are inconsequential, Baron. We have broken the Pact. The enemy know this now, I am sure. They will not let us prevail. If, by some chance, we manage to defeat the greyling hordes vomited forth from the Pits, they will obliterate us. Remember, Kumbha. Remember what we saw."

"I remember," the giantess replied. "And even then, I voted to fight against it. Why, Makara told us—"

"Enough riddles," said Jelaïa. "You talk of wanton

destruction, of desolation and ruin, but nothing tangible. Tell us what happened down there. Tell us what we face. Only then can we truly begin to fight back."

Brachyura fixed her with his black eyes. Searching, probing. Finally, he gave an almost imperceptible nod.

"Very well. I will tell you of the day we entered the Pit." He looked past Jelaïa, staring at nothing, willing the memory to return.

"I will tell you of the day we met our doom."

CHAPTER 7

SURVIVAL OF
THE FITTEST

*"My children. My poor children. What have they done to you?
Ostracised. Punished. Forced to flee the temple I helped build.
All because you stayed loyal to your patron and continued to
honour the Pact. I see you now, your armour broken and your
homes destroyed. I see you now and I weep. Let me help you rise
from the gutter and take back what once was yours."*

MITHUNA, THIRD OF THE TWELVE, 426 AT

❧

"WE'RE BEING FOLLOWED," said Jeffson calmly,
as they turned the corner into another dark
alley. "Two men, maybe three. Armoured."

"By the Pit!" swore Taleck. "How did they find us?"

"I'm not sure they were looking for us per se, Sir Knight.
We are entering one of the more unsavoury parts of Morlak.

I fear we may simply be in the wrong place at the wrong time."

"And where is everyone?" asked Syrella. Jeffson was impressed to see that the Baroness applied her disguise to her whole demeanour; her shoulders hunched slightly to make her seem smaller, her left foot dragging behind her to give her a partial limp.

"Locked up inside their homes, my Lady," he said. "Or somewhere else far, far from here. Remember what Vohanen told us. Without the town guard or the Knights of Kriari to patrol the streets, crime is on the rise. A lot of these places look abandoned." He inclined his head towards one of the shops, its door and windows boarded up. Someone had pried one of the planks away from the smallest window to try and get inside. A faded wooden sign hanging overhead indicated it had once been a bakery.

"Despicable," said Syrella. "This will be my first act once I am returned to power. We will make the streets of Morlak safe again. Everyone should be able to feel secure in their own home."

Jeffson only nodded, his acute hearing picking up a muffled jingle of metal somewhere ahead of him. "I think we may be surrounded, my Lady. If you would be so good as to stay between Taleck and me?" He slipped his knuckle knives onto his hands and flexed them experimentally. Taleck drew his short sword, his face grim.

"You may make yourselves known, gentlemen!" Jeffson shouted into the darkness.

"Fine," came a voice from the shadows. "But you really are no fun at all." A lanky figure in full plate stepped out into the alley a few paces ahead of them. A thick layer of grime and rust covered the interlocking sheets of metal, while the left vambrace and gauntlet were missing entirely. A pasty, thin-lipped face sneered at them in disdain.

"An old man, a priest, and a whore," he said, shaking his head in disappointment. "I had hoped for better playthings." He made a circular motion with his right hand and two more Knights of Mithuna appeared behind Jeffson, cutting off all hope of retreat.

"You appear to be out after curfew," the knight continued with mock regret. "Tut-tut-tut. That is not good. Not good at all. Lady Syrella del Morlak herself expressly forbade any sort of travel through the lower town after sunset. And the penalty for disobeying the Baroness is imprisonment or death." One of the other knights gave a short bark of laughter that made him sound like a bad-tempered dog.

"Apologies, M'Lord," said Syrella in a frail, worried voice. She attempted an awkward curtsy, grasping the hem of her threadbare peasant skirt and bobbing her head. "We've just arrived today, you see. Me an' me da are takin' this priest to see me mam; caught herself a cold, poor thing."

"The guards at the gate have orders to inform all who pass through of the curfew," the knight said, one hand dropping casually to the longsword at his side.

"Ain't nobbudy told us, M'Lord."

"That is … unfortunate. They will have to be punished. Of course, we could let you go—" he sighed theatrically "—but where's the pleasure in that?"

"How about we make them run, Frexin? Give them a few minutes head start?" mused another of the knights. He was as tall and pallid as the others, blue veins visible under marble skin.

Frexin pretended to think for a moment. "I think not. We tried that a couple of nights ago with that family and one of the children nearly got away. The Baroness would not have been pleased. No, I think we will kill them now and dump the bodies somewhere. Besides, this is a dangerous neighbourhood, especially after dark."

He smiled a predatory smile and drew his blade.

Taleck was quivering with rage. "You are Knights of the Twelve," he growled between clenched teeth. "What are you doing? Since when did slaughtering innocent travellers become part of your creed?"

Frexin's smile fell from his face, two dark spots colouring his cheeks. "*Innocent?* Do not talk to me of innocence, old man. My fellow knights and I have lived for years in squalor, begging for scraps of food, poor, shunned, and homeless. Only the strongest survived. Those who followed our 'creed' were the first to die; those who refused to steal and kill, who refused to put their own needs before those of others."

He sniffed and spat onto the cobblestones. "We few who remain now follow a different creed. We call it survival of the fittest. And our actions have been vindicated, as Mithuna herself has absolved us of all crimes."

"Delusional," said Taleck. "How can Mithuna absolve you of anything? She has been missing for three hundred years."

"How do you know that …" Realisation dawned. "Of course. The bewildered expression, the stench of ale on your breath, the short sword held clumsily like you have no idea what to do with it: a Knight of Kriari. I should have seen it sooner." The smile returned, stretching his thin lips into a taut line. "That is where you are wrong, *Brother*. She has returned."

Frexin leapt forwards, his longsword flicking out like a serpent's tongue. Taleck parried hastily with a clang of metal and a flash of sparks. Jeffson tore his eyes away from the clashing blades and sized up the two knights blocking the alleyway behind him.

They have made no move to attack me, he thought. *They must not perceive me as a threat.* He swept his gaze over the two armoured forms, looking for a sign of weakness. Plate armour was such cumbersome protection. It reduced speed and agility and had far too many weak points; between the joints, under the armpits, and … behind the knees.

He dived at the two knights, rolling smoothly between them and lashing out with the sharp blades of his knuckle knives as he passed. The aim of his left arm was slightly off, the weapon skittering uselessly off the knight's greave. His other opponent was not so lucky. Jeffson cut through the thin layer of leather behind the knee and deep into the flesh beyond. With a surprised yell, the knight crashed to the ground. Quick as a flash, the balding manservant whipped round and hammered his knuckle knives into the fallen knight's face, the spiked tips punching through his skull into his brain.

Jeffson came to his feet to see the other knight staring at him, wide-eyed. "You … you are no priest!" the man stuttered. Jeffson backed away slowly, bloodied knives raised. He had lost the element of surprise, and things were about to become a lot more complicated.

He spared a quick glance at Taleck. The old veteran had

been pushed back against the wall of the bakery, blood trickling from a shallow cut on his cheek. Frexin was attacking relentlessly, his sword arm moving in a series of thrusts and flourishes that left no opening, especially for the reduced reach of Taleck's short sword.

I need to finish things quickly, he thought, and launched himself at his opponent, hoping to take him off guard again. But this time the enemy was ready for him. The knight turned, taking the blow on the shoulder, and brought his armoured knee up hard into Jeffson's stomach. Jeffson let out a *whoosh* as the air exploded from his body, and he tried to stagger away, but the knight was faster, his hand wrapping around Jeffson's wrist and pulling him into a crushing embrace.

The knight's hands locked behind Jeffson's back and he found himself trapped against the rusty breastplate with his cheek pressed painfully into the other man's chest. Jeffson struggled to free himself, but it was like trying to bend an iron bar. The knight said nothing, just started to squeeze, pushing the remaining air from Jeffson's lungs. He coughed, fighting to draw breath. Black dots appeared on the edge of his vision as the knight looked down on him impassively.

Then suddenly, without warning, he was released.

He sank to the ground, wheezing and filling his aching lungs with air. Something wet and sticky dripped onto his back. Looking up, he saw that the Knight of Mithuna had his hands pressed against a ragged wound in his neck, bright blood welling through his fingertips, his mouth opening and closing soundlessly like a fish.

"Why ..." the knight started to say, then he toppled forwards onto the cobblestones. Behind him stood a squat, broad-shouldered figure, its features hidden in the shadows of its hooded riding cloak. One gloved hand held an enormous double-bladed axe, the tip covered in blood. The word 'Brachyura' was inscribed in angular script on the haft.

Jeffson looked at the weapon, confused. "Aldarin?" he said tentatively.

"Pit, man, I did not save your life to be mistaken for that arrogant scrier," grumbled the figure, pushing back the hood of its cloak. Hard, grey eyes the colour of storm clouds stared out from a noble face, marred only by a badly-broken nose.

"Sir Caddox, Knight of the Twelve. At your service. Apologies if I do not help you up, I only have the use of one hand at the moment. Broke some bones after an unfortunate … misunderstanding."

"What—" Jeffson began, but Caddox cut him off. "It can wait." He pushed past the kneeling manservant, striding confidently towards the far side of the alley where Taleck was still pressed against the wall, holding back Frexin with wide, sweeping cuts. Blood ran in rivulets down his left arm.

"Three Orders of the Twelve reunited," boomed Caddox, causing Frexin to wheel round in surprise. "A momentous occasion."

"What? Who in the Pit are you? Stay out of this, it does not concern you."

"Caddox, Knight of Brachyura. And I'm afraid it does concern me. I took an oath, many years ago, to defend those in need. Attacking an old man seems to qualify, methinks? Leave the Knight of Kriari alone and come test your mettle against a more worthy opponent."

Frexin smiled his predatory smile and wiped the sweat from his brow. "I do not know you, Knight of Brachyura, but you are meddling in things you do not understand. I would suggest you leave here now, before—"

He shrieked as Syrella, forgotten and ignored, ran out of the shadows and rammed a long dagger into his unarmoured left side. Taleck gave him no time to recover, batting aside Frexin's longsword and plunging his own weapon through the fallen knight's eye. Frexin spasmed as the short sword entered his brain, then crashed to the ground with a clanking of rusty metal.

"That was ... not honourable," remonstrated Caddox, sheathing his battle-axe under his riding cloak.

Taleck tested his injured left arm gingerly and winced in pain. "Agreed, Sir Caddox, but I fear honour is a rare commodity now that the greylings have resurfaced."

"Aye, and it is not just the greylings. Brachyura also walks these lands once again. I have experienced his power first hand; the ancient legends are no exaggeration. Strong as an ox and fast as a hare. Has Kriari shown signs of life?"

"No, nothing yet. Although, if this man Frexin is to be believed, Mithuna has returned."

"Hmm, unfortunate," Caddox replied, running his hand through his short blond hair. "The Knights of Mithuna are among the fallen. The odds are not in our favour."

"Why are you here?" interjected Jeffson brusquely. He had retrieved his wide-brimmed hat and stood staring stoically at the Knight of Brachyura, arms crossed.

"Jeffson ..." cautioned Taleck.

"No, he is right," Caddox said. "My presence in Morlak is no secret. I was sent here by the Conclave of Brachyura. The First Priestess, Praedora, had a vision. Something to do with the Morlakian Pit. I have been trying to enter the inner city for days to discuss the matter with the Baroness, but the gates remain shut."

Jeffson looked at the knight with renewed interest. "The Pit? It is no more. We destroyed the dam at Terris Lake. The whole ravine is flooded, nothing remains."

"Indeed? That is auspicious news! Then it appears that my work here is done. I can return to Kessrin and tell Praedora that Morlak is safe."

"You could do such a thing, but it would be a lie," Syrella said softly, her right arm covered in blood, her long black hair in tatters around her face. "For you see, Sir Knight, the Order of Mithuna has stolen the Barony from me, and we are fighting to take it back."

"My ... my Lady," stammered Caddox, sinking to one knee. "My apologies. I did not recognise you."

"Yes, well, that was rather the point. Rise, Sir Knight. We are all among equals here. Sir Taleck and Jeffson came to assist me, and we have more knights outside the city awaiting our command."

"I see. Then I was not sent here for nothing. Maybe we were wrong, maybe the priestess's vision was not of the Pit but of Morlak itself! In any case, I cannot stand idly by while the Barony is in peril. To leave you now would be an act of unjustified cowardice. I am not quite the fighter I was, but you have my support. Morlak must not be left in the hands of Mithuna."

Jeffson did not appear swayed by the Knight of Brachyura's elegant speech. "And why, exactly, should you be trusted, Sir Knight? Lady Syrella has been betrayed twice over the last month; once on the road to Fallow's End, and a second time on our trip north to Dirkvale. Taleck is right.

Honour is a rare commodity. And trust even rarer. Where is your armour? Where are your other knights? Why, you could have taken that axe from a dead initiate, or maybe even killed one yourself."

Caddox stiffened at hearing this, lightning flashing in his storm-cloud eyes. "I do not wear my armour, *friend*, as I cannot." He threw back his cloak. His left hand was bound tightly to his chest with leather straps, the fingers covered in bandages. "Brachyura crushed my hand nearly a month ago and I have yet to regain full use of my fingers. Maybe you can buckle on a full suit of plate armour with one hand, but I cannot. As to my identity, notwithstanding the fact that I have just saved your life, I will also swear by the Twelve that I am who I say I am." His voice became low and dangerous. "And if that is not enough, maybe a trial by combat would be the best way to resolve things."

Jeffson remained expressionless. "I do not think that will be necessary, Sir Knight. For if you are a Knight of Brachyura, then you must have met both Sir Aldarin and Sir Manfeld many times. I was present at the siege of Arelium, so I too know them well. Describe them to me, if you would?"

"The scrier? Tall, olive-skinned, broken nose. Thinks he knows what is best for everyone, paints himself as an orphaned pariah. And Manfeld is the elder of our Order, a bald, scarred man in his sixties with a white moustache. A bit archaic, but a capable commander. Is that sufficient?"

"I think so. Lady Syrella, I believe the choice should be yours. What is your decision?"

The Baroness was scraping Frexin's blood from her arm with her nails. "I think, Jeffson, that you are wise to be careful. However, we will not get far in our battle against the greylings if we stand divided. Why, if memory serves, it was that very error that nearly led mankind to destruction four hundred years ago. Sir Caddox, we would be honoured to have you join us."

The burly knight nodded. "Then I would suggest we move on; it would be a pity for another patrol to come down here and find us talking over the bodies of three dead Knights of Mithuna."

"Follow me," said Jeffson, brushing past the knight and taking a right down another poorly-lit alleyway. After a few more minutes navigating the winding warren of cobbled streets, they reached *The Crimson Wing*, a sizeable one-storey building on the edge of a cramped square. Candlelight filtered softly through two glazed windows, and the image of a red sparrow swung on a painted sign hanging overhead.

Jeffson pushed open the door without a word and entered the tavern. It was empty save for a paunchy, dark-skinned Da'arran standing behind the bar, wiping an empty ale mug. He was dressed in flowing pantaloons, his shaved pate gleaming with sweat. A gold earring hung from his right ear, and a gold band pierced his nose. A fine chain linked the two, running across his right cheek.

He caught sight of Jeffson and let out a yelp of surprise, his eyes bulging out of their sockets. The mug he was polishing slipped from his fingers and hit the ground hard, shattering into a thousand fragments.

"Y … you," he stammered. "I thought you were dead. Have you come here to kill me?"

Jeffson smiled thinly. "Lady Syrella, Sir Knights, may I present to you Ner'alla. Owner of *The Crimson Wing*, and the man who murdered my wife and child."

CHAPTER 8

PEACE

"I think perhaps our own lack of fear contributed to our downfall. For a hundred years, we fought battle after battle and nothing could defeat us. We were wounded, of course; a lucky arrow or a chance blow, but all except the most grievous of injuries healed within days. And Kumbha could always be called upon if the circumstances were particularly dire. We put far too much credence in our own immortality."

BRACHYURA, FOURTH OF THE TWELVE, 426 AT

&

BRACHYURA CHECKED THE straps on his armour for the third time as he waited for the last of his brothers and sisters to arrive. He was perched on a boulder far above the Morlakian Pit; the gaping, oppressive maw a black scar on the floor of the ravine below. It was a sweltering summer's day, and sweat trickled down from his hairless scalp onto his ornate gorget and breastplate.

"It's always the same people who are late," complained Mithuna from her spot on another rock a few feet away. She huffed irritably as a strand of her grey hair fell in front of her face. She concentrated for a moment and slowly her hair began to recede, from shoulder-length, to square-cut, to stubble. "Damn heat."

"There must be heat for there to be cold," Zygos replied, arching a stern eyebrow. "Spring and Summer must follow Winter, the seasons must remain in balance, otherwise crops would die, rivers would run dry, trees would—"

"I wasn't talking about the changing of the seasons, Brother. You always take things so literally."

Zygos sniffed and returned to the book he was reading, his eyes darting across the pages at inhuman speed. Further down the ridge, Kriari, Simha, and Guanna appeared to be wrestling or partaking in some other ludicrous contest of strength. They looked so alike that they could be triplets: same long manes of hair, handsome faces, and impressive physique. Big-boned Shala watched them from the shadow of a pine tree, shouting words of encouragement to egg them on. She threw a pine cone at Guanna who yelped as it clipped his ear.

Children, Brachyura thought. *We are hundred-year-old demigods, and yet we still act like children.*

"Don't be too hard on them," said Kumbha, sensing his thoughts. "They are just excited. It is a propitious day. One that has been years in the making. Everything we have been working towards, everything we have strived for, culminates with this."

"And yet, certain members of our group still fail to arrive on time," groused Mithuna.

"They'll be here," Brachyura said. "Some have further to travel than the rest of us. Luridae is in Da'arra now, Makara in Klief, Mina somewhere along the western coast, and Dhanusa ... wherever he is."

"There!" said Kumbha, pointing to the opposite ridge. A group of figures was slowly making its way down the steep incline. Sunlight flashed off golden plate.

"Mina and the others. Let's meet them at the bottom."

"Two more minutes," said Zygos, licking his index finger and turning a page. "Let me finish one more chapter. We had to wait for them, it is only fair that they should wait for us."

Makara was living proof that the Twelve were not exempt from old age. He was already well past his prime when Brachyura had first met him and seemed even older now; his bent, wizened frame looking so fragile it was remarkable that he had made it down to the edge of the Pit without toppling over. The half-moon spectacles perched precariously on his hooked nose only added to the impression of a doddering old man.

In fact, nothing was further from the truth. Brachyura was on good terms with his brothers and sisters, but he only really *admired* one of them. Makara embodied the best of each of the Twelve: Dhanusa's tactical expertise, Zygos's ability with numbers, Kumbha's empathy, Brachyura's engineering, Mithuna's resourcefulness, and so on. And

Brachyura had seen the eldest of the Twelve fight during the Battle of the Northern Plains. Makara had barely moved, yet each precise movement of his steel-tipped ebony cane had left one of the enemy dead.

Makara was the glue that held the Twelve together, a role bolstered in part by his extraordinary gift: the ability to locate and speak to his brothers and sisters over great distances, his throaty voice croaking in their ears like the crackling of dry parchment. Since the defeat of the greylings and the dispersal of the Twelve throughout the nine Baronies, all relied on Makara to keep them abreast of current affairs, to relay information from one member of the Twelve to another, or to arrange for them to meet in person. He was their eyes and ears, a treasure trove of knowledge and counsel. The loss of his life or his gift would be disastrous.

"You're late," he said with a wry smile as Brachyura reached the shadow of the wall surrounding the Pit. Behind Makara, a full contingent of the Old Guard stood to attention, spear tips polished to a bright reflective sheen, vermilion cloaks flapping in the breeze. Their officer held his basket sword high in salute, beads of sweat moistening his wafer-thin moustache.

"PRESENT ARMS!" The officer bawled with a well-practised wave of his sword. A hundred spears were thrust forwards.

"Impressive," murmured Mina sarcastically, toying with a ringlet of her hair. "Make them dance next."

"My thanks," Brachyura said to the officer, ignoring his sister. "My thanks for your presence here today, for maintaining my wall, for being our first line of defence against the greylings of the Pit. The men and women of the nine

Baronies sleep safe in their beds, knowing that you stand here, watching the dark."

"You honour us, Lord," the officer replied, his eyes glistening. "All has been made ready for your arrival, and we await your command."

"The honour is mine, guardsman. And yet, I must ask you to leave us now. My brothers, sisters, and I will be descending into the very bowels of the earth. I do not know what we will find there, but it would be best if you and your men were at a safe distance."

"But, my Lord, what if you need our help?"

Booming laughter exploded from Kriari's immense chest. "If *we* need your help, little one? If there is something down there that the twelve of us combined cannot handle, I do not think your one hundred men will make any difference."

"Hush, Brother," said Kumbha reprovingly. "Courage comes in many shapes and forms, and should not be mocked."

"Of course, Sister." Kriari bowed low to the officer. "Please forgive my impertinence, young guardsman."

"Think … think nothing of it," stammered the man, visibly flustered. "We will, of course, vacate the site immediately. Send word to Fallow's End if you need us." He sheathed his sword and signalled to his spearmen to form up behind him.

Mithuna watched them leave. "You should not bow to them, Brother," she said to Kriari. "Nor apologise to them. We are not their equals. We are their leaders."

"That is not—" Brachyura began, but Makara cut him off.

"Enough bickering. We have wasted too much time as it is. You know why we are here. Mithuna, show them."

The Third of the Twelve pulled out a crumpled scroll from a pocket sewn into her padded jacket. Brachyura recognised it immediately. He had seen hundreds of similar scrolls over the last few years. It was all part of a great plan set in motion by Mithuna and Luridae to end a hundred years of attrition. The enemy were no longer to be killed but to be captured. Those who could not speak were given scrolls; the threshers and brood mothers, who had a rudimentary knowledge of the human language, were taught a single word and its meaning: PEACE. And then they were released, free to scamper back to the Pits and hopefully pass the message on to whatever higher power was masterminding the attacks on the nine Baronies.

Mithuna unrolled the scroll and held it up for all to see. The word PEACE was stained with black ichor but, underneath it, two words had been added in a flowing, cursive text: Morlak. Midsummer.

"Astounding!" said Zygos, leaning closer to peer at the parchment. "Look at the writing. The juxtaposition of the letters. The elegance. I would surmise the hand that held the quill belonged to a being of considerable intellect."

"It could, of course, be a trap," said Guanna, adjusting the round buckler strapped to his forearm. "The perfect occasion to eliminate all of us in one fell swoop."

"Yes, I had considered that possibility," pondered Makara, "and you may well be right. But are you not all tired of this incessant fighting? For every underground cave we clear, another is found. Villages situated near forests that have been scoured clean a dozen times are reporting new sightings. I sometimes feel that for every greyling we kill, two more appear to take its place …. It is exhausting. Never-ending. If there is a chance for peace, no matter how slim, should we not take it?"

"We should," Brachyura replied. "And we will. We all agreed to come here. There is no turning back now. Mina, did you bring the rope?"

"Yes, Brother. The same as I have been using for my new weapons project. It's been substantially reinforced. If each of my brothers and sisters uses their own individual rope, it should hold their weight."

"What do you mean *should?*"

"Well, I haven't been able to test them, but they can take the strain of a wound ballista, so there is no reason for them not to. And I suppose that if your rope snaps and you plummet to your death, then you won't be around to berate me, will you?"

"Fair enough. It'll have to do. We'll descend in pairs to minimise risk. Mithuna and her knights have scouted all of the Pits many times; there will be openings leading into the network of tunnels. We just have to find one. Ready?"

Eleven heads nodded in near-perfect harmony.

"Very well. Then let us go once more into the dark."

They were expected. A pinprick of light in the depths of the Pit took shape as they got closer: torchlight seeping from the mouth of one of the tunnels. A brawny thresher stood watch, almost as tall as Brachyura himself, one giant hand resting on the head of an obsidian hammer, the other holding a guttering torch. "Uuuu-mann," it growled as Brachyura reached the entrance, Kriari at his side.

"Uuuu-mann. Come."

"Wait." The Fourth of the Twelve pointed upwards, where Mithuna and Guanna were beginning to rappel down the side of the Pit.

The thresher scowled and barked a series of short, unintelligible syllables. "Hurr-rry."

Luridae and Mina were the last to descend. The Eighth of the Twelve hardly seemed to need the rope at all, practically floating, his dark-skinned sandalled feet only occasionally brushing against the sides. The tunnel mouth was barely wide enough to contain all of them, forcing them to huddle together. The thresher cocked its head inquisitively.

"My thanks," Brachyura said. "We are at present all accounted for; we can proceed."

"Come." The thing heaved its hammer onto its shoulder and set off down the tunnel at a loping gait.

"Guanna, you're with me. We'll take point. Kriari, Simha, protect the rear. Makara in the centre. Forwards."

They set off in pursuit of the thresher, following five or six feet behind, a slight incline taking them deeper and deeper into the bowels of the Pit. Brachyura unholstered his double-bladed axe and heard the swish of Guanna's sword leaving its scabbard.

Despite all the walls he had built, despite all the greylings he had fought, this was the first time Brachyura had entered one of the Pits. The air down here was stale and smelt faintly of rotten eggs. Sulphur. Not a good sign. His eyes took in the claw marks on the walls and the detritus that littered the rocky floor. The tunnel was most definitely greyling-made. The striations left by the claw marks told him that the greylings had dug upwards, meaning they had come from somewhere below him and tunnelled their way to the surface. But how long ago?

"Shala, how old are these tunnels?" he called back behind him.

"I ... I don't know," the Sixth of the Twelve replied. "I can't connect to the earth. It's like I'm being blocked."

Brachyura felt a knot tighten in his stomach. "Makara? Can you speak to us?"

The elder brother concentrated for a moment, then shook his head.

"So, our gifts do not work down here. That is most unsettling."

Kriari laughed. "Pffft. We do not need petty magic tricks to deal with a bunch of greylings. Strength of arms will suffice."

"Hmmm. Perhaps. Dhanusa, leave one of your arrows every hundred feet or so. If our guide decides to leave us down here, I do not want to be imprisoned without a way out."

The next hour was a long, plodding trek through a series of tunnels, each one more twisting than the last. The smell of sulphur grew so strong that Brachyura could taste it in his mouth. He began to think it could be a trap. Maybe the thresher was leading them into an ambush or was hoping to leave them lost in the dark? Dhanusa's supply of arrows had long since run out, and their only hope now lay with Makara's formidable memory.

"Here," barked the thresher suddenly, his guttural voice magnified ten-fold by the echoes of the tunnel. It had led them to the upper level of a vast underground cavern, so impossibly huge that the far side was lost to the darkness. Scores of stalactites hung down from the natural ceiling like a stone forest, slick with dripping water. And carpeting the floor below them, chittering and shrieking, were thousands of greylings. Threshers carrying torches strode among them like drovers herding cattle, occasionally lashing out with a well-placed foot or barbed whip. The cacophony was deafening.

"What's that?" shouted Kriari over the chaotic din. He was pointing with his short sword to something in the centre of the cavern. Brachyura squinted, willing his eyes to adjust to the dim light. He could make out a group of twelve brood mothers — the obese, slug-like creatures that birthed the lesser greylings — clustered around what appeared to be an archway made up of massive slabs inscribed with whirling runes and symbols.

At first, he thought he could see straight through the arch and into the shadows beyond but quickly realised that wasn't quite right. It was the archway itself that was filled with undulating darkness, ripples emanating from its centre similar to when a stone is dropped into the middle of a lake. Brachyura felt himself inexplicably pulled towards that darkness; a sense of longing and something else, something familiar. He did not need to look at his brothers and sisters to know that they felt it too.

"Well?" insisted Kriari.

"Our destination," Brachyura replied, looking for a way to reach the cavern floor. A short distance away, a narrow path zig-zagged down from their vantage point. "Follow me."

They reached the bottom and adopted the same circular formation that had worked so well during the Battle of the Northern Plains. Brachyura found himself between Kriari and Mina, his brother protecting his left flank with his imposing tower shield while his sister defended his right with her two-handed blade. The chittering of the greylings was even louder here, a wall of sound that pounded incessantly at his aching brain. Wrinkled faces leered at him, spat at him. One of the closer creatures picked something off the ground and threw it at him, splattering his sabatons with foul-smelling faeces.

Yet none of them moved to attack.

"To the archway," he said to the others, raising his voice. They began to move, and the sea of greylings parted to let them pass. As they approached the circle of brood mothers, the dark liquid filling the archway became more agitated; bubbles popping and bursting, the pulsing ripples intensifying. An oval-shaped protuberance formed in its centre, flowing, transforming. Two smaller ovals appeared inside the first.

Brachyura gasped. A face!

The chittering stopped immediately. The cavern was deathly silent save for the steady dripping of the stalactites and the weak, plaintive mewling of the brood mothers. With a strange sucking sound, a grey-skinned figure emerged from the archway, leaving the bubbling blackness behind. It was almost human in shape, close to nine feet tall and clearly female, with disproportionately long twig-like arms and legs that tapered into spidery fingers and clawed toes. Her head was completely hairless, her almond eyes tinged yellow. She was naked but for two thin strips of fabric wrapped around her breasts and groin.

"Hello," she said to Brachyura, favouring him with a smile that revealed a set of triangular teeth. "Thank you for coming." There was a slight lilt to her speech, and she stressed the wrong syllables as if reciting sounds rather than words.

"I am—" he started to reply.

"Brachyura," she said, turning to his companions and naming them each in turn. "Guanna, Kriari, Mithuna, Simha, Dhanusa, Makara, Shala, Mina, Luridae, Zygos, and Kumbha. You are all welcome here."

One of the brood mothers whined and she placed a consoling hand on its cheek, soothing it.

Mithuna coughed loudly. "We have come here at your behest … my Lady," she said. "To discuss terms of peace."

The creature smiled again. "I am no Lady, Third of the Twelve. I am the weaver, the stitcher, the seamstress. I am the one who guides. The one who shapes. The one who leads. I am the mother, the father, the god, and the general. I am nothing, and I am everything."

Mithuna furrowed her brow, unsure of how to respond.

"Now, I will not waste any more of your time," the weaver continued. "I have something to show you." She strode off towards the far end of the cavern, her clawed feet clicking on stone. None of the greylings moved, but thousands of eyes were riveted to her face. Some were weeping openly, others trembling with shock and excitement. Whatever this creature was, she was venerated like a god.

The air grew hot and thin as they approached the rear of the cavern. The Twelve all started to sweat profusely. The stench of sulphur was overwhelming. They could make out the far wall now, split by a jagged fissure from which spilled a dark crimson light. Brachyura wiped his forehead with a gauntleted hand.

The weaver, showing no visible signs of discomfort, reached the cleft in the rock and stepped through to the other side, beckoning the others to follow. Brachyura was forced to turn sideways to shuffle through the crack. What he saw on the other side would remain etched into his brain forever. He dropped his axe, his mind aflame as he tried to comprehend what he was seeing.

He was standing on the edge of a lake of sluggish magma that stretched off into the distance. Fifty feet away, gazing down at him, was a colossal serpent. Only the beast's head and ruby-scaled upper body were visible, but it was without a shadow of a doubt the largest living creature Brachyura had ever seen in his long life. Its diamond-shaped head was well over a hundred feet long, covered with hundreds of inter-locking scales and topped with a pair of spiralling horns wider and taller than a dozen trees combined. Plumes of smoke billowed from slitted nostrils, mixing with the steamy haze of the lake. The thing's eyes were two balls of incandes-cent yellow fire, flickering and burning like miniature suns.

"A wyrm," the weaver said. "We found it resting, deep within the earth. It killed so many of us. Thousands. Hundreds of thousands. Until we learnt how to stop it. How to control it." She clenched her hand into a fist and the wyrm opened its mouth, letting out a roar that shook Brachyura to his very core.

There was nothing that could stand against such a beast.

It could annihilate armies in minutes. Destroy whole cities. There was only one thing he could say.

"Tell us what we must do."

࿓

Brachyura fell silent, his story told. Kumbha stood and went to take his hand. The others looked at each other in shock, trying to understand what they had just heard.

"You are right," Loré uttered sadly. "If what you say is true, then all is lost."

Jelaïa was looking pensively at Kumbha. "That's not the whole story though, is it?" she asked slowly. "What were you saying, my Lady? Before Brachyura cut you off. Something about Makara?"

The golden-haired giantess let go of her brother's hand. "Thank you, Baroness, for asking the right questions. I was going to say that there is something my brother does not know: before Makara left us, he entrusted a secret to me, and to me alone."

A spark of hope flickered in the swirling blackness of her eyes.

"He told me how to win."

CHAPTER 9

A ROLL OF THE DICE

"The uninitiated believe that seduction is the art of giving people what they want. Nothing could be further from the truth. Seduction is a game of psychology, not beauty. You must create the illusion of attraction while keeping yourself well beyond reach. Until they pursue you feverishly. Relentlessly. And lose all control."

VERONASSANDRA, PRIESTESS OF MITHUNA, 424 AT

NER'ALLA REACHED SLOWLY under the bar and brought out a vicious-looking cudgel, its tip studded with nails. "Come now, Nissus, you know that's not true," he said to Jeffson. "If you really thought me guilty of such a heinous crime, I'd already be dead. Why don't we all have a glass or two or Arelian red and discuss things civilly, like gentlemen?"

"It's Jeffson now, not Nissus. I gave that name up long ago. Bring us a *Morlakian* red. And make it a bottle."

Ner'alla bobbed his head nervously and disappeared into one of the adjoining rooms. Jeffson removed his hat and motioned for the others to join him at one of the bar tables.

"All these secrets and hidden names are getting annoying, *Nissus*," said Syrella, ignoring the sound of clinking bottles and muffled curses coming from the other room. "Especially if we are to trust this man you call a murderer."

Jeffson sighed. Something caught his eye on the far side of the bar, half-hidden in the shadows. A human-shaped figure, three or four feet high. A child. He squeezed his eyes shut tight, and when he opened them again, the figure was gone.

"Jeffson?"

"There is not much to tell, my Lady," he said, forcing himself to speak calmly. "I worked for a time here in Morlak, offering my services to those who needed them. I met a woman, Cerra was her name, the most beautiful, caring, generous person in all the nine Baronies. I did not deserve her, and I knew it. So, I decided to change, to better myself, to try and become someone worthy of her."

Ner'alla returned with a dark green bottle and a set of glasses, which he set down wordlessly on the table. Jeffson nodded in thanks and poured himself a generous measure of wine. He swirled the liquid around and around the glass, lost in thought. No one spoke, waiting silently for him to continue.

"I began to refuse contracts. We built a house, not here in the city, but out in the countryside, on the road south to Lostthorn. We had a child together. A daughter."

He drank deeply from the glass of wine.

"But, of course, there were always those who did not believe I could leave my former life behind. People like Ner'alla, who continued to try and rope me into certain … unsavoury practices. Things I no longer wished to do. I refused them all. One of the contractors was displeased with my answer. He voiced his displeasure by burning my house down … with my wife and child locked inside."

He knew what was coming now and tried to steel himself against it, but it was no use. Memories hit him like a tidal wave. The room swam out of focus, replaced by a wall of bright yellow flames. A wooden cabin consumed by fire, a blazing inferno that lit up the night sky. He had arrived just in time to see the roof cave in, collapsing in a shower of sparks.

Nothing could survive that. Nothing and no one.

But he had tried anyway, getting so close that his skin had begun to blister. He had called their names until the smoke had burnt his lungs and stung his eyes. Even after the fire had died down, a part of him had still hoped to find them alive. A slim hope shattered by the discovery of two charred corpses, arms wrapped around one another in a final embrace.

"I am sorry." The deep voice of Ner'alla drew him back to the present. The stocky Da'arran was weeping, his face a mask of grief. "I am so, so sorry."

Syrella went to place her hand on Jeffson's arm, but he moved it away out of reach.

"It is not your fault," he said in a voice void of emotion. "It is my own. I was a fool to think that my old life would let me go. It was my selfish desire for normality that led to two beautiful, innocent people being killed. I will never make that mistake again." He took another sip of wine and looked up at Ner'alla, his eyes hard. "But you still owe me, Ner'alla. Not just for that but for all the debts you've accrued over the years. And I am calling those favours in. I am aware you have a way into Morlak keep. I need you to share that with us."

Ner'alla nodded and tugged at his gold earring. "I do, yes. You know I do. The same passageway you took yourself during the Canderdash affair."

"I knew it!" exclaimed Syrella, bolting upright in her chair. "I knew it was you! By the Twelve, I should be furious, but all I can think about is how livid she was! Livid!"

Ner'alla turned to her, his mouth dropping open. "Nissus called you Lady Syrella … you are *the* Lady Syrella, the Baroness of Morlak?"

"Why, of course. How many other Lady Syrellas do you know?"

"But … why would you want to break into your own keep? I don't understand."

"Luckily, you do not need to," cut in Jeffson. "Just answer my questions. Is there really no other way in? I was hoping to avoid that particular route this time around."

"Why is that?" Syrella asked.

"Well … there is no easy way to say this, my Lady. It's a sewer pipe. Runs out from the ground floor latrines and under the ramparts, down into the lower city. The soil is too hard for a cesspit, and it's much more efficient than having the stuff carted away. All that's needed is a slight incline and gravity takes care of the rest."

"I see. And what happens if something comes down the pipe as we are going up it?"

"Well, that depends," said Ner'alla. "If it's just one man's, um, *waste*, you'd be all right. Problem is, the latrines on the higher floors aren't linked to the pipe. The contents are collected and emptied every morning by hand, unless things have changed recently." He plucked the bottle of wine from the table and refilled their empty glasses. "In which case, you will die an extremely smelly and very unpleasant death."

"Gonna take a while to get fifty Knights of Kriari up there," said Taleck sourly. He had removed his leather jerkin and was wrapping a cloth around the deep cut in his arm.

Ner'alla glanced at Jeffson. "Do you want to tell him or should I?"

Jeffson drained his second glass and drummed his fingers on the table. "It's not wide enough, Sir Knight."

"What?" said Taleck, his eyes narrowing.

"It's not wide enough. To be honest, I'm not sure it's even wide enough for me. I scraped my arms and elbows on the side of the pipe last time, and my body's not as thin as it once was. There is no way even the smallest Knight of the Twelve would get more than a few feet before becoming stuck. Stuck in the dark, unable to move, waiting for them to empty the latrines."

"You knew this!" snapped Taleck angrily. "You've known all along that this was the only way in. How is this going to help us stop Mithuna and her knights?"

"I do not know that it will, Sir Knight. However, that was never my intention. My first and most important priority was to find a way to free Sir Reed. The sewer passage will allow me into Morlak keep. Reed is just as thin as me, and that was *before* spending weeks in a cell. I'll be able to bring him out the way I got in."

"And how will you find your way from the lower latrines to the prison?" asked Syrella sceptically. "Do you even know where the cells are situated under Morlak keep?"

"Well, no, but—"

"The knights may not fit into that pipe, but I most certainly can." Jeffson started to protest, but she raised her hand to cut him off. "No, hear me out. Three things." She began to tick them off on her fingers as she talked. "One: I know the layout of the keep better than any of you. Two: once inside, I will be mistaken for the usurper and, unless we run into the real imposter, we will be able to travel unhindered throughout the lower levels. And three: I owe Merad Reed my life. A debt that I would like to repay."

Jeffson rubbed his chin thoughtfully. "Maybe, my Lady. *Maybe*. But no one will believe you are the Baroness if you go in looking like that."

Syrella waved her arm irritably. "Details. A canvas bag pulled behind us with a comb and a fresh change of clothes."

By the Twelve, thought Jeffson. *She's right. I will have a greater chance of reaching Reed if she comes with me. But will I be able to bring them both out again safely? That remains to be seen.*

"Very well. You've convinced me. But if you are captured, my Lady, you are on your own."

"Agreed," Syrella replied, holding out her arm. Jeffson took it and they grasped wrists.

"STOP!" shouted Taleck, pounding the table hard enough to make the glasses rattle. "You are forgetting what is at stake! Bjornvor entrusted me with the purging of our garrison. My fellow knights are waiting for me back at camp. We have travelled far, wagered much on this endeavour. I will not be pushed aside. Lady Syrella, do you not wish to regain your lands and title? To take back what these traitors have stolen from you?"

"Of course I do," Syrella said sadly. "More than anything. But even if I manage to convert some of the town guard to my cause, we cannot take on the Knights of Mithuna by ourselves. It would be a massacre."

The five companions sat for a moment in silence.

"There may be a way," said Ner'alla slowly. His eyes were lingering on something hanging over the bar. A paper model of a sparrow, painted crimson red. "Dangerous, foolhardy, fraught with peril. But not impossible."

"Oh, no," said Jeffson, following his gaze. "Absolutely not. I broke my arm last time. I thought I told you to have those horrible contraptions burnt. Don't tell me you kept them? They were the worst—"

"We'll do it," interrupted Taleck. "Whatever it is, we'll do it."

Caddox grunted in consent. "I do not know what in the Pit I have got myself into, but I agree with old ram's head, here. Tell us what it is."

Ner'alla smiled for the first time. "I can do better than that," he said, his eyes glinting mischievously. "I can show you."

∽

Thrust, return, pivot. Thrust, return, pivot. Reed sent the imaginary spear whistling over his head. He was stripped to the waist and covered in sweat, his wiry torso marked with numerous nicks and bruises. An ugly purple scar, barely healed, zig-zagged across his ribs. A permanent reminder of how close he had come to losing everything.

Thrust, return, pivot.

"What *are* you doing, Reed?" came a voice from the other side of the cell bars. Nidore was watching him, a perplexed smile on his face. The blond-haired noble was holding a tray containing a heap of dried fruit and what looked like a chicken leg.

"Keeping busy," Reed replied, out of breath. "Not much else to do. Captain Yusifel always used to say: 'A body is like a sword, it must be maintained with care, or it will rust'." He rolled his shoulders and bent to examine the tray Nidore had slipped under the bars. "Chicken! By the Twelve, you have outdone yourself! Thank you."

Nidore looked pleased. "It's been getting easier and easier over the last few weeks. I don't quite understand what's going on, but Mithuna is not happy, and the Baroness's servants are bearing the brunt of her displeasure. There is something unpleasant in the air, like the gathering of clouds before a storm. People are leaving the upper city in droves; the guards are abandoning their posts. The keep must be half-empty by now, the corridors dusty and silent."

"Hmmm," murmured Reed, his mouth full of chicken. Nidore visited him nearly every day now and rarely empty-handed. Food, water, clean clothes, fresh bandages … Reed would never have survived the last few weeks without the young del Conte's help.

"How about a game of Hazard?" asked Nidore hopefully, removing a small leather pouch from his belt and rattling the dice inside. "You owe me a rematch after the thrashing you gave me yesterday."

Reed squatted down on the floor close to the bars and picked at a piece of chicken stuck between his teeth. "Thrashing? I may occasionally talk to a rat when I'm feeling lonely, but I haven't gone mad just yet, Nidore. And my memory is working just fine. We must have played this Pit-spawned game half a dozen times and I haven't managed to beat you once."

"It's not my fault," Nidore replied with a hurt expression. "It's a game of luck, you know, there's no skill to it."

"No skill? Is that supposed to make me feel better?"

"Well, yes, it is. What shall we bet this time? Titles again?"

"Titles it is. I believe I lost 'Captain of the Old Guard' to you last time, so you have a choice between 'Commander of the Southern Pit' or my knighthood."

"Tricky. Listus didn't have time to grant you a holding, did he? So, you're pretty much Lord of nothing at the moment. I'll take the other one, Commander of the Southern Pit. Best of three. And if you win, I'll sign the del Conte estate over to you. Fair enough?"

"Fair enough," said Reed, picking up the dice. He realised he was enjoying himself. What had started as an attempt to sway Nidore to his cause had morphed over the last few weeks into something more tangible, a genuine bond of friendship even.

An image flashed across his vision, a black-fletched arrow whistling past Syrella and taking her handmaiden in the eye.

No, not friendship. *Never* friendship.

Although it was true that Nidore had changed. He had started paying attention to his appearance. His blond hair was tied back in a carefully styled ponytail instead of hanging wild and loose around his face. The rough patches of stubble had been shaved clean. His thin cheeks had filled out somewhat, softening his careworn features.

But what had changed most were his eyes. When Reed had first seen him in northern Morlak, those eyes were dull and cold, as lifeless as a corpse. A glimmer of newfound energy sparkled there now, a tiny flicker that Reed hoped to nourish until it burst into flame.

"Number?" said Nidore.

Hazard was a deceptively simple game of chance played with two dice. The thrower chooses a number, then tries to roll it. Depending on how the dice fall, they either win, lose, or roll again.

"Five," said Reed firmly and sent the dice spinning across the floor. "So why is Mithuna in a huff?"

"*In a huff?* I don't think one of the Twelve, a living demi-god, could be described as being 'in a huff.' She's … discontented, let's say. Bad news from her allies."

"Oh?" He picked up the dice to throw again.

"Yes. Look, I shouldn't be telling you this, but Mina, Last of the Twelve, attacked Kessrin. And failed. The greylings were routed and Mina was … killed."

Reed dropped the dice in surprise. One of them bounced away and rolled under the bed. "What? Killed? Is that even possible?"

"Apparently. Several sources have confirmed it. One of the towers of Kessrin keep collapsed on her."

"Well, that would probably do it," said Reed sardonically, crouching down next to the bed and searching for the lost die with a groping hand. "So, what now?"

"I'm not sure. You won't be surprised to know that I am not really part of Mithuna's inner circle. I'm a bit concerned about what that means for you, though. You're supposed to be bait. Jelaïa and Aldarin were seen in Kessrin, about as far away from Morlak as you can get. They probably have no idea you are even *in* Morlak, let alone a prisoner here. Verona will have to try something else …"

"… which makes me expendable," Reed finished, throwing the dice and cursing as he lost.

"I fear so. I wish I could tell you why, but Verona hasn't spoken to me in days."

They played for a while in silence.

"My father loved this game," said Nidore suddenly, cupping the dice in his hands and staring at their chipped and battered sides. "We used to play sometimes, in the evening, once my mother had gone to bed. Just the two of us. As I grew older, it was the only thing we still did together, whenever he wasn't off hunting or whoring or whatever else he did to get out of the house …" he trailed off, lost in his memories. Reed waited quietly for him to continue.

"He talked a lot. About politics, the running of the estate … I realise now he was trying to teach me in a strange, roundabout way. He believed that no success in life was due to pure luck, that a clever man could always find a way to turn the odds in his favour. Seven." He let the dice fall from his hands without looking and they clattered onto the floor. A three and a four.

"Like this dice game for example. He abhorred cheating: sleight-of-hand, loaded dice, that sort of thing, but he knew there was invariably a way to gain the advantage. So, he paid one of his servants to roll the dice every day for a week. Thousands of throws. Thousands upon thousands. Guess which number came up the most."

Reed glanced down at the fallen dice. "Seven?"

Nidore gave a melancholy smile. "Seven. He's a terrible husband, Reed. A terrible father. But I am not sure he's a terrible person. And I miss him. I miss Mother. I miss Jelaïa. I know I have done bad things. Unpardonable things, and I will have to pay for them." He stood up, pocketing the dice.

"I am going to get you out of here, Reed. We're leaving Morlak before the whole place tears itself apart."

Reed let out a long breath that he hadn't realised he had been holding in. "Thank you, Nidore. Thank you. I do not know what the future holds, but if we make it back to Arelium safely, I will do what I can to plead your cause to Praxis and your father."

Nidore nodded and held out his hand. Reed grasped his wrist. The noble was turning to leave when the creaking sound of hinges from the end of the corridor heralded the arrival of a new visitor. Reed quickly grabbed the tray of food and pushed it under the bed away from prying eyes. He smelt the overpowering scent of crushed flowers and strawberries, and groaned.

"Reed," came the sultry voice of Verona. She moved closer to the cell bars and Reed could see that the Priestess of Mithuna was not doing well. Her once lustrous black hair was greasy and unwashed, her eyes sunken deep in her face. Two red welts marred her bare arms, and a purplish-yellow bruise covered one cheek. "Reed and Nidore. What are you doing here, my love?"

Nidore averted his gaze. "Just checking on him," he mumbled. "Just making sure he's all right. No one else does."

Verona frowned. "That's not your job. I do wish you wouldn't go wandering around the keep like this, Nidore. If it hadn't been me who found you down here, you would be in serious trouble." She turned to Reed and flashed him a smile. "It is good to see you again, though, my dear Reed. Prison life seems to agree with you." She gazed admiringly at his naked chest until he snatched his undershirt from the bed and pulled it on over his head.

"You're such a spoilsport, Reed. Not amusing at all. Anyway, no time for idle chit-chat. Big things are happening. Great, wonderful things. And so, our plans must change. Yonis? Come here, please."

The Knight of Mithuna slunk out of the shadows and leered at Reed. "Yes, my Lady?"

"Release the prisoner and bring him with us. It is time for him to prove his worth."

And Reed, with a final worried glance at Nidore, allowed himself to be led away from the prison cell that had been his home for the last few weeks and out into Morlak keep.

CHAPTER 10

BROKEN CROCKERY

"Kumbha is well on her way to making me obsolete! Do you know how long it's been since someone asked for my services? Four days! I'm running out of things to do, Xandris! I've washed my instruments a dozen times, cleaned my surgery, organised and categorised my extensive collection of plants and herbs … I think I will come with you to Kessrin. It's not like I'm needed here."

FIRST HEALER OF ARELIUM, 426 AT

"I DO NOT WISH to contradict you, Sister, but whatever Makara told you was false," said Brachyura sternly. "How can you not remember? The decision to sign the Pact was not made on a whim; we spent hours down there on the shore of that lake, sweltering in the heat, debating. Twelve of the greatest strategists to have ever lived. We devised battle plans using catapults, trebuchets, ballistae. We discussed the fires of Brachyura, the incantations of Shala, the transformations of Mithuna. We even briefly talked of flooding the Pits or evacuating the Baronies entirely. It was all useless. The wyrm is invincible."

"And Makara agreed."

"Then what—"

"My mother used to tell me that if you cannot solve the equation, then maybe it's the equation *itself* that is wrong," said Jelaïa, drawing imaginary numbers on the table with her finger. "Perhaps you were aiming at the wrong enemy."

"Or barking up the wrong tree," grunted Orkam.

Kumbha was nodding emphatically. "Quite right. Makara believed that the weaver could be the key to the problem. She stated herself that she had learnt to *control* it. Not how to *tame* it. What would happen if that control was released? What would happen if the weaver was killed?"

"Then this ... wyrm ... of which you speak would run rampant and annihilate us all," said Loré.

"I am not so sure. My particular gift enables me to heal others but, like all our gifts, it comes with a price. I feel the pain of those I heal. Every broken bone, every open wound. It has given me a certain understanding of these things, an empathy. The wyrm was suffering, I am sure of it. Whatever the weaver was doing to keep it compliant was hurting it. What would you do if you could take revenge on those who have caused you pain?"

Loré ran a hand down his healed cheek. "I would destroy them," he said fervently.

"Exactly. So why would the wyrm not do the same?"

"Even so," rumbled Brachyura in his deep voice. "We

do not know what gifts the weaver may have, nor where she might be found. You are clutching at straws, Sister."

"We do have one lead. The secret that Makara told me in confidence ..."

"Yes, Sister?"

"... When we first saw the weaver. When she touched the brood mother. Makara *heard* her. He heard her in his mind. Something whispered in an alien tongue. Both the weaver and Makara have the same gift; they can project their thoughts."

Brachyura was silent for a moment as he analysed this new piece of information. "This ... this changes everything. This is how the greylings could coordinate their attacks. This is how they managed to draw our forces into ambushes, how they managed to avoid those of our own ..."

"The tactics used at the siege of Arelium," Aldarin added. "The way they encircled the Old Guard at the Pit. There was always a guiding hand."

"She even told us so herself. *I am the one who guides. The one who leads.* Why did Makara not share this?"

"He was afraid of how the Twelve would react," Kumbha replied sadly. "I know you admired him, Brother, but others thought him weak. Senile. He feared that at best he would be laughed at — mocked for another ridiculous eccentricity — and at worst mistrusted, imprisoned, or accused of collusion."

"He should have told me," said Brachyura softly.

"What would it have changed? We would still have signed the Pact. I agree, there are many things that we should have done differently, but we cannot dwell on the mistakes of the past. His gift gives us a chance to find the weaver.

To be effective, the link between minds must work both ways. Makara told me that he would hide away somewhere in Klief. If we can find a brood mother, if we can capture it alive and bring it to him, then maybe he can use it to find the location of the weaver."

"That's a lot of ifs," said Derello. "Where would we start? We don't even know where to find a brood mother!"

"I do," Sir Gaelin said grimly. "We'll find one in Talth."

⤚

Gaelin's words were enough to set plans in motion. A punitive expedition into Talth now seemed to be the most viable strategy. Even Loré was easily convinced. The problem became logistical in nature: the allied army needed to travel hundreds of miles in the shortest possible time.

Ships could arrive in Haeden in just a few days, but the Kessrin navy was still recovering from the Battle of the Bay of Doves. A single seaworthy carrack remained — the *Summer Dream* — supported by a smaller flotilla of caravels and auxiliary vessels. Sufficient transport capacity for two to three hundred men. The rest would have to travel by land. Weeks of forced march and, once in Talth, they would have to assault the town itself. The two walls encircling the outskirts and the inner keep were still intact; another series of obstacles to overcome.

Gaelin could help with this. The Knights of Guanna were engineers, much like those of Brachyura, although their primary focus was assault rather than defence: ladders, grappling hooks, catapults, siege towers, and the like. Great quantities of wood would be needed and, although the greylings had burnt the trees surrounding the town of Talth itself, the forests closer to Haeden should still be untouched. A job for the Knights of Brachyura and their axes. They could gather lumber there, then use wagons to transport it to the city walls. They would have to be the first to arrive in Talth.

The Barons of Kessrin and Talth, Kumbha, Brachyura, and his knights would take the ships, roughly one hundred and twenty initiates and their horses; animals trained since they were foals to travel by sea. This first group would form the tip of the spear, retaking the coastal village of Haeden from the greylings, then pushing inland towards Silverlake in search of exploitable woodland.

The Arelian and Kessrin foot soldiers would head north over the River Trent and pass through the western Redenfell Mountains. Brachyura suggested an ingenious method to save time: half the men would sleep in wagons during the day while the other half marched, then the two groups could switch places at dusk, allowing those who had walked to sleep, and those who had slept to march through the night. Fresh oxen, horses, and supplies could be commandeered from the northern farmsteads A twenty-day marathon would thus only take ten.

Jelaïa gripped the arms of her chair in frustration, careful not to let the disappointment show on her face. It was a sound plan, with one unfortunate side effect: she was to be separated from Aldarin again. She toyed with the idea of saying something, a reason for her to accompany him, but everything she thought of sounded petty and childish. In any case, her own aims and desires had become irrelevant once she had accepted the mantle of Baroness. Duty was the most important thing now. Duty above all else.

She looked around the table at the others. Each and every one of them carried their own burden. The loss of a parent, a lover, a friend, a father. Beliefs shattered. Dreams forever broken. And yet, none of them was hesitating to step into the darkness once again. This is what the Twelve cannot comprehend. Strength and cohesion through solidarity and friendship.

With a scraping of chairs, the meeting came to an end. Barons, captains, knights, and demi-gods filed out of the room, hurrying away to organise the expedition to Talth. Jelaïa lingered by the table, her fingers tracing the pencil-drawn Barony of Arelium, from the River Stahl down to the Great Southern Plains and the Pit. All of it hers.

"Jelaïa?"

Aldarin stood in the doorway, helmet under one arm. "Do you have a moment?"

"Of course," she replied, smiling to hide the worm of trepidation squirming in her stomach. "How have you been?"

"Well, thank you. Brachyura has been keeping me busy. He is constantly telling us that he is here to guide, not lead, but ordering people around for three-hundred years has left its mark and I think he is finding it hard just to watch from the sidelines. And the paperwork! By the Twelve. So much paperwork."

"Hah. I know what you mean. I relied on Praxis to share the load, but now ..."

"Yes. I heard. Do you think the things people are saying about him are true?"

"No … I … Actually, I suppose I don't really know. That he would betray us? It's possible. He spoke to me several times of his frustrations with my father's policies and of the importance of choosing one's own path. But murder? An alliance with the greylings? That sounds rather far-fetched, even for him."

"Agreed. But then again, I was fooled by Verona. Perhaps I have been too trusting. I will try to speak to Praxis myself; there should be ample time during the journey north."

"What do you mean?"

"Derello didn't tell you? He believes it is too dangerous to keep Praxis here. He's bringing him with us."

"Oh. No, he didn't. That's odd. I hope his discovery of Praxis's treachery is not leading him to be overly suspicious."

Aldarin did not reply. Seconds of silence stretched to a minute.

"I … wanted to talk to you about something," the big knight finally said. "Something important." He took a step closer to Jelaïa, and she found herself drawn into his ocean-blue eyes.

"I have asked Praedora for permission to step down as temple master, as soon as a suitable replacement can be found. I only agreed in the first place so as not to disappoint Sir Manfeld, but he was unaware of the oath I had already taken, the one I gave to you down in the smithy before all of this began, do you remember?"

"Yes," Jelaïa replied, so quiet it was almost a whisper. The worm was gone, replaced by a feeling of growing warmth. "You talked of reinstating the garrison of the Knights of Brachyura. You promised …"

"I promised I would return with you to Arelium. Is that still what you want?"

"Of course, Aldarin. I meant what I said. Everything seems easier when you are around."

He nodded and took another hesitant step towards her. She could smell the oil he used to maintain his interlocking sheets of armour, mixed with the salty tang of the sea. "Jelaïa, I—"

"Aldarin!" interrupted an exasperated voice from outside. "Get a move on! They are waiting for us and I can't navigate these winding streets by myself. I'm blind, remember?"

The knight jerked backwards as if he'd been caught doing something wrong. "My Lady," he said formally to Jelaïa, bowing at the waist. "I must leave you yet again. We will finish this conversation another time." He bowed again and turned awkwardly to leave.

"Aldarin?" Jelaïa called after him.

"Yes, my Lady?"

"I look forward to it."

He smiled broadly. "So do I, Jelaïa. So do I."

It didn't take long for Jelaïa to find where Loré del Conte was staying. She just had to follow the angry cries and the sounds of broken crockery. As she made her way up the path to a fine-looking guest house, a servant pushed past her, his doublet stained with red wine. "Careful," the man confided. "His lordship is in a terrible mood."

Wait until he hears what I've got to tell him, she thought as the servant scampered off down the road.

Xandris and the healer were sitting on the terrace, drinking tea and playing a complicated game of cards that Jelaïa didn't recognise. "My Lady!" Xandris exclaimed, bouncing to his feet as she approached. "How nice of you to come and join us. Some tea, perhaps? Derello has it imported directly from Quayjin; it supposedly costs an absolute fortune!"

"Another time, perhaps. I am here to see Loré."

"Ah, right. Well, good luck. He doesn't seem to be in the best of dispositions." As if to prove his point, a porcelain dish sailed overhead and shattered on the gravel path.

Jelaïa touched her amulet for luck and took the stairs up to the first floor. She entered Loré's room without knocking. Del Conte was pacing back and forth, muttering to himself, his limp a thing of the past. A bedside table lay in pieces against the far wall, surrounded by fragments of glass.

"My Lady," Loré said hotly as she entered. "That young fop of a Baron is not letting me see Praxis. He's our steward, Jelaïa, it's completely unreasonable."

"Well, I—"

"And Kumbha, he's taking her with him! Wants her all to himself, leaving me to herd the foot soldiers and baggage train like a lowly quartermaster. Who does he think he is?"

Jelaïa took a deep breath. "Enough, Loré."

"Prancing around here like he owns everything and everyone—"

"LORE. ENOUGH."

Lord del Conte's jaw slammed shut.

"Good," Jelaïa continued. "You will not speak of Derello in such a manner. We are guests in his city, and I will not have you criticise our host."

"Yes, my Lady."

"And Kumbha, Eleventh of the Twelve, is not a trophy to be paraded around the nine Baronies. She is quite capable of making her own decisions, and accompanying the others on the *Summer Dream* is the logical choice."

"Yes, my Lady."

"Now sit."

Loré searched around for a chair, found an upturned stool and righted it. He sat down sullenly.

"Loré. There is something I need to tell you."

"Yes, Baroness?"

"I know you are my father."

Loré looked at her in shock. "How ... I mean, who told ..."

"Praedora. As is her right. I have known for several weeks now. And I have played this meeting over and over in my head, trying to think of what to say." Jelaïa's hand drifted to her amulet. "The answer, when it came, was quite liberating. You are not my father."

Loré's face screwed up in puzzlement. "I'm not sure I understand."

"I mean, you are part of me, I came from your loins, but you are not my father. My father is the man who taught me to ride my first pony, who came and held me close at night when the thunderstorms made me cry, who carved our names into a tree on the outskirts of Kaevel Forest. He is the man who helped me to be just, to be kind, and to be firm. My father is Listus del Arelium and always will be. Nothing can change that."

"Jelaïa—"

"I haven't finished. So, we now have two choices. Either we can keep this between us, and I remain Baroness of

Arelium, with you as my closest advisor. Or we can let the people of Arelium know what has been done. Listus's reputation will be dragged through the mud, as will your own. I will confirm the story's veracity and step down as Baroness. The people can then decide who they trust to govern Arelium."

Loré leant back, one hand stroking his healed cheek. "Everyone will know," he said, half to himself as if mulling it over. "Nidore will know."

"Yes."

"Listus's reputation ... besmirched. Mine own too."

"Yes."

He made a clicking sound with his tongue. "It is an easy decision. I have been given a second lease on life, Jelaïa. Kumbha has made me whole again. And this time, I want to do better. You have the makings of a fine Baroness. Let us keep things as they are."

Jelaïa felt a wave of relief. "Very well," she said. "Then let this be the last time we speak of this. I will see you on the road."

"I ... Know that I am proud of you, Daughter."

"Loré?"

"Yes?"

"Never call me that again." And with that, Jelaïa left del Conte to his broken furniture, walking briskly back to her own quarters to prepare for the long trip north to Talth.

CHAPTER 11

THE CRIMSON WING

"Praise the Twelve! Well, all of them apart from Mithuna. There's something wrong with that one. I never know what she's thinking or where she's running off to. Gives me the creeps. Call me a heretic if you want, but I don't think she has our best interests at heart. She is definitely loyal to her brothers and sisters … I'm just not sure she's loyal to us."

FINAL SERMON OF PREACHER KLENDON, 121 AT

❧

"**A**BSOLUTELY NOT," SAID Caddox when he saw what Ner'alla wanted to show them. "I would rather climb up a sewage pipe a thousand times than use one of those Pit-forsaken things."

Ner'alla had led them down to the cellar and through an opening concealed behind a stack of ale casks. They had emerged into a vaulted stone chamber, lit by a couple of gut-tering torches fixed to the far wall.

Before them, covering the floor and piled high against the walls, were rolls of cotton fabric dyed a shade of red so dark it was nearly black, as well as long poles of spruce, and supple branches of willow approximately five feet in length. In the room's centre, suspended from ropes anchored to the ceiling, hung a gigantic pair of wings, sheets of fabric stretched taut over ribs of wood. Syrella stepped forwards, her hand caressing the soft cotton.

"What do you call it?" she asked, green and blue eyes shining in wonder.

"A Crimson Wing," said Jeffson. "A glider that harnesses the power of the wind. Used at the right time in the right place, it enables a man to fly."

"Preposterous," snorted Caddox. "Look how flimsy it is! You'd have to be mad to even attempt such a thing!"

"I have used the Wing several times, Sir Knight," Jeffson replied. "It was often the only way to reach some of the more inaccessible areas of the nine Baronies. If handled correctly and prudently, there is a fairly low risk of injury."

"What's that supposed to mean?"

"Well, I broke my leg once, but it was the fault of capri-cious weather conditions, not the glider itself. The wind changed direction at the last minute and I landed in a tree instead of a nice flat field of corn."

Caddox shook his head in disbelief and went to examine the glider more closely.

"How many are there?" said Taleck. He looked pale, his left arm hanging at his side, fresh blood trickling down his forearm from the wound somewhere under his leather jerkin.

"Twenty-four," said Ner'alla proudly. He indicated the rolls of packed fabric. "Once dismantled, each one is compact enough to be carried on one's back. I can have them smuggled out of the city after the curfew is lifted tomorrow morning, and one of my men can show you how to assemble and fly them."

"What about weight? Jeffson's used one, but he's as thin as a reed. What about an armoured Knight of Kriari?"

"Ah, yes. That may be problematic. I would say two hundred pounds, two hundred and fifty at the most. Any more than that and you'll plummet like a stone."

"Pit," complained Caddox. "Well, that settles it. My set of plate weighs close to eighty pounds, not counting my axe."

"Unless we leave our shields and armour behind," said Taleck slowly, his eyes on the glider. "Short swords only and maybe breastplates. That would make us light enough."

"By the Twelve, man, can you hear yourself? So, *if* you manage to dive off some cliff above Morlak and *if* you manage to land on the garrison roof without breaking both your legs, you will end up being two dozen knights, unarmoured and shieldless, against who knows how many Knights of Mithuna and, of course, Mithuna herself! Where would you even be jumping from?"

"Oh, that's an easy one," said Ner'alla. "There's only one peak that's positioned just behind the upper city and high enough to attempt such a thing."

He grinned, his teeth white against ebony skin.

"The Spike."

❦

They stayed overnight in one of Ner'alla's many guest rooms.
The following morning, they returned to camp, joined soon
after by Ner'alla's man; a short, stocky Morlakian with a
missing leg and a stubbly grey beard, driving a cart loaded
with the Crimson Wings.

It was decided that both teams would attempt to enter
Morlak simultaneously. Jeffson and Syrella would go through
the sewage pipe, find Reed, and get out again by whatever
means necessary. Taleck and his knights would land on the
roof of the garrison and aim to eliminate or otherwise contain whoever they found inside, hoping that the element
of surprise would make up for their lack of numbers and
weapons.

Caddox, after much cajoling, had been persuaded to
join them, although he still looked at the dark red gliders
with a mixture of disgust and trepidation. Vohanen appeared
to have no such qualms, laughing so hard during Taleck's
explanation that the older knight had to stop and wait for
him to quiet down.

"By the Pit, Taleck," wheezed Vohanen, wiping a tear
from his eye, his shoulders still shaking. "Wait until Bjornvor
hears about this! And he called *me* the reckless one. Hiking
halfway up the Spike with a bunch of gliders! You crazy son
of a whore!"

"If I may finish?" said Taleck testily. "There is no other
way. You've seen for yourself. The gates to the inner city are
barred shut, and the walls are manned day and night. If we
wish to stop the Knights of Mithuna, this is our best bet.
Now, let us—" He paused, his mouth twisting. His gaze

lost its focus and he swayed on his feet. Vohanen rushed forwards to catch him before he fell.

"What's the matter?" asked Syrella anxiously. Taleck's eyes had rolled into the back of his head, his mouth opening and closing soundlessly.

"Get that jerkin off him," said Jeffson sharply. "And give me some room. Sir Krelbe, I'll need dry linen, boiling water, and lemon juice if you have any." The dour-faced knight looked over at Vohanen, who nodded.

One of the other knights slowly removed Taleck's jerkin. There was a strip of fabric bound tightly around his left bicep, wet and slimy with a yellow liquid. Jeffson delicately unwound the makeshift bandage and almost gagged as he was hit by the sickly-sweet odour of rotting flesh. The wound was only a couple of inches wide but deep and surrounded by angry red streaks. A sluggish trickle of pus dribbled from the torn skin.

"Infection? Already?" said Syrella. She had removed her disguise and was once more dressed in animal furs, a dash of mascara highlighting her remarkable eyes. She drew a hand-kerchief from her pocket and pressed it to her nose, leaning closer to the wounded man.

"It's too fast," agreed Jeffson. "I'm no healer, but I saw Taleck bind the wound shortly after the skirmish." He steeled himself and took a tentative sniff but could only detect the smell of putrefaction. "It could be poison or flakes of rust from the longsword."

"What can be done?" asked Vohanen, his face lined with concern.

"I'm not sure, Sir Knight. If the infection is local, I can attempt to cut away the diseased skin and tissue—"

"Don't tell me, you've done this sort of thing before."

"Yes."

"And?"

"And what, Sir Knight?"

"Did the patient survive?"

"He did not. Though I do not believe it was due to my intervention."

Vohanen scratched at his beard and looked away towards the edge of the campsite. Parts of distant Morlak could be seen through the treeline, the snow-capped summit of the Spike rising behind it, a flash of white in the early morning sun.

"The rules of our order dictate that with Taleck no longer fit to lead, command should be passed to the next most senior Knight of Kriari," he said. "Krelbe, we're the oldest. It's down to you or me. How about it? Fancy taking over?"

"Not for all the wine in Morlak," said Krelbe unequivocally. He set down the pot of hot water he was carrying and passed over a roll of lemon-soaked linen.

"Duly noted." Vohanen scanned the half-circle of knights grouped around the fallen Taleck. "Then the burden of responsibility falls to me. Jeffson, do what you can."

The manservant licked his lips. "Hold him steady," he cautioned. Four knights held the unconscious man firmly, while a fifth pried his mouth open and wedged a piece of wood between his teeth.

"Syrella, your knife, please," said Jeffson, holding out his hand. He dipped the blade in the boiling water, wiped away the worst of the purulent secretion with a piece of linen and then began to cut away the necrotic tissue around the wound.

Taleck moaned, his skin hot and feverish. Fresh beads of perspiration dripped from his forehead down into his beard. His jaw tightened, clamping down on the wooden stick in his mouth. Suddenly, he convulsed, writhing under the steady hands of the knights.

"Just a moment longer," said Jeffson, removing the last visible part of infected skin. Dark blood flowed from the laceration now, staining his fingers red. He cleaned what he could with the last of the water and covered the wound with several strips of linen while the surrounding knights looked on in silence.

"I believe I have done all I can," he said, wiping a sheen of sweat from his brow with the back of his hand. "But he can't be left alone. Some of us will have to remain here, to make sure the wound is kept clean and the patient stays out of trouble."

"Aye, he will not be happy about missing out, poor man," said Vohanen. "I'll find someone to look after him. They can use Syrella's wagon. A couple more will have to stay with the horses; there are not enough gliders for all of us in any case. Hey! Ner'alla's man! Whatever your name is! We only have two hours left if we want to get into position over the keep before midnight. How about you show us how it's done, eh?"

The Morlakian, who had not moved from the cart since he had arrived, climbed laboriously down from the driver's seat. He grabbed some wooden poles and one of the big canvas bags from the back. As he hobbled over, they could see that he was missing not only a leg but also two fingers from his right hand.

Caddox gave a low whistle. "By the Twelve, man, what happened to you?"

"Wolf."

"Really? Must have been a big one. And what should we call you?"

The man seemed to panic slightly at this, his eyes roaming the campsite for a moment before replying.

"Err ... Stick?"

"They call you Stick?"

"Yep."

"Like a ... stick?"

"Yep."

Jeffson, seeing the slowly mounting terror in the man's eyes, interceded smoothly. "Delighted to meet you, Stick. Would you allow me to explain to these gentlemen how the gliders work?"

"With pleasure, M'Lord," Stick replied, visibly relieved. He opened up the canvas bag and dumped its contents onto the ground. Vohanen motioned for the other Knights of Kriari to gather round.

"The poles here are made of spruce," Jeffson said. "Light and flexible. They'll form the triangular skeleton. The red canvas needs to be stretched over the edges and the crossbar; then we use the smaller bits of willow to reinforce the canvas and keep it nice and tight. Like a sparrow wing, you see? Add some loops of hemp to make a harness and you're ready to go."

"*Ready to go?*" repeated Caddox incredulously. "How do we take off? How do we fly?"

"Fly?" smirked Stick. "Who ever said anythin' about flyin'? You'll be fallin', Sir Knight, not flyin'. The fabric will only slow your fall and let you aim for a landing spot."

"Indeed," Jeffson agreed. "And that will only work if there are enough air currents to provide sufficient lift. My last trip was *not* an enjoyable experience."

"Madness," muttered the Knight of Brachyura softly, shaking his head.

"Oh, come on, Caddox, it's the only way into the keep," said Vohanen, giving him a playful punch on the shoulder. "I'm sure you have faced worse things than this!" The older knight looked better than he had in weeks, revitalised by the prospect of some activity at last.

Jeffson and Stick spent the next two hours showing the knights how to assemble the gliders, how to pilot them by shifting one's weight and, most importantly, how to land. There were only two ways to do so: the first — and safest — was to stall the glider by pushing the nose up and hitting the ground upright. The second was to slow the glider as much as possible, then cut through the rope harness, releasing the pilot at speed. Obviously, something to be attempted only if there was no other option.

They ate a hasty midday meal of dried meat and fruit. Two of the older knights volunteered to stay behind with Taleck, who had still not regained consciousness. They would also be keeping a watchful eye on the cache of armour and tower shields, all far too heavy to equip those using the gliders.

Vohanen approached Jeffson as he was helping Stick climb back onto the cart. "So, this is where we part ways, my friend," he said, extending his forearm to grasp wrists. Jeffson took it, his grip tight.

"It would seem so, Sir Knight."

"If you can get out again through the sewage pipe, I suggest you do so. Return to *The Crimson Wing*. If for some reason that fails, make for the Great Hall. We will try and find you there."

"Agreed."

"I … I do not know what the future brings, Jeffson, but I hope to see you again. I …"

"Yes, Sir Knight?"

"I apologise for some of my behaviour towards you. I fear I have, once again, let my prejudices influence my actions. For a long time, I thought you were nothing more than a common thief. A thief, a liar, and a murderer."

Jeffson smiled thinly. "I am all of those things, Sir Knight."

"Aye, perhaps you are. But I had forgotten that you were also the person who came to me after Avor's death. After the flooding of the Pit. I was thinking some dark thoughts that morning, Jeffson. Dark, terrible thoughts. You told me—" he paused and took a deep breath, "—you told me I owed it to my son to carry on. To carry on, to remember him, and to remember him to others. For as long as the memory of those we have loved and lost remains, then a small part of them lives on … and they are never truly gone."

He released Jeffson's wrist and averted his eyes, gazing down at his steel-shod boots.

"I thank you for that, my friend," he said in a hoarse whisper.

Jeffson nodded and pulled himself up onto the driver's

seat. "You are a good man, Sir Knight," he said. "May we meet again, in this world, or the next." And with a crack of the reins, he sent the cart trundling back towards Morlak.

~

The Great Hall of Morlak was similar to that of Arelium; a rectangular, high-ceilinged room with the heraldic banners of the Barony's vassals lining the walls.

At least, that must have once been the case. Now those banners lay crumpled on the floor in tatters or shredded into thin strips. An imposing iron throne dominated the far end of the hall, its arms and legs decorated with thorned roses. Mithuna, disguised as Syrella del Morlak, lounged nonchalantly on the cushioned seat, one smooth leg hooked over an armrest. Before her, two knights in mottled armour were pummelling each other with their gauntleted fists. The clang of metal resonated off the stone walls.

"Ah, Reed!" said Mithuna, her eyes lighting up as he approached. "You are alive! Excellent! See how my knights vie for my affection. What chivalry! Now, I hope you have not forgotten your manners. Will you not kneel before your Baroness?"

Reed muttered something in reply.

"Kneel," said Yonis, kicking him in the back of the calf and forcing him to his knees. Verona sank to the ground next to him.

"That's much better."

"Can we stop this stupid charade, Mithuna?" sighed Reed tiredly.

"No, I don't think so. I rather like wearing this skin.

And it costs an awful lot of effort to change form, tires me out for days."

One of the duelling knights sidestepped an obvious lunge and punched his adversary in the jaw, knocking him out cold. He turned and bowed stiffly to his patron with a creak of rusted joints.

"Very good, very good," said Mithuna, clapping her hands together. "Perseverance and subterfuge, two qualities I greatly admire. For a body is like a sword, is it not, Reed? It must be maintained with care or it will rust."

Reed's head shot up. "What did you say?"

Mithuna beamed at him, the expression somewhat alien on Syrella's face. "Oh, *come on*, Reed, I do wish you would stop taking me for a fool. Three hundred years ago, I was sent to gather information on the greylings. I was a *spy*, Reed. For *years*. In fact, the Pact probably only exists thanks to me. Did you really think I would not have you watched while you languished down there in your little cell, plotting and scheming?"

Nidore blanched. "My Lady—" he began.

"Oh, be quiet, you useless excuse for a man! You're even worse, latching on to whoever shows you an ounce of affection like a love-starved barnacle! Pitiful. You're not even worth the effort. I did enjoy you looking so proud and happy when you stole the food that I had ordered to be left out for you. You have been a welcome distraction in these difficult times."

She smiled to herself.

"Difficult times?" said Reed, rising to his feet. "Ah, yes. How fares your sister, Mina?"

Mithuna's smile fell from her face, and she turned her

gaze on Reed. Her eyes melted, the transparent liquid running down her cheeks like sticky tears. In their place formed two orbs of shining blackness, cold and hard.

"DO NOT TEST ME," she shouted, bounding to her feet. Her voice hit Reed like a blow to the skull. He shook his head, trying to clear the ringing in his ears. Something red and tangy dribbled onto his upper lip as his nose started to bleed.

"This is not a game," she continued, as the echoes died away. "This is treachery. Sedition. Rebellion. You are playing with things you do not understand, and there will be consequences." She paused. "Mina would have survived, you see, Reed? The Pact was quite clear. The Twelve are not to be harmed. We are to facilitate the greylings' return, then we will be free to go, to live our lives as we please. And your stupid human allies, in their despicable arrogance, took that chance away from her."

She stepped down from the throne and began to pace slowly towards him.

"Luckily, those responsible will be punished. They have set off on some foolhardy journey to Talth, whether to reclaim it or avenge it, I am not sure, but it matters not. Those loose ends will soon be well and truly finished off."

She moved closer, her purple dress brushing against the flagstones. One hand fell to her belt, caressing the pommel of a sheathed dagger.

"That is bad news for you, I'm afraid. The last of the bloodline of Arelium and the Knights of Brachyura are far from Morlak, too far to lure them here by using you as bait, so we no longer need you. Although, I have been told that Syrella is looking to mount some reckless rescue expedition."

She drew the dagger and tapped the tip against her lips in mock reflection.

"I suppose we can keep *part* of you around for a bit longer, you never know. But we don't need *all* of you, do we? Yonis, his right hand, please."

Reed's eyes widened as he realised what was about to happen and he turned to run, but the knight was faster, grabbing his arm in a vice-like grip and yanking him towards Mithuna, his right hand outstretched.

"No!" yelled Reed. "Don't do this Mithuna. You talk of being above games. Above childish squabbles. Do not lower yourself to petty revenge!"

He forced himself to stare into her eyes, searching for some trace of compassion, of empathy. Anything he could use.

He found nothing but endless darkness.

The knife came down.

CHAPTER 12

FLOTSAM

"Look, I can't take all of you. I'm sorry. I just don't have the room. Women and children first, no extra baggage: only take what you can carry. The rest of you will have to stay behind. And may the Twelve have mercy on your souls."

LORD TAILE BANSWORTH, 426 AT

⋘

THE *SUMMER DREAM* crested another wave and Praxis felt his gut heave in protest. He scrambled across the cabin, reaching the bucket in the corner just in time. His stomach clenched, and he vomited a stream of yellow-brown bile, flecks of the stuff becoming stuck in his beard.

He wiped himself clean as best he could. *This would be easier if my hands weren't tied together,* he thought acidly, cursing his own stupidity for the hundredth time. He had underestimated Derello, like so many others before him. And now he was paying the price; trussed up like a chicken and forced to participate in some ludicrous expedition to Talth.

He had been bound with a length of rope that looped around his forearms then snaked along the floor to a metal ring. Praxis had spent the first day of his captivity trying to untie himself and ended up with nothing to show for it except a broken fingernail. These sailors knew their knots.

The cabin door opened and Hirkuin entered, stepping gingerly over the half-full bucket.

"Seems like you're keeping yourself entertained," the guard captain said, chuckling at his own joke. "Boats really aren't your thing, are they, Praxis?"

"Not when they are moving."

"I still don't understand why Derello insisted you be brought with us. You're taking up valuable cabin space. I could have used this room as storage. An extra hundred crossbows."

"He thinks I'm dangerous."

"Are you?"

The walls moved, the ship banking to port. Praxis felt a new wave of nausea churn in his stomach. He teetered sideways, nearly losing his balance.

Hirkuin laughed. "I think you've answered my question. The Baron is asking for you. If you would follow me?"

Praxis held up his bound hands.

"Ah, yes. Hold still." The Kessrin took his sailor's knife and cut through the rope. Both men glanced down at the sharp blade.

"Try it," Hirkuin said. He was no longer smiling. "The

Baron gave specific instructions for you not to be harmed, but if you attack me, I will have no other choice but to … defend myself."

They stared at each other for a moment, then Praxis held his hands up in mock surrender. "Fine. *Fine.* Lead on."

The deck of the *Summer Dream* was overflowing with Knights of Brachyura. Praxis was engulfed by a seething hatred at the sight of all these pompous fools, laughing and joking, unperturbed by the roll of the ship.

They call me a murderer, Praxis thought bitterly. *But I only did what was asked of me and only when it was essential. What these hypocrites did to the temple of Zygos after the Schism was far beyond simple necessity.*

He followed Hirkuin to the starboard rail, where Aldarin and Derello were conversing quietly. A caravel whisked past them, part of a larger flotilla of armed escort ships circling the convoy. The Kessrin shoreline was just visible in the distance, mile upon mile of rocky creeks and crags.

Aldarin caught sight of Praxis and frowned. He said something to Derello and walked away towards the prow. The Baron waited patiently, the sea wind ruffling his hair. He was once again wearing his chainmail. Praxis was beginning to wonder if he would ever wear anything else.

"Thank you, Hirkuin," Derello said. "You can leave us. If Praxis tries anything, I'll just signal for the helmsman to turn hard to starboard. Knock him into the water. I seem to remember he's not the strongest of swimmers."

"I think you are referring to our flight from Kingfisher Isle, my Lord?" Praxis said innocently. "Just after I saved your life?"

"And that is one of the few reasons you are still alive."

Derello took in Praxis's dirty beard and sickly complexion. "It appears you still haven't found your sea legs. The nausea results from your eyes and ears telling your brain different things. Your eyes say that you're standing still, but your ears think that you're moving. Try fixing the horizon."

Praxis concentrated on the far-off cliffs and, to his surprise, felt slightly better.

"Do you remember the story of the two inner wolves?" said Derello with a touch of melancholy. "One representing who we truly are, the other how we are perceived by those around us? You told me that both were equally nourished. At the time, something didn't feel quite right. You answered too quickly, without thinking. You were the first to do so. Generally, people take a minute or two to mull it over. But you are not like most people, are you?"

Praxis squirmed under the Baron's gaze. He wanted so much to confess everything. The continual subterfuge was exhausting. Overhead, the gaudy purple sails billowed as they caught the wind.

"I've lost a lot of sleep because of you," Derello continued, his eyes still probing. "Loré is unequivocally convinced that you murdered Listus del Arelium, and his evidence is quite compelling. I keep playing my memories over and over in my mind. You stopped Mina from killing me on Kingfisher Isle. You helped us fight the krakens. I can't believe you did all of that out of pure self-interest."

It would be so easy to tell him the truth, Praxis thought. But he couldn't. "I suppose my trial will give me the opportunity to explain myself," he said instead.

"Ah yes ... the trial. You are right, I strongly believe that all people are innocent until they are proven guilty.

However, …" Derello looked to the prow where Brachyura was standing, unmoving, staring at the white-flecked swell, "I have since spoken with the two members of the Twelve who have returned to us, and they have told me of a more efficient way. All of them are proficient judges of character, but one of them, Makara, can take things a step further. His gift enables him to enter the mind of another."

"That sounds … aggressive."

"From what I understand, it is painless. The Twelve themselves used this method to communicate over great distances. A trial would take more time and could lead to the wrong result. Between Loré, who advocated for you to be executed without delay, and myself, who argued for a more conservative approach, it seems the perfect middle ground. I am sorry. But then again, if you are innocent, you have nothing to fear, have you?"

"Unless the Twelve are hiding things from us. I find it ironic that you all choose to trust them so easily after they betrayed humanity. Not that my opinion matters. Where is Makara?"

Derello sighed. "I think that information is best kept from you, Praxis. You speak of trust and you are right. I have been far too trusting recently. You will know when the time comes."

"HAEDEN! NORTH-WEST!" came the cry from the crow's nest. The flat line of the horizon was now broken by a trio of green landmasses: the southern islands of the archipelago known as the Shattered Hand. To starboard, a dark brown streak on the coastline could only be the port of Haeden.

"You will have to return below decks, Praxis," Derello said, beckoning to a couple of knights.

Praxis baulked at the idea of going back to that windowless, vomit-stained prison. "Just a few more minutes, Derello. Please? The fresh air is helping clear my lungs and my mind."

"Didn't I just tell you I have been too trusting? What's to say you won't try to escape?"

"Escape to where? We're on a *boat!* What am I going to do, jump into the sea? There's nowhere to go."

"Baron!" Brachyura called from the prow. "We need you! Something's wrong!"

"Pit!" Derello said in exasperation, banging his fist against the ship's rail. "Fine. You can stay." The two knights hadn't moved. "Watch him," he said to them. "If he so much as breathes the wrong way, shove him back into his cubby hole."

Haeden was approaching. Praxis could now make out twenty to thirty buildings of varying sizes, with a crescent-shaped rubble seawall protecting a fleet of fishing boats moored close to the shore. Hirkuin pushed past him, yelling at a group of sailors to remove the tarpaulin covers from the ballistae lining the deck. Lord Bansworth trailed after the Kessrin captain, straining under the weight of three enormous steel-tipped bolts. The disgraced vassal had strapped an almost comically large breastplate over his pink-and-purple silk shirt.

Flotsam bobbed in the water near the village, bumping against the hull of the *Summer Dream* and its escorting caravels. No, not just flotsam. Praxis leant over the rail as far as he dared to get a closer look. What he had thought to be a broken barrel was, in fact, the horribly bloated corpse of a woman, its distended stomach keeping it afloat, its hair trailing out behind it like some nightmarish seaweed. The current carried the corpse over to another floating body, that of a young child, and they spiralled around each other like in some macabre dance.

Praxis turned away in disgust. "Hirkuin!" he called. "Bodies! In the water."

"I told you. The town was attacked," Bansworth huffed irritably. "We barely escaped with our lives. The corpses are the villagers I could not take with me. They were forced to stay behind."

"I thought you managed to save all the women and children."

"No ... I tried. I really tried. There was just not enough room."

"MOVEMENT!" yelled the barrelman from his perch.

Hirkuin sent a sailor running to fetch him an eyeglass. "Can't be greylings," he said, half to himself. "It's the middle of the day, with a cloudless sky."

Praxis scoffed. It always amazed him how so many of those around him never took the time to stop and *think*. The Twelve themselves had underestimated the enemy once, and hundreds of years later people continued to make the same mistakes. Praxis had spent countless hours reading about the greylings; first during his training at the temple of Zygos and then in Listus's extensive archives. He had come to realise something. The greatest strength that the enemy possessed was not their numbers but their *adaptability*.

How long was it since the greylings had returned to the surface? Weeks? Months? All that time spent above ground.

Would they not begin to grow more resilient? Praxis had heard of Da'arrans living in snow-covered Morlak and Morlakians working in the sun-drenched deserts of Da'arra. Why should it be different for other species? He scanned the shoreline and was unsurprised to see a half-dozen armoured threshers emerge from the buildings where they had been hiding.

Hirkuin gauged the distance. "Ballistae! On my mark!" The *Summer Dream* edged closer. "Wait … Wait". The threshers advanced towards the seawall.

"Wait … NOW!" Three almost simultaneous clangs rang out as the ballistae crews sent the bolts thrumming over the waves. One bolt missed entirely. The other two reduced a pair of threshers to pulp, drilling through their bodies with gruesome results.

"RELOAD!" Hirkuin yelled.

The caravels swooped in. They were armed with smaller, lightweight ballistae, one on either side. They would need to sail closer to the shore if they wanted to use them effectively. The threshers were tearing at the ropes holding the protective sheets of metal to their bodies.

"What are they doing?" asked Hirkuin, watching through his eyeglass.

"PULL THE CARAVELS BACK!" boomed the deep voice of Brachyura from the prow. The threshers, now wearing only loincloths, were running full tilt at the seawall. Behind them, a mass of greylings poured forth from the village buildings. One of the caravels fired, but the artillery crew had aimed poorly, and the bolt passed harmlessly over the attackers.

The first thresher reached the end of the seawall and *jumped.*

The helmsman of the closest caravel saw the danger and span the wheel, but it was too late. The thresher sailed thirty feet through the air and crashed onto the deck. It roared a challenge, decapitating a Knight of Brachyura with a sweep of its arm. It was soon joined by one of its fellows.

Hirkuin spat out a curse and ran over to one of the ballistae. "Stop the other threshers!" he ordered, aiming down the sights. He exhaled slowly, feeling the *Summer Dream* move beneath him, then fired. His bolt hit a thresher just as it was leaping from the seawall, plucking it out of the air.

Praxis watched apprehensively as the greylings reached the sea. *What will they do now?* he thought. *They can't swim.* Another bloated corpse bumped against the side of the ship and, in a flash of lucidity, he understood why the greylings had thrown the dead into the water.

Oh no.

He saw the first greyling bound onto the lifeless body of a villager and then onwards, hopping to a floating crate, a dead guardsman, an upturned barrel, and finally onto the stern of the caravel, its claws digging into the hull. A score more followed, using the scattered detritus like stepping stones. Some misjudged their jumps or were hit by waves, but the majority managed to reach the boat unharmed.

And while we sit back and do nothing, the enemy continue to overcome their weaknesses, Praxis marvelled, as a greyling eviscerated the helmsman, causing the caravel to list to starboard.

Brachyura was marching along the deck, unbuckling the straps of his ornate armour. "Helmsman. Bring us within forty feet if you would. Hirkuin. Concentrate your ballista fire on the seawall. Lord … Apologies, I forget your name."

"B … Bansworth, Lord," the gaudily dressed noble stammered, his visage showing a mix of fear and admiration.

"Bansworth. Right. You know this place well. I would think you are the perfect candidate to lead the counter-attack. What say you?"

"Yes, Lord. It would be an honour." Bansworth saluted, bowed, saluted again and hurried off to have the rowboats lowered into the water.

"Strange man," muttered Brachyura. He removed the last piece of his armour and set it down on the deck in front of him and, after a moment's hesitation, reluctantly put his axe down beside it. "You!" He called out to a passing sailor. "No one touches the axe. Understood? Helmsman! How far?"

"About fifty feet, Lord!"

Brachyura nodded and stretched his powerful limbs. Hirkuin and his artillery crews were firing on the greylings still ashore, but the bolts were proving less effective against the smaller creatures. There was a splash as one of the rowboats hit the water, eight knights packed tightly in the little vessel like herrings in a barrel. Bansworth stood at the stern, his sword drawn.

"Closer!" Brachyura ordered. Praxis could hear the sounds of battle, carried to him by the wind. One of the threshers was down while the other had managed to commandeer a knight's battle-axe and was wielding it one-handed with surprising skill. Greylings swarmed everywhere, biting and clawing.

With a rush of air, Brachyura launched himself from the

deck of the *Summer Dream*. He landed close to the surviving thresher, tore the axe from its hand and used it to remove its head from its shoulders. "Form up on me," he said coolly, shaking the black ichor from the blade. "Let us deal with the stragglers."

It was an impressive display of prowess, enough to captivate the attention of Praxis's two guards … which gave him the opportunity he had been waiting for.

Now! he thought, as he climbed quickly onto the ship's starboard rail. He jumped and experienced a half-second of freedom before a hand grabbed the heel of his boot and pulled him back on board. He hit the deck hard.

Hirkuin stared down at him, his moustache bristling. "Innocent or not, you are not making a very good case for yourself," the guard captain said sternly and dealt Praxis a heavy kick to the head that sent him spiralling into unconsciousness.

CHAPTER 13

THE VALUE OF SORROW

"Why is it that you want to risk your life for these people? People you have never met? Where does all this sense of duty come from?"

"From you, Father. I am your son."

EXCHANGE BETWEEN VOHANEN AND AVOR, 426 AT

"WHERE IN THE PIT ARE WE?" yelled Vohanen to Krelbe over the biting wind. Dusk was fast approaching, and once what little light remained was gone, the mountain trail would become even more treacherous.

Krelbe threw his hands up in exasperation. Swirling eddies caught the loosely packed snow on the path in front of them, creating an icy mist shaped from a thousand miniature snowflakes. To their rear, more knights struggled up the winding trail, fur mantles and braided beards speckled with white. The long wooden poles strapped to their backs protruded over their heads, making their silhouettes look almost alien, like a parade of strange, man-sized insects.

Far, far below them, on the lower slopes, Vohanen could just make out a cluster of distant blurs. The horses and the two knights left to guard them. Above, the jagged peak of the Spike, partially obscured by the low-hanging clouds, loomed over them menacingly. Luckily, they would not have to go that far. Stick — or whatever his real name was — had told them that they only needed to climb about halfway to the top.

"THERE SHOULD BE A TREE WITH TWO TRUNKS," Vohanen shouted, scanning the white vista. He blinked irritably as wet specks of snow were blown into his eyes. The tree supposedly marked a fork in the path that would lead to a ridge overlooking Morlak keep; the launch point for the gliders.

"TO THE LEFT," called out Krelbe, gesturing towards a vague V-shaped smudge up ahead. A wolf howled, its high-pitched cry mingling with the whistling wind. An answering howl echoed off the rocks somewhere to their left.

Vohanen trudged through the snow, bending close to Krelbe to speak into his ear. "Don't like the sound of that. Let's get the men moving."

Krelbe sniffed dismissively. "Not sure there's anything to worry about. We've had wolves in Dirkvale before; they always steered well clear of the temple and surrounding woodlands, even in winter."

"Aye, but in Dirkvale they could find other sources of food. Look around you, what do you think is left to eat around here?"

"Well, berries and grubs and such—"

"*Us*, Krelbe. We are all that's left to eat around here. Remember Stick's missing leg. Get the men moving."

Krelbe turned away, muttering to himself, just as a dark, limber shadow bounded out of the swirling snowflakes to their right and slammed into his side, bowling him over. A snarling maw bit into his arm, sharp teeth piercing the animal furs and the flesh beneath. Krelbe cried out in pain, his other hand struggling to pull his short sword from its scabbard.

Vohanen shrugged off his backpack, removed his ram's head horn and drew his own weapon. He approached cautiously, observing the struggle, waiting for an opening. Krelbe changed tactics. Balling his hand into a fist, he punched the wolf hard on the muzzle. The creature yelped and relaxed its jaw, allowing the knight to pull his arm free and roll away. Vohanen leapt forwards, stabbing into the wolf's back, crunching through flesh and bone, and pinning its writhing body to the hard ground beneath.

Six more wolves rushed to meet them, led by an enormous one-eyed alpha male, its grey-furred body covered in scars. It swerved past Krelbe and pounced on an unsuspecting knight behind him, tearing a chunk of muscle from the man's neck. A spray of blood splattered onto the white snow — hot and steaming in the cold air.

"SHIELD—" Vohanen started to cry, then stopped himself with a curse. Pit! The shields were back at the campsite, along with their steel breastplates. They would have to try something else.

"CIRCLE!" he yelled, running towards the dying Knight of Kriari, his braided beard jingling. The alpha male was on top of the fallen warrior, claws digging into his arms, muzzle buried in the man's neck.

"For Kriari!" Vohanen barked, slicing down at the alpha's unprotected back, but it twisted at the last minute, as if warned by some sixth sense, and dodged backwards.

Krelbe was shouting himself hoarse over the wind, pulling and prodding the knights into formation. Another wolf pounced. Krelbe lashed out with a steel-capped boot and scored a lucky hit on the creature's soft belly. It fell back, whining.

Vohanen stared down at the dead knight. The corpse's face had been so badly mauled, he couldn't even tell who it was anymore. He looked away with a shudder. A meaty hand clapped down on his shoulder and pulled him backwards into the relative safety of the defensive circle.

"We need to kill the alpha," said Caddox, his face tinged with red from the cold.

"And how do you propose we do that?"

Caddox shrugged and drew his battle-axe from its sheath with his uninjured hand. "One of us needs to act as bait."

Vohanen tightened his grip on his short sword. "Well, that'll have to be me, won't it? If what you say is true and Brachyura has returned, he will be most displeased if I get you killed. If I fall, you can tell Krelbe he's in charge."

And without waiting for Caddox to reply, he pushed his way out of the circle of knights. The wind slowed for a moment and he took a closer look at the beasts tracking them. The wolves were lean and mangy, their ribs visible beneath their taut skin and patchy grey fur. They were starved and desperate.

One of the males began to slink forwards, only to be

stopped in its tracks by a low growl from the alpha. Yellow eyes fixed the knight with a shrewd intelligence.

"Come then!" said Vohanen with as much courage as he could muster. He found he was sweating despite the cold. He could feel the gaze of his men on his back. Now was not the time to show weakness.

"COME ON!" he yelled, baring his teeth in an animal-istic snarl. "I am Vohanen, Knight of Kriari! Come, taste my blade!"

The alpha attacked, lightning-fast, its jaws stretched impossibly wide. Vohanen brought his short sword up, but he was too slow. One hundred and fifty pounds of fur and muscle hit him in the chest. He felt like he had been punched by Kriari himself. He staggered backwards, tripped, and landed hard on his back, his sword slipping from his hand into the snow.

The wolf sprang after him with a howl, its teeth aiming for his neck. Vohanen flung his head to one side and the animal missed his jugular by inches, tearing a great chunk out of his beard instead.

"PIT!" he shouted in desperation. He grabbed hold of a handful of fur under the wolf's neck and pushed as hard as he could in an attempt to escape. The slavering maw was directly over his face, thick gobbets of drool dripping down into his nose and beard. The stench of rotten meat filled his lungs and made him gag.

Then, with a loud *thunk*, the pressure on his arms and chest was released. With a final heave, he shoved the dying wolf aside and stood up, his head spinning. The alpha lay in a pool of its own blood, a butterfly-shaped axe buried in its back. The other wolves had disappeared, using the whirling snow to fade away into the shadows.

Caddox ripped his weapon free and wiped it clean on the remains of the beast's fur.

Vohanen spat to clear the vile taste from his mouth. "Took you long enough," he grumbled, bending to retrieve his short sword.

"You are most welcome," glowered the Knight of Brachyura. Shaking his head in irritation, he started up the slope towards the distant two-trunked tree.

Vohanen remained near the fallen corpse of his fellow knight as the others passed him by, a few murmuring their thanks or pausing long enough to clasp wrists. After a while, he crouched down and drew the dead man's short sword, placing it on his chest and wrapping the stiff fingers around the hilt.

"May you go in peace to meet your ancestors," he said reverently in a low voice.

"We just gonna leave him here, then?" Krelbe was waiting at a respectful distance, the wooden poles swaying above his head. He held Vohanen's glider pack and ram's horn in his hands.

"What would you have us do?" Vohanen rasped. "How long do you think it would take to get a fire going in this weather? We can't burn him, and the ground's too hard to bury him. We have to abandon him."

"Abandon him to the wolves."

"Yes. I am sorry, Krelbe, but I do not have the power to choose how and when we die. Otherwise, I would be dead and my son would still be alive." Vohanen marched over and grabbed his pack, hoisting it onto his back and setting off after the others without another word.

He soon heard the crunch of booted feet on snow as Krelbe came up behind him. They walked on in silence, reaching the V-shaped landmark and turning off the main trail in the direction of one of the wider ridges overlooking Morlak keep.

"Here's your ram's horn back," said Krelbe finally. "Why do you carry that thing around with you all the time anyway? It's just weighing you down."

Vohanen gave the horn an affectionate rub. "Family heirloom. Been passed down from father to son for generations. My grandfather told me that it's so old, Kriari probably once heard it himself!"

"Hmmm. You can believe what you want, I suppose. So, tell me, do you think that wolf got worried when you told it who you were?"

"What?"

"All that 'I am Vohanen, Knight of Kriari' stuff. Probably was right terrified, hearing that."

"Krelbe …"

"Come taste my blade!" said Krelbe in a surprisingly good impression of Vohanen's voice. "Must have been quivering in its boots, poor thing."

"Krelbe, shut up."

"'Course, doesn't really have boots, does it? Quivering in its paws, maybe? In its fur?"

"All right, all right. I'm sorry I snapped at you. Now shut up."

"Yes, Sir. Can't wait to tell Evie though. And Jeffson. An eyebrow will be cocked, I'm sure … oh, look, we've arrived."

"Pit," said Vohanen with a low whistle. Ner'alla had chosen their spot perfectly. The ridge was roughly eighty feet long, a dark spur of granite protruding from the surrounding snow. Beyond it lay the town of Morlak. Night had fallen, and the lower city was lit by thousands of distant lights, blinking like fireflies. A sinuous line of fire ringed the glowing dots — the braziers atop the curtain wall. Above, they could make out the inner city, dark and silent, save for the dim glow emanating from the upper floor windows of the keep and garrison.

Vohanen walked over to Caddox, who was struggling to remove his pack with one hand.

"Apologies for earlier and thank you," he said, helping the other knight to slip the strap over his bandaged arm. Caddox inclined his head. "Think nothing of it. Now send someone over here to give me a hand, would you? There's no way I'll manage to assemble this Pit-spawned contraption by myself."

They worked quietly for half an hour, attaching the fabric to the wooden frames, testing the harnesses, checking for loose knots. And once they had finished, Vohanen had them check everything all over again.

"Right," he said. "I'm fairly sure that these won't come apart when we jump. Can't promise anything about what will happen when you land, though."

There were a few nervous chuckles.

"It is time," he continued, more seriously. "And now I must ask you if you really wish to do this. You did not volunteer to come, and you did not choose me as your leader. What we are about to do is risky, unplanned, and, quite frankly, stupid. There is no shame or dishonour in turning back."

Twenty-two pairs of eyes stared back at him. No one spoke.

"Very well. Then remember what, er, Stick told you. A fast run along the ridge. Keep your head level with your shoulders and your feet up. Get a feeling for updrafts and make sure your turns are slow and steady. Aim for the roof of the garrison. If you miss the roof, aim for the courtyard. Stall your glider to land and, if all else fails, cut your harness." He looked up at the night sky. The low-hanging clouds were still there, blotting out the moon and stars. Harder to be seen, but harder to see.

"Those of you who know me are well aware that I'm useless at speeches, so I'll be brief. You should be proud. Proud to be who you are, proud to be Knights of Kriari. Since the time of the Twelve, we have defended Morlak from its enemies, and we will continue to do so until the last of us draws his final breath. Your ancestors look upon you now. Do not show them your fear. Show them your courage! Show them your strength! For Morlak! FOR KRIARI!"

"FOR KRIARI!" came the answering cry. Men unsheathed their weapons, a glittering line of swords raised high.

I must lead, thought Vohanen. *I have to be the first to jump.*

He took a deep breath and slipped into the harness of his glider. Immediately, the wind began to tug at his back, pulling him into the air. Before him, the runway of dark stone stretched off into oblivion. He took another deep breath and started to run. Forty feet remaining. Thirty. He was fighting to keep his feet on the ground now, bounding more than running.

Twenty.

A manic laugh escaped his lips. Terrible thoughts rushed into his head. Had he secured the harness? Tightened the knots? Were his men ready? Questions swirled round and round like a whirlwind. He faltered, starting to panic.

What was he doing? This was madness!

Ten.

"I believe in you, Father," whispered the distant voice of Avor, cutting through all fear and doubt. "I believe."

Vohanen smiled.

And jumped.

CHAPTER 14

THE CHAINED MAN

"I do not like the word 'risk'. It implies a lack of planning or, even worse, a lack of sufficient statistical analysis. Let us talk instead of probabilities. If the probability of retrieving information is high and, inversely, the probability of losing an asset is within acceptable parameters, then there is no logical reason for us not to proceed."

ZYGOS, SEVENTH OF THE TWELVE, 121 AT

J ELAÏA TWISTED UNEASILY in the saddle, the leather fender rubbing against her raw thighs. Her snow-white palfrey whinnied in protest. "Sorry," she whispered, patting the beast's neck. "I know you're tired. I'm tired too."

The combined Kessrin-Arelian forces stretched out behind her like a snake, close to a thousand men traipsing through the windswept scrublands that bordered the

north-western edge of the Redenfell Mountains. Following
the rank-and-file, several hundred wagons lumbered along
gracelessly, filled to bursting with sleeping soldiers and crates
of supplies. Outriders dressed in the red and white livery
of Arelium patrolled the flanks, galloping up and down the
column carrying missives to the unit captains.

   Loré del Conte and his vanguard formed the head of
the serpent; a score of Arelian and Kessrin nobles on barded
warhorses, their multi-coloured pennants fluttering in the
breeze. They had spotted no sign of the greylings since cross-
ing over into Talth, but it always paid to be vigilant. Jelaïa
could see Loré chatting and joking amiably with two of his
vassals, a different man to the angry, petulant one she had
spoken to back in Kessrin.

   Since leaving the maritime capital ten days ago, they
had dined together every evening in Loré's tent, often
accompanied by Orkam, Xandris, and the healer. True to
his word, del Conte never referred to their earlier conversation, using the time instead to regale his guests with tales of
his tempestuous youth, tales that often involved an equally
mischievous Listus del Arelium. Jelaïa realised just how close
the two men had been and how alike they were.

   It was during one particularly wine-filled evening that
they learnt that the healer's name was Belen, and that he and
Xandris had met when the latter had purposely ingested a
few too many apple seeds so that he could spend more time
in the healer's presence and eventually become his appren-
tice. The two were a good fit, each relying on the other's
strengths to compensate for their own weaknesses.

   A cloud of dust appeared half a mile up the trail, quickly

revealing a single horseman, riding hard. Orkam. He skid-
ded to a halt before Loré, his stallion pawing the ground.

"Found them, Sir Loré," he said. "About a mile from
here, camped on the edge of a pine forest. But there's a problem. They are under attack."

"Under attack?" scoffed Loré. "Who would dare attack
a hundred Knights of Brachyura and two of the Twelve?
'Twould be folly!"

"That's just it, my Lord. They aren't there. Didn't see
more than twenty men fending off a sizeable force of greylings. They need help."

Aldarin! thought Jelaïa, nudging her horse closer to the
group.

"Pit!" swore Loré, securing his helm. "Cavalry! On me!
Diamond formation. Lances loose. Half-canter. Squire!
Bring me a lance!"

"I'll be coming too," Jelaïa said firmly.

"My Lady—"

"No discussion, Loré. I'm coming." She pulled her axe-
shaped medallion out from beneath her riding cloak and left
it hanging there, within easy reach.

"Understood, my Lady. Orkam, your horse looks
exhausted. Stay here with the outriders. If you see anything
strange — *anything* — you send a rider straight away."

Loré accepted his lance from the returning squire, gripping the shaft just below the vamplate. He wheeled his
warhorse around and accelerated into a canter. Jelaïa followed, the wind whipping through her hair. After several
hundred yards, the terrain began to slope downwards and
pine trees came into view, with acres of forest stretching out
in all directions.

Loré tapped his horse's flanks and lowered the visor of his helm, motioning for his men to do the same. The squire riding to his left unveiled the snarling wolf's head banner of Arelium. The faint sounds of battle could be heard now, coming from somewhere down near the edge of the forest. Jelaïa could see a semi-circle of knights, caught unawares and unarmoured, fighting desperately to keep a swarm of greylings at bay. They were defending a scattering of tents and two rows of cut tree trunks stacked seven feet high.

"LANCES!" yelled Loré, crouching low and tucking his lance under his arm for support. Less than a hundred yards remained.

"CHARGE!" he bellowed, coaxing his horse into a gallop.

"FOR ARELIUM!"

Jelaïa cracked open her medallion and let three drops of Aldarin's blood fall onto her tongue. She had felt the pain of the fires of Brachyura many times now but still underestimated the sheer physical agony as the raw power of Aldarin's memories crackled through her body like lightning. She swayed in the saddle, her vision blurring.

Father, she thought, searching for distant memories of the only paternal figure she would ever acknowledge, the man who raised her, the man who had shaped her into the person she was today: Listus del Arelium. One came unbidden. A juggler throwing daggers into the air, her father smiling and tossing a gold coin. The pain receded.

Her sight snapped sharply into focus, now tinged with a hint of blue. She saw the cavalry charge crash into the rear of the enemy lines with the force of a tornado. Greylings shrieked in pain and surprise as they were trampled under hoof. Lances punctured skin and bone with ease, impaling dozens of the creatures. Loré had spied a larger prey and aimed his own weapon at one of the threshers. The thing's hard, leathery skin was protection enough against spears and swords but defenceless against the unstoppable force of a steel-tipped lance. The thresher was caught half-turning to meet the Arelian threat, and the lance entered its side, burrowing through its innards and exploding from its stomach.

The cavalry charge had barely slowed, cutting a line deep into the midst of the greyling attackers. Loré dropped his blood-spattered lance and drew his sword, decapitating one of the creatures as it leapt at his squire. The emboldened Knights of Brachyura pushed forwards courageously, wielding their axes with a skill born from years of training.

Jelaïa scanned the battlefield, her eyes alighting on one of the more heavily-armoured threshers. With a twist of her wrist, she sent an azure blaze flashing from her fingertips. The fires of Brachyura melted the rusty metal in an instant, reducing it and its unfortunate wearer to a pile of molten slag. Greylings rushed in, jabbing at her palfrey. She made a sweeping gesture with her burning hand and a circular curtain of flame surrounded her, roasting the creatures' grey flesh black.

The stench of burnt meat assailed her nostrils. Out of the corner of her eye, she caught a glimpse of Loré, his visor raised, his mouth agape, before the ebb of battle swallowed him up again. She lifted her burning hands once more but found she had run out of targets. The enemy refused to approach, preferring to take their chances with the swords of the cavalry or the axes of the knights.

Suddenly, one of the threshers bellowed something

inarticulately and the surviving greylings broke off the attack, fleeing into the trees.

"AFTER THEM!" shouted Loré, bloodlust distorting his features. He slammed his visor down again and set off in pursuit, supported by his retinue.

Jelaïa concentrated for a moment, calming her nerves and feeling the burning sensation slowly drain from her aching limbs. She dismounted and walked over to what appeared to be the leader of the Knights of Brachyura, a chalky-haired veteran organising the triage of the wounded.

"Lady Jelaïa del Arelium," she said, curtsying perfunctorily. "What's going on?"

The man bowed deeply in return. "Baroness, we are honoured. It is good that you arrived when you did, we were severely outmatched." He looked past her, where two young knights were carrying bodies from the battlefield to a shallow grave a few yards away. "Once the wagons arrive, we can load up the lumber and leave this Pit-forsaken place."

"Where are the others?"

The knight wasn't listening, watching as the dead bodies tumbled down the earthen slope.

"The others?" prompted Jelaïa.

"I … yes. Apologies. 'Tis the first time I have lost men under my command. Not an easy thing. We heard reports that a large host of greylings had been sighted near Silverlake. Thousands strong. Brachyura and Derello decided it would be best to go out to meet them on open ground rather than let them return unimpeded to Talth. They left this morning."

"Leaving you in charge. It must have been a decoy, a way for the greylings to seize your supplies. Are they really that devious?"

"It would appear so. If I remember my teachings correctly, they have been using such tactics for some time, as
hard as it may be to believe. I was not left in charge, however; I do not hold the rank of temple master. Sir Aldarin
had the honour of commanding our forces here."

Had? Jelaïa's heart skipped a beat. "I do not see him
among you. Where is he?"

"Sir Aldarin is … It would be better if you saw for yourself." He motioned for her to follow him, skirting around a
pile of greyling bodies. One of the creatures was still moving
feebly, emitting a mewing sound. He crushed its skull with
the butt of his axe.

They reached an opulent blue and white tent pitched
on the edge of the treeline, a sea serpent banner flying from
its highest point.

"Lord Derello's tent," the knight said, lifting the canvas
flap. The interior was large and spacious. A round table,
half-hidden under a plethora of maps and parchments,
dominated the centre of the room, surrounded by military-
style chairs. The floor was covered by an expensive-looking
rug while a curtained area off to one side contained a single
bed and travelling chest. Jelaïa's gaze was drawn to an object
that was at odds with the rest of the furniture: an iron post,
five feet high, which had been driven into the dirt at the far
end of the tent.

"It was where we kept the prisoner," the knight said
slowly as if reading her mind.

"The prisoner? You mean Praxis?"

"Yes. Derello would entrust him to no one else."

Jelaïa felt a jitter run down her spine. The tent suddenly

became very small, oppressive even, smothering her. *I need some air,* she thought. *I need to get out.*

"Praxis has escaped? How?"

The knight raised the canvas behind the metal post. Someone had sliced through the leather ringlets and guy lines used to anchor the tent exterior to the pegs. "He had some help. Someone cut their way inside."

"Who?"

"We don't know, but he was cunning. Aldarin had set up an acceptable perimeter, with regular patrols. Whoever got him out was clever enough to find a way through the net."

"And now Praxis is free."

"Not quite, my Lady," the knight replied with the ghost of a smile. "That's why Aldarin's not here. He went after them."

⚜

Praxis cursed as another low-hanging branch caught him in the face. The figure in front of him brought a finger to his lips, telling him to be quiet.

Easy enough for him to say, Praxis thought, *he hasn't got his hands chained together.* He didn't know why they had to keep silent; they'd left the allied camp a good half-hour ago. Surely they were out of range of any Kessrin patrols?

Praxis didn't know much about the man who had saved him. He appeared to be a Knight of Zygos or someone who had enough knowledge of their call signs and code names to imitate one perfectly. He had spoken very little since slithering under Derello's tent to cut Praxis free from the post

holding him captive, only ordering him to follow closely
and soundlessly.

It could be another trap, of course. Another ploy by
Derello to test Praxis's loyalty or extract a confession. But
Praxis found he didn't care. After days locked up in the hold
of the *Summer Dream* followed by a bone-jarring ride across
country in the back of a supply wagon, he was ready to risk
anything to escape.

The Baron had come to see him a handful of times, his
demeanour oscillating between angry, hurt, and confused.
Hirkuin was never far behind, staring at Praxis like he was
something foul that he had just scraped off his shoe. Their
short conversations had always ended in the same way, with
Derello storming off to sulk. With time and a lot of hard
work, Praxis *might* have convinced the young Baron of his
innocence, but this most recent development was considerably better.

"How much further?" he whispered to his silent companion. No reply. He started to move cautiously forwards,
then stopped. What was that? A faint metallic clinking
sound, muffled by the dense foliage. His ally had heard it
too and stood frozen to the spot, his head cocked to one
side. Listening.

There. Again.

"We are being followed," Praxis hissed. "And they are
gaining on us."

"Pincer," the other man replied and disappeared behind
a tree.

For a minute, Praxis thought that he had gone mad,
and then he remembered the dry voice of his drill instruc-
tor all those years ago, rattling off a list of attack patterns. A

two-pronged attack, then. He looked down at his chained hands. A serious handicap but not unsurmountable.

Aldarin's thickset frame came into view. The knight was ploughing through the undergrowth at speed, branches cracking and splintering as they came into contact with his armour. He drew to a halt, panting.

"Praxis. Stop. Enough hiding," he said, breathing hard. "Do not do this. It but further proves your guilt."

"Aldarin. You do not understand. I *am* guilty. Guilty of following orders. Guilty of maintaining the Pact. You may think that makes me a traitor, but it is you and those of your order who have betrayed the Twelve. And by doing so, you have most assuredly doomed the entire human race to extinction."

A soft rustle of leaves from a tree to Aldarin's left. Not long now.

"You are better than this, Praxis — if that is even your real name. You speak of treachery, of upholding the Pact, and yet you did not turn Derello over to Mina. I believe you are conflicted, and if so—". Aldarin saw something in Praxis's eyes and ducked. A throwing knife whistled overhead and embedded itself in a nearby tree trunk. The Knight of Zygos sprang from his hiding place, a needle-like dagger in each hand. Aldarin reeled backwards, deflecting the blades with his gauntleted hands, his axe still strapped to his back. A desperate kick crunched into his assailant's knee, forcing him to retreat.

"Oathbreaker," snarled the Knight of Zygos, echoing Mina's words in the Great Hall of Kessrin. Aldarin didn't reply, pulling his axe free. The fallen knight attacked again, but this time Aldarin was ready for him. His axe sang, cutting deep into his opponent's arm just above the elbow. The man screamed and dropped his daggers, pressing his hand to the wound in an attempt to staunch the flow of blood. Aldarin advanced.

Now! thought Praxis as Aldarin turned away from him. He ran swiftly forwards, bending to pick up one of his ally's fallen daggers and, holding it clumsily in his chained hands, pushed it with all his might into the unprotected spot behind Aldarin's knee. Praxis felt the knife cut through the chainmail and bite into the flesh beneath. He gave the blade a vicious twist for good measure and was rewarded with a cry of pain. He let go, leaving the hilt protruding from the wound.

Aldarin whirled to meet him, but his injured knee gave way and he lost his balance, hitting the ground hard. Praxis looked down at him in disgust.

"Useless. Beaten by a chained man. You are so head-strong, Aldarin. Always rushing into things without taking the time to think them through. Now, where is that other dagger so we can finish things?"

"ALDARIN?" came the worried voice of Jelaïa.

"HERE!" Aldarin replied. Praxis kicked him hard in the mouth. His ally approached and tapped him on the shoulder. "We must go. Now."

"No. Twice this man has eluded us. Never again."

"Too risky. The woman is a priestess of Brachyura. She'll carbonise us. I have orders to bring you back alive. Come. Now."

"Orders? Orders from whom?"

The knight looked at him strangely. "Why, from our patron, of course. Zygos, Seventh of the Twelve."

Praxis ground his teeth in frustration. Pit! Why was Zygos so eager to meet with him? Eager enough to set him free? Whatever the reason, he couldn't ignore such a prestigious summons.

He smiled his half-smile at Aldarin and stamped down hard on the wounded man's knee, eliciting an agonising moan.

"Serendipity, my friend. Serendipity, once again. But we are taught that there is balance in all things. For every lucky escape, an unfortunate death. Your time is coming, Aldarin, and when it does, I hope I will be there to see the light leave your eyes."

And with one last glare of hatred, Praxis left Aldarin writhing in the dirt and followed his liberator north towards Zygos and his freedom.

CHAPTER 15

MEMORIES OF QUAYJIN

"Every single Morlakian has his role to play in society. I, as Baron, provide my subjects with guidance and protection. My policies aim to reward the hard-working and punish the sluggards. I serve the people and, in turn, they serve me. And that includes emptying my latrines."

BARON DEL MORLAK, 406 AT

❧

"BY THE PIT! It's so much worse than I expected," said Syrella, clapping her hand over her nose and mouth.

She was standing with Ner'alla and Jeffson in the shadow of an abandoned shopfront less than six feet away from the inner wall. They were close enough to see the circular shape of the sewer grate and smell the revolting miasma vomited forth from the drainage pipe. A green-brown sludge dripped through the holes in the grate, accumulating at the bottom of an earthen ditch that followed the curve of the ramparts. Far above, the faint tinkling of metal and the thud of leather boots signalled the passage of another patrol.

"I wonder where it all goes?" said Jeffson curiously. He was wearing a black tarpaulin over his clothes, the sheet of water-resistant cloth pulled tightly around his wrists and ankles by a series of drawstrings. Syrella was similarly attired and also wore a cap to protect her hair.

"Dunno," Ner'alla replied. "Never really thought to find out. Probably ends up down near the bottom of the outer city, if they just let gravity do its work. It's where most of the poorer homes are, close to the warehouses. Unfortunately, being knee-high in waste is the least of their problems."

"That can't be right," Syrella said, frowning. "I have been to those neighbourhoods many times; it's not that bad."

"Have you, my Lady? By yourself? Disguised as you were yesterday?"

"Well, no, as part of an official—"

"Right, yeah. You see, my Lady, when it's a *planned* visit, the town guard come down the day before and make things a bit more presentable."

"What's that supposed to mean?"

"It means they start by rounding up all the orphans, beggars, and other street rabble. Cart them off to some place where they won't be seen or heard for a while. Then they make the residents clear up the sh... the waste run-ning down the gutters and overflowing onto the cobbles. And lastly, perhaps most importantly, they set up a nice, easy route for you; no side trips down any of the alleys, no way to veer off the beaten track. Once all is in place, the del Morlak family arrives, under heavy guard, gives out a few loaves of bread and grasps a few wrists … the cleaner ones."

"I see," said Syrella in a clipped tone, anger plain on her face. "Another idea of my father, the late Baron, I would surmise?"

"Yes, my Lady, if the rumours are true. He thought it would be best not to upset the Baroness by showing her any of the more undesirable parts of Morlak."

"And one more thing he *forgot* to tell me. By the Pit, he really was setting me up to fail, wasn't he?"

"My Lady?"

"Never mind, it was a rhetorical question."

"Retto-what?"

"They are moving," interjected Jeffson, his eyes scanning the top of the wall. "Are you sure that's the last patrol for the evening?"

Ner'alla squinted at the cloudy sky. "Can't be sure," he said slowly, tugging fretfully at the golden chain on his cheek. "Moon's being shy tonight, it's making it difficult to keep track of the time. And, um, well, my contact in Morlak keep has gone silent."

Jeffson made a tutting sound. "You should have told us this earlier, Ner'alla. How long since he checked in?"

"'Couple of weeks," the Da'arran replied in a small voice, looking down at his boots.

"So, the last guard patrol schedule you have is from …"

"Two weeks ago."

"And the schedule for the emptying of the latrines?"

"Two weeks ago."

"Ner'alla!"

"I do have the key to the grate though!" He delved into

one of his many pockets and fished out a rusty-looking key. "And I mean, come on, why would they change anything now, right?"

Jeffson snatched the key from Ner'alla's outstretched hand. "This is *not* ideal."

There was a burst of muffled laughter and both men turned to see Syrella leaning against the wall of the shop, her hand over her mouth to stifle the noise and her shoulders shaking with mirth.

"By the Twelve, gentlemen, this rescue mission is certainly turning out to be something special. The Red Sparrows fly again!" She wiped a tear from her eye and straightened her tarpaulin cap. "Well, Vohanen must be halfway up the Spike by now. I don't see how we can afford to wait any longer. We'll just have to make the best of it, won't we? Shall we proceed?"

Ner'alla gave an embarrassed cough and nodded. "The grate only locks from this side, so you'll have to keep it open if you're thinking of coming back out this way. I'll keep watch here as long as I can, and if any of the town guard or those mean Knights of Mithuna turn up, I'll do my best to stall them. Oh, and you'll be wanting these."

He produced two strips of fabric from another of his many pockets. "Masks dipped in the juice of limes," he explained. "Like lemons, but smaller. Plenty of lime trees in Da'arra but not much demand for them further north. In any case, a lot of my men tell me it's good for blocking out the smell. That and, well, let's just say you want to have something that covers your mouth, so nothing gets in there by mistake."

Jeffson gave a long sigh. "I am beginning to think we

should have taken a glider, my Lady. Vohanen and his knights seem to have the better part of the deal." He accepted one of the proffered masks and tied it across his nose and mouth.

"Dress and makeup?" he said in a muffled voice. Ner'alla threw him a small waterproof bag filled with Syrella's things. He caught it deftly and attached the drawstring to his ankle. "Very good. Ready, my Lady?"

"Not really."

Jeffson turned and looked Ner'alla squarely in the eye. "Let us hope that we do not find any unplanned surprises, for if we do, and I survive, I will be back to burn your tavern to the ground." He set off without waiting for a reply, Syrella falling in step behind him.

They reached the grate. The stench was overpowering despite the lime masks. Jeffson opened the lock, the screech sounding unnaturally loud in the quiet of the night. Crouching, he peered into the pipe. A dark tunnel stretched away from him, angled slightly upwards towards two small circles of light. The latrines.

Lying down on his stomach, he used his hands to pull himself into the pipe, his shoulders brushing against the sides.

An even tighter fit than last time, he thought. *Either the pipe has become smaller, or I have become fatter.*

He began to crawl, trying to ignore the horrendous smell and the slick slime that rubbed against his protective clothes. He heard a gagging sound from a few feet behind him, signalling that Syrella had entered the pipe. There was no room to turn his head, barely enough space to move his arms. He concentrated on the spots of distant light, pushing one elbow forwards and then the next, dragging his body inch by inch closer to his salvation.

Something wet and sticky dropped down from the roof of the pipe and spattered onto his cheek. He could feel it, glistening there, but there was no way to wipe it off. An irresistible urge to vomit came over him, and he swallowed with difficulty.

The last time things had been different. He had been younger, brash and fearless, with that feeling only youth can bring; of being unstoppable, invincible, ready to take on the world. He had been up the pipe in minutes, laughing to himself. He wasn't laughing now.

After what seemed like hours, he reached the top of the pipe and the lower floor latrines: a wooden box with a hinged lid into which two round holes had been cut. Dragging his hand forwards, he pushed against the lid to open it and free them from this nightmare.

Nothing happened.

Jeffson was not one to panic — he prided himself on it, in fact — but when he felt the wood resist him, a kernel of dread, small and heavy like a ball of lead, formed at the bottom of his stomach. He paused a moment and then pushed again, harder this time. The lid refused to move.

Pit!

He thought back to what he had said to Taleck. *Stuck in the dark, waiting for them to empty the latrines.* A child's laughter echoed in the confines of his mind. Painful memories, pushing their way to the surface as they always did when he began to lose his composure.

He closed his eyes. There was a way out of this, as there was for every situation. He was no longer that smiling, impetuous youth but, what he now lacked in physical strength and resilience, he made up for with experience. He had travelled the world, from shore to shore. He had seen the oasis of Da'arra, the towering temples of Klief, the tranquil Zen gardens of Quayjin.

Wait! That was it! Quayjin!

He had learnt much there, in that remote eastern Barony, far beyond the borders of Morlak. The people of Quayjin placed great value on the harmony between body and mind. Their soldiers eschewed traditional weapons, preferring to focus on unarmed combat. They believed that, with enough concentration, the palm of a hand could be as destructive as any sword.

Jeffson dug deep, struggling to remember. He focussed on his right hand, opening and closing it to make a fist. His body was a river of energy, flowing from his head to his toes. He imagined himself diverting that river, waves of water running from his chest and arms to his hand, feeling the pressure build at the tips of his fingers.

His eyes snapped open and he sent his arm hurtling forwards, palm first. The lid slammed open with a crack of splintered wood and a current of fresh air rushed down into the opening, crisp and cool. Jeffson grasped either side of the pipe and hauled himself upwards, slithering out of the box and onto the floor like a stinking worm.

He rolled onto his back, exhausted … and stared into the wide eyes of one of the keep's servants, a young lad of no more than seventeen with a swathe of greasy hair and a runny nose.

"Intru—" the boy started to say, before Jeffson grabbed his leg, pulling him off his feet. The servant hit the ground hard, his head bouncing off the packed dirt. He blinked groggily a few times, then his eyes rolled into the back of their sockets and he was still.

Jeffson ripped the mask from his face and inhaled a lungful of fresh air. "You may come out, my Lady," he said. "The coast is clear."

A bedraggled Syrella appeared, caked with mud and other, more unsavoury matter. She removed her mask and spat twice.

"I am. Never. Ever. EVER doing that again," she said vehemently.

Jeffson stood. Behind the unconscious servant, he could see a rickety trolley: a couple of planks nailed together with wheels screwed underneath. On the trolley sat six buckets, filled to the brim. He did not need to move any closer to guess their contents; he could smell it already, the nauseous stench of excrement similar to what he had just crawled through.

"The upper floor latrines," he muttered. "They were about to empty the upper floor latrines!"

Syrella looked at him with a mixture of panic and anger. "You mean, we were nearly—"

"Buried, my Lady. Under all of that."

"I am going to kill that Pit-spawned Da'arran," she swore, fiddling with the drawstrings of her protective clothing. "I'll start by ripping that chain off his face and throwing it into one of those buckets!"

"His information has proved to be a trifle unreliable," agreed Jeffson. "If I may suggest a more suitable punishment, my Lady?" He glanced down at the servant. "He could, for example, take this poor man's job for a couple of weeks? It would allow him to gain a better understanding of what we have been through."

Syrella smiled briefly. "An excellent idea! I'll keep that in mind." She finished untying the drawstrings and wriggled out of the tarpaulin, letting it fall to the floor with a soggy squelch. "Now, hand me that ... Jeffson, what are you doing?"

Jeffson had spun round to face the wall, a red flush creeping slowly up his cheeks. "You are in your ... underclothes, my Lady."

"So, you are human after all! I thought you unflappable! Wait until Reed hears about this! Send my things over to me, would you?"

Without looking, Jeffson removed the bag from his ankle and kicked it backwards towards her.

"The stairs down to the prison are on the ground floor, the same level as we are on right now," Syrella said as she dressed. "Only a couple of minutes away. Sometimes there's a guard at the top, and there will almost definitely be one at the bottom." There was the sound of a corset being done up. "How do I look?"

Jeffson turned and gazed upon Lady Syrella del Morlak, the White Rose. She had chosen a burgundy dress trimmed with white fur. Her black hair cascaded over her left shoulder, leaving the right side of her neck bare and accentuating the pale curves of her neckline. Her dress was complemented by a silver necklace, set with amethysts, and a pair of studded earrings.

"You look ... like a Baroness, my Lady," he said, a hint of admiration softening his usual dry voice.

"Good. That's what I'm meant to look like. Now, take off those awful clothes so we can get out of here."

※

They ended up leaving the unconscious servant propped in a sitting position on the box, his trousers round his legs and his back leant against the wall. With any luck, from a distance, it would seem that he was using one of the latrine holes.

The corridor on the other side of the door was quiet and dark, the torches unlit. Faint moonlight filtered in through a row of narrow glazed windows.

"This way," Syrella said in a hushed tone, turning left. She led them down a series of empty corridors until they reached a sturdy-looking door with a grated aperture.

"Unguarded. Where is everyone?"

"Either hiding or fled," replied Jeffson. "Whoever this usurper is, they are not doing a very good job of maintaining the castle's corridors or its occupants." He gave the door a tentative push and it creaked open, revealing a set of well-worn stairs leading down into the blackness.

They proceeded cautiously. Jeffson took out his knuckle knives and pulled them on over his fingers. At the bottom of the stairs, they nearly ran into a scruffy guardsman, leaning on his spear in front of a locked iron gate. The gate protected the entrance to a roughly-hewn tunnel cut straight into the bedrock. A single torch sputtered and flickered in the damp air, casting strange shadows on the wall.

"M'Lady," stammered the startled guard, standing up

straight and clacking his heels together in some sort of salute. "I did not expect to see you down here again so soon!"

Jeffson shot a sidelong glance at Syrella and quickly hid his hands behind his back.

"You forget yourself, *guardsman*," the Baroness said imperiously. "It is not for you to question my motives. The last time I checked, this is my keep. I may come and go as I please."

"Of course, M'Lady, apologies," the man replied, bowing his head. "It's just ... is this some sort of test?"

"What are you talking about, guardsman?"

"Well, M'Lady, you told me to allow no one through to see the prisoner, under absolutely no circumstances, no matter who they were. And now you come back down here asking to be let through. Are you testing me?"

Syrella's eyelid flickered. "No, of course not. I meant no one apart from me. Now, hand me the key and step aside."

The guardsman licked his lips. "Can't do that, M'Lady, need the password first. That's what we agreed."

"Password, what—"

Jeffson stepped forwards and lashed out with his fist, clipping the guardsman on the chin. The man collapsed with a jangle of rusty chainmail. "You were taking too long, my Lady," Jeffson said, rummaging through the man's pockets. He produced a small key, which he used to unlock the barred gate.

"A moment longer and I would have convinced him," Syrella replied with an almost child-like pout.

"I do not doubt it, my Lady, but every minute wasted here puts us in more and more danger." He lifted the torch from its bracket and walked down the tunnel. It led to a single, unmarked cell; a cave with a set of bars across one end and an opening high on the opposite wall. The floor of the cell was covered in damp straw and what looked like the remains of a rat's carcass. Bolted to one wall was a wooden bed and lying on that bed, his body wreathed in shadow, his salt-and-pepper hair long and unkempt, was Merad Reed.

He raised his head at their approaching footsteps, and the pain and weariness etched into his features vanished, replaced by joy and relief.

"Jeffson? My Lady? Is it ... is it really you, this time?" He squinted at them as his eyes adjusted to the light. "Yes, yes it must be you, she could not imitate both of you. How is this possible? I had begun to lose hope!"

Seeing that Reed was alive, Jeffson felt a rush of happiness, warming him like a glass of mulled wine. His lips twitched into a half-smile.

By the Twelve, he had missed this stubborn, grumpy man.

"Good evening, my Lord," he said, forcing himself to keep his tone calm and neutral. "We have come to take you away from this unpleasant place, unless, of course, you are not yet tired of it?"

"Not yet tired? Pit, Jeffson, you haven't changed at all, have you?"

"I live to serve, my Lord."

"What did you mean by 'imitate?'" asked Syrella, coming closer to the bars. Reed stared at her.

"My Lady. You look ... you look ..."

"Yes, yes, you can compliment me later. Imitation?"

"Yes, my Lady. Mithuna, one of the Twelve. She is your imposter. She can mimic your form; I do not know how. She is very ... convincing."

Jeffson hung the torch on the wall and bent to unlock the cell door. "So, what those Knights of Mithuna said was true. She has returned. That will make Vohanen's task more difficult. I should find a way to warn him."

"Vohanen?" Reed's brow creased in incomprehension. "He's here too?"

"He's the one that started all of this, my Lord. Though I fear he does not realise what he has let himself in for. I hope we will not have to fight our way out."

"As do I," said Reed sadly, rising from the bed and moving into the light.

Syrella gasped in shock as she saw the bandaged stump at the end of his right arm.

They had taken his hand.

CHAPTER 16

ALDARIN'S REPLY

"The family of the man whose leg we had to amputate came to see me today. They were angry. Incensed, even. They had heard of my gift, but rumour and speculation had distorted the truth about what I could do. I tried to explain to them that the wound was self-inflicted. That there were some things I simply could not heal. They left even angrier than before."

KUMBHA, ELEVENTH OF THE TWELVE, 31 AT

✍

"**A**LDARIN!" JELAÏA CALLED again. She bit her lower lip in frustration. At first, it had been easy enough to follow the knight's trail. He appeared to have moved in a straight line through the forest, destroying anything that got in his way. But then the trail had passed through a trickling stream and she had lost him.

He's angry, she thought. *I need to find him.*

"ALDARIN!"

"HERE!"

Finally.

Her palfrey gave a crotchety whinny, exhausted. Jelaïa swung herself out of the saddle and hitched the reins to the trunk of a nearby pine. "You stay here," she murmured. Taking hold of her medallion in one hand, she moved towards Aldarin's voice, quickly spying a faint glimmer of silver among the green of the undergrowth. He was lying on the ground with his back to her, his articulated gauntlets and a bloody dagger next to him. He turned his head as she approached, his eyes lighting up as he saw her.

"Jelaïa, I thought for a moment that your voice might have been a hallucination. How did you get here?"

"I followed you," she replied, examining the wound in his knee. It was still bleeding, albeit sluggishly.

"I find myself rather indisposed," he said, following her gaze. "Due in part to my own stupidity. Not only did I rush off without waiting for reinforcements, but I then took to the field of battle without first making a careful study of my surroundings. I did not adhere to the teachings of my patron. Brachyura will be most displeased."

"I won't tell him if you don't. Who stabbed you?"

"Praxis," Aldarin replied grimly. "Acting in concert with a Knight of Zygos. A man with orders to take the traitor to meet Zygos himself. There is now no doubt in my mind that Praxis betrayed us. That look of contempt when he twisted the knife … I fear he may well be the man who murdered your father."

"Oh …" Jelaïa said softly. There was no real surprise at

hearing the news. She realised it was probably because she had subconsciously come to the same conclusion herself.

"Where are the men who accompanied you?" Aldarin continued. "I am not in any serious pain, but I do not think I can walk too far unaided. I will need help removing my armour and getting back to camp."

"I ... There's only me. I rode with the vanguard and when we arrived, the lumber camp was under attack. We routed them, but Loré took it upon himself to chase down the stragglers."

"I see. That is unfortunate. You will have to go back and get help."

"Nonsense. I'm quite capable of removing your armour myself. It's that wound I'm worried about. It's still bleeding."

"Jelaïa, it would not be proper for you to—"

"Aldarin," she replied. "Shut up. Roll over onto your stomach."

He complied, grumbling, and she knelt down, carefully removing the sabatons and then unbuckling the greaves and cuisses, sliding them down his legs and over his feet. The wound in the back of his knee was narrow but deep.

"How bad is it?" he asked.

"I'm not sure a bandage will be enough to stop the bleeding. I do have an idea, but it's going to hurt."

"Do it."

She opened her medallion and dabbed the smallest possible smear of liquid onto one finger before sticking it into her mouth. Pain flared up behind her eyeballs. She placed her left palm onto his knee and slowed her breathing. Careful ... careful ... Her hand flickered blue for an instant and Aldarin yelled out as she burned the wound to close it.

"Pit, woman! You could have warned me!"

He was wearing an expression somewhere between annoyance and admiration. She laughed.

"What's so funny?"

"You are! I like it when you swear, it reminds me that you're not quite so perfect after all. You can go and see Kumbha once we get back. Now roll onto your back, let's take your breastplate off."

She bent over him, searching for the clasps and buckles. A strand of chestnut hair fell across her face and she blew at it irritably. Then a calloused hand gently caught the stray lock and pushed it back behind her ear.

She stopped what she was doing and looked down at Aldarin, her heart racing. She became aware of her hands on his chest. His ocean-blue eyes were sparkling. They were all she could see.

"My Lady …" he began tentatively. She leant forwards and kissed him softly, relishing the tingling sensation that spread from her lips to her body, coursing through her like the fires of Brachyura but painless and pure. She felt his arm wrap around her and his hand caress the nape of her neck.

This was what she wanted. Not a protector. Not a guardian.

This. This perfect moment.

He released her reluctantly. "I have been wanting to talk to you for some time now about what you said to Brachyura. When you came to my aid."

"Oh, so you heard that?"

"I did. I was not sure what to reply at first, and then, when I was, events always seemed to conspire to keep us apart."

He caught her hand in his own. "I wanted to say … me too."

She smiled, and the constant oppressive weight of her legacy suddenly seemed considerably lighter.

"I gathered as much," she said, giving his hand a squeeze. "Now, much as it pains me to say it, we should have that wound looked at by someone more qualified than me."

He grinned. "Oh, I'm feeling much better."

"Nevertheless, I would not want to be seen as one who would take advantage of a wounded man."

"Jelaïa?"

"Yes?"

"Maybe just a little longer?"

His lips found hers and the worries of the world faded away.

They returned to find the camp in an uproar. The baggage train had arrived, joined moments later by the disheartened host of mounted knights and an infuriated Baron del Kessrin. Soldiers were rousing their sleepy companions from the flat-bottomed wagons that would now be used to transport the timber to the battlefield.

Jelaïa helped Aldarin down from her palfrey and handed the reins to a passing stablehand before making her way through the logistical bedlam to the exterior of the command tent and an impromptu reunion between the allied leaders.

"They led us on a wild goose chase," Derello was saying to Loré, waving his hands in the air. "Through the ruined village, out onto the shores of the lake and back into the forest. Bad terrain for the horses. We had to dismount and follow them on foot."

"They have employed such tactics before," rumbled Brachyura. "I should have thought to leave more men to guard the lumber. 'Twas lucky you arrived when you did, Sir Loré, or we would have nothing left to assault the walls of Talth."

"As you both know, I have fallen prey to similar enemy stratagems," Loré replied. His armour was covered in dirt and ichor. "We continue to underestimate them, despite all we have seen them do, I … Ah, my Lady, there you are! I was about to send out search parties. Where have you been?"

"Chasing after Praxis," said Jelaïa. "And failing to catch him. Aldarin overheard him speaking with the man who set him free. A Knight of Zygos. It would appear that Zygos himself gave the order."

Brachyura and Kumbha exchanged a glance. "That is regrettable," the bald colossus said. "For our brother was one of the first to agree with the Pact. He is not … evil as such, simply … "

"Unfeeling," Kumbha added.

"Yes. He is emotionally detached. Governed only by pure, hard logic. If he is gathering the members of his Order to him, then he is planning something."

"That may well be," said Gaelin, standing protectively in front of Kayal. "But this changes nothing. We cannot afford any more distractions. We must press on to Talth."

"Agreed. If Praedora and Aldarin allow it, I would counsel sending a small squad of knights north. They may be able to pick up the trail."

"Kessrin should be a part of this," said Derello. "Hirkuin, you will accompany them. Pick three or four of your best men and requisition some horses. I want you ready to leave within the hour. Try and find yourself a hot meal while you're at it. Now, let's get that lumber stored and the men moving; there's still a couple of days travel through enemy territory before we reach the capital."

The group dispersed quickly, all save Jelaïa and Praedora who found themselves alone together. The blind priestess was studying Jelaïa with her milky-white eyes. "Something's changed, Jeli. I can't explain it, but you *feel* different."

"I don't know what you mean," the Baroness replied hurriedly, trying to change the subject. "Would you like me to escort you somewhere, to your tent perhaps?"

"No, no, I'm fine right here. It's strange this blindness. I can't walk more than three feet before tripping over something, yet I knew it was you and Aldarin approaching earlier. And I can sense Brachyura when he is close by. Another puzzle to solve. Speaking of you and Aldarin, have you finally had your little talk?"

Jelaïa laughed. "Is it that obvious?"

"Not to others perhaps, but to me you're shining like a beacon. It's about time. I couldn't take much more of Aldarin moping around like a dejected puppy."

"*Praedora!*"

"What? He was in such a hurry to get back to Kessrin, I thought he was going to swim there himself. I'd never seen him so excited."

"By the Twelve, I wish he'd said something sooner."

"Yes. I don't think that's really his forte. The initiates of the temple are primarily men so, apart from the occasional visit to the outlying villages, not a lot of … mingling goes on, if you see what I mean."

"Um. Yes. I haven't … mingled much myself."

"Oh, I wouldn't worry about that. Everything seems to work itself out in the end. And if you need some help, I'd be happy to give you a few pointers. I've done a fair bit of mingling myself over the years."

"Praedora …"

"I told you. A lot of men in the temple. Not a lot of women. It wasn't hard to be the centre of attention. Why, one time I—"

"My Ladies," interrupted Aldarin cheerfully. He had left the infirmary and was no longer limping.

"What were you talking about?"

"Nothing," they both answered, almost simultaneously. Jelaïa let slip a giggle.

"Hmm. I find you both quite perplexing at times. I suppose there is still much for me to learn. Kumbha has treated my knee, her gift is beyond astounding. See for yourselves."

Jelaïa peered round his leg and saw that the wound was gone, reduced to a red patch of blotchy skin. "Incredible!" she marvelled. "There's nothing there! It really is miraculous. Our army will be unstoppable!"

"There are limitations. The use of her gift leaves her extremely fatigued. Loré told me that she slept for several days after healing him. Furthermore, the injury must be recent and not self-inflicted. Oh, and it appears that troubles of the mind are unaffected; she has been unable to cure dementia, for example."

"Self-inflicted …" said Jelaïa, turning to Praedora. "So …"

"I went to see her," the first priestess replied in a tired voice. "She knew what I was going to ask, of course. And, to her credit, she tried. She did her best to heal my sight. But, as you can see, she was not successful."

"Oh, Praedora, I'm sorry."

"It is what it is. I am not overly distraught about it. I made my choice, and I knew the consequences. The only person responsible for my current situation is myself. It is for my sisters that I am disheartened. All save Niane awakened to their gift before we found them and had no one to guide them or warn them. They did not choose to lose their sight; it was taken from them. I had thought for a fleeting moment that there might be a way to help them."

Jelaïa found her aunt's hand and squeezed it. "You did what you could. You found them, brought them back to the temple, gave them a new home and a new purpose. I spent some time with them during my training, and they seemed happy."

"Thank you, Jeli. I suppose we cannot all be as lucky as Loré."

"No," Jelaïa said bitterly. "We cannot."

❧

"How much further?" asked Praxis testily, as they came to yet another forest clearing, one that looked near-identical to the past three. He had managed to break the chain linking his hands with a sharp rock, but the manacles were still attached to his wrists, rubbing the skin raw.

His brother knight didn't reply, only waved him forwards with his uninjured hand.

They had bound his other arm tightly, packing the wound with a mixture of moss and earth, but the Knight of Zygos had lost a lot of blood. Praxis could see the thin sheen of sweat on the man's brow.

Perhaps he is delirious, he thought. *He could be leading us round and round in circles.* The thick clouds blanketing the sky hid the sun. He had no idea in which direction they were going. His gaze fell on the trees bordering the clearing.

Doesn't moss grow on the southern side of the trunks? Or was it the eastern side? Pit! He should have paid more attention during his training. There was no other choice but to press on.

After what seemed like hours, the closely grouped pines began to thin out, pushed aside by large jagged rocks erupting from the earth like crooked fingers. On the far horizon, a solitary mountain peak jutted up out of a sea of green.

"Nearly there," grunted the Knight of Zygos.

"Why are we not going south to Nightvale?" asked Praxis. "Surely it would be better to return to the temple rather than to whatever hunting lodge or campsite you are taking me to."

"Nightvale? Pit, how long have you been undercover?"

"Too long. Over ten years."

"Hmm. Then you don't know. The temple in Nightvale is no more. We were discovered eight years ago. A combined force of Knights of Brachyura and Guanna came at us from all sides. A slaughter. Close to a hundred dead, including the priestesses. Must be fewer than twenty of us left now."

"That's ... I didn't know. So where is the temple now?"

"Here."

The knight had led them to a mass of rocks grouped

around the entrance to a cave. Two of his brothers stood guard, crossbows ready. They stepped aside to let the travellers pass.

Praxis shuddered as they descended into the inky blackness. "Underground? Really?"

The other man shrugged. "It's the easiest way to avoid prying eyes. The Knights of Guanna rarely patrol this deep into the forest, but there's no way to be sure." He picked up a torch from a wicker basket and lit it using a nearby brazier, motioning for Praxis to do the same.

The sloping tunnel led to a vast network of subterranean caves of various shapes and sizes, some filled with water or too small to be functional, others used by the Knights of Zygos to store supplies and equipment. Praxis passed one high-roofed cavern lined with wooden cots; another opening revealed a long, tapering space converted into an archery range. Praxis was quietly impressed by how his fellow knights had managed to make this place their own in such a short time.

"This is where I leave you," his companion said abruptly, stopping before a wide craggy opening in the rock.

"Thank you. And thank you for setting me free."

The man scowled, cradling his wounded arm. "I was only following orders. I don't understand what our patron sees in you. If it had been up to me, I would have left you to rot."

Charming, thought Praxis, watching the man leave. He ducked prudently through the opening. The cave he found himself in was quite different from what he had seen so far. Ornate tapestries covered the natural walls, and several plush woven rugs were spread out over the floor. A set of bookshelves, weighed down with scrolls, took up the entirety of one side. In front of them stood a man with sharp, angular features and silvery hair, his hands leafing through a slim leather volume.

"Ah, Praxis," he said, closing the book with a snap. "You have returned."

"Master Aldos," Praxis replied, bowing low. "I have. Returned to find our Order much changed."

"A minor setback. Balance, initiate. Balance in all things. Our trials will make us more resilient."

"Yes, Master."

"Don't 'Yes, Master' me, I'm a bit more astute than Listus del Arelium; I can tell you don't believe me. That was always your problem, Praxis. You lack faith. Now, wait here."

He pulled aside one of the tapestries, revealing an alcove, and disappeared from sight. Praxis frowned. It was Aldos who had given him his instructions all those years ago, who had directly told him to facilitate the greylings' return and hasten the destruction of Arelium.

Praxis had tried to do both those things but had failed to eliminate completely the del Arelium bloodline and had now lost his control over the Barony. To add insult to injury, his ploy to sway Derello to his cause had similarly backfired. Had Aldos brought him back to praise him or to kill him? He glanced down at the dagger in his belt, taken from his liberator. Hopefully, he would not need to use it.

A creaking of wheels came from the alcove, and the temple master reappeared, pushing a wheelchair much like the one Merad Reed had used when recovering from his punctured lung. Praxis gasped when he saw the chair's occupant.

It was Zygos but not the proud, charismatic demi-god he had seen many times in the various illustrations and statues of his temple. What sat before him now was a ruin of a man. Both pairs of arms and legs were gone, while his face was covered in pockmarks and lacerations. Hair was missing from the left-hand side of his head, laying bare a bruised scalp.

Only the eyes were untouched: black and fathomless. Zygos turned his gaze on Praxis and, just like with Mina on Kingfisher Isle, he felt the Seventh of the Twelve drill into his mind, peeling back the layers of his soul.

"Praxis. How good of you to join us."

"Lord." Praxis sank to one knee, bringing his head level with his patron. "You have found your way back to us."

"I have. Although not in the way I had planned," Zygos sighed. "Once the Pact was signed, we searched for the best means to exile ourselves from the nine Baronies for three hundred years. It was Shala, Kumbha, and Makara who devised what was thought at the time to be a perfect solution. Statues. Using Kumbha's understanding of the human body and Shala's mastery of the elements, we conceived the perfect way to hide in plain sight. Each chose a suitable site, either our temple or another significant location." He coughed, staining his lips red.

"Aldos, some water if you please? Thank you. I chose the temple of Zygos. The perfect place: surrounded, admired, and protected by hundreds every day. Unfortunately, I failed to take into account man's stupidity." Aldos held a glass up and Zygos wet his lips.

"The Schism. What fools you were. Our instructions were clear. And yet you failed us. You *squandered* the gift we gave you. So much knowledge. So much power. The Knightly Orders could have ruled the nine Baronies. And instead, you threw it all away." He shook his head in frustration. "Not only that, but when your idiotic *brothers* destroyed my temple, my statue was ripped from its pedestal and broken into pieces. When I awoke from hibernation, I nearly died from the pain." He closed his eyes, remembering. "If Aldos had not had the foresight to keep the temple watched, I might never have been found, slowly starving to death in the dark."

"I … am sorry, Lord," Praxis said and was surprised to find he meant it. "What is it you wish of me? Why have you called me to your side?"

Zygos smiled a twisted smile. "You carry something of great importance, Praxis. Information. The greatest weapon there is. Aldos tells me that some of my brothers and sisters are refusing to honour the Pact. We cannot allow that to happen. You are going to help me stop them; and for that, I need you to tell me what you know. I need you to tell me everything."

CHAPTER 17

A TITANIC STRUGGLE

"People often ask me how difficult it is to fly one of the Crimson Wings. Well, let me tell you. Flying the Pit-spawned thing is easy. It's landing that's the hard part."

'STICK', 419 AT

❦

THE ICE-COLD WIND tore into Vohanen's face and beard like a dagger, digging into his cheeks and pulling at his ears. He clipped a tunnel of rising air and veered off-course. Muttering a curse, he shifted position in the harness, slowly resetting the nose of the glider towards the flat roof of the Morlak garrison hundreds of feet away.

He only hoped that his men were not far behind. The rushing sound of his descent blocked out everything else, and he dare not twist his head around for fear of upsetting his trajectory. With a whoosh, something appeared on his left, and he risked a quick sideways glance. Caddox flew past him, his face contorted with effort, his uninjured hand clutching a borrowed dagger. He dipped lower, faster than Vohanen, his glider perfectly aligned with the garrison roof.

By the Pit, I will not be beaten by a one-armed Knight of Brachyura! Vohanen thought and adjusted his weight to lower his angle of descent.

Immediately, he began to pick up speed, the keep approaching at an alarming rate. Ahead, Caddox had cleared the inner wall and was nearly at the garrison, dropping his legs and leaning backwards in an attempt to stall his glider.

Vohanen shot towards the ramparts and began to sweat as he realised his mistake. He had angled too low. He saw Caddox land, the knight slashing through his harness as his boots touched the roof. Desperately, he tried to pull his own glider up, but it was too late. He was not going to hit the roof.

Perspiration dripped down his forehead. His hands felt wet and clammy in his gloves. He tightened his grip on his short sword and dropped his legs to increase drag. He passed over the inner wall and the hot air from the braziers filled his Crimson Wing, giving him a tiny amount of lift.

His glider was stalling, but he was still going too fast. The garrison wall filled his field of view. He crashed into the hard stone with a sickening crunch that sent a jolt of pain through every bone in his body. The glider shattered, bits of broken wood and pieces of torn fabric cascading down into the courtyard below. He flailed wildly with his free hand and found an inches-deep fingerhold in the old mortar of the wall. His feet scrabbled for purchase, but the cold night air and damp weather had made the stones slimy and wet.

A gust of wind caught the shattered remains of the glider still attached to his back and he felt himself being pulled backwards. If he didn't act fast, his arm would be wrenched from its socket. Desperately, he slashed at his harness, trying to ignore the rapid pounding of his heart. The last strands of rope parted, and the devilish contraption, finally free, fell away into the night.

Vohanen laughed out loud as he felt the great weight lifted from his body. Slamming his sword back into its scabbard, he lodged his second hand next to the first. And there he hung, his ram's horn digging painfully into his side. The top of the wall was tantalisingly close, only four or five feet away, but he had no way of reaching it. His boots skittered across the slippery slabs of stone.

Pit!

His biceps, already weakened by the skirmish on the mountain path, sent warning tingles up to his brain. He glanced down. There was nothing below him to break his fall save for the mangled remains of his glider, and that would not be enough to stop his ribcage from exploding through his chest. Other gliders sailed over his head. One passed by almost level with him, missing the roof entirely. It floated round the side of the wall and out of sight.

The tired fingers of his right hand could no longer retain their grip and he gasped as his remaining arm took all of his weight. Rivulets of sweat poured down his face. He could taste the salt in his mouth.

Avor, I have failed, he thought silently as the last of his energy drained away.

Then a gauntleted hand of burnished silver shot over the edge of the roof and latched onto his wrist. The patrician features of Caddox appeared, something akin to concern on his features.

"Well, come on, then, I can't hold you forever, old man."

Vohanen slammed his booted feet into the wall and allowed himself to be pulled slowly upwards, sweating and cursing, inch by laborious inch. He crested the top of the low parapet that ringed the garrison roof and collapsed in a heap on the other side, breathing so hard he thought his lungs would burst. Caddox lowered himself down next to him.

"By the Twelve, that was cutting it closer than I would have liked," he said. "Apologies for the delay."

"Your gaunt—" wheezed Vohanen. He paused to get his breath back, gesturing tiredly at the knight's argent gauntlet and breastplate poking through the folds of his riding cloak. "We … said … no … armour."

"No, you told *your* men not to wear armour. I do not take orders from you. I'm already injured; there was no Pit-spawned way I wasn't going to bring my plate with me. I got Jeffson to help me with the breastplate before he left, and then I strapped the gauntlet onto my uninjured hand when we landed, which is why it took me some time to come to your aid."

Vohanen felt a spark of anger but hesitated. It would probably not be the most honourable of actions to berate the man who had just saved his life.

"So … you had your breastplate on the whole time?"

"Yes."

"Yet you still let me take on the alpha wolf by myself?"

"Ah, yes. Thought it would be a good chance to prove yourself to the men. Lead by example, as it were."

Vohanen gently massaged the burning muscles of his left arm. "Hmm. We do not agree on much, Sir Caddox, but I must admit, I think we are better off with you than without you." He looked up at the starless sky. "Moon's still hidden. I have no idea how much time we have left, but we're committed now. Let's take back our garrison."

The roof was littered with gliders, most of them smashed beyond repair. Clearly, he was not the only one to have had a bumpy landing. His men were covered in bruises and abrasions but, somewhat miraculously, had no broken bones. Krelbe was among the unlucky ones, his cheek scraped raw, the beginning of a black eye forming under his left orbit.

Vohanen did a quick headcount. Seventeen, not counting Caddox or Krelbe. He had lost three. Three knights and one more up on the windswept mountain. They had yet to face the Knights of Mithuna and already their losses were high. He hoped Bjornvor would understand.

"Gather round," he ordered quietly. "Now, against all odds, we seem to have landed unnoticed. Quite how we managed it I don't know, but I suggest you all say a quick prayer of thanks to the Twelve when we're done here."

Krelbe scowled but said nothing.

"We are outnumbered and unarmoured — well *mostly* unarmoured," Vohanen glared pointedly at Caddox, "so all we have in our favour is the element of surprise. Most of you have already been stationed here, or visited here, so you know the layout. Top floors are storage, then the training hall. The living quarters are below that, then the meeting hall, mess, and kitchens on the ground floor. We'll start with the training hall, then go room-to-room through the sleeping area. Questions?"

Silence.

"Very well. Oh, one more thing."

He strode over to the flagpole set into the middle of the garrison roof. The twin-headed heraldry of Mithuna fluttered in the night breeze. A single stroke of his short sword was enough to sever the counterweight and the flag plummeted to the ground.

No one spoke, but he could see a lot of grim smiles and appreciative nods.

I'm getting quite good at this leadership thing, he thought, and motioned for his men to follow him off the roof and down into the garrison.

⁊

The top two floors, much as Vohanen had expected, were unoccupied. They passed rows of salted meats, bags of flour, loaves of hard bread; enough for the men of the garrison to survive the harsh Morlakian winter. Some of the stores had been needlessly vandalised or soiled, proof that the Knights of Mithuna had been here.

Krelbe paused before one of the doors and beckoned to Vohanen. "Armoury," he whispered. "Might be something left." He entered slowly, his eyes darting left and right as if expecting something to leap at him from the shadows.

The place had been pillaged. The dozen or so sets of half-plate that had been stored there were missing, as were most of the short swords. Broken spears were piled into a pyramid in the centre of the room like the kindling for a bonfire.

"Here!" came the excited murmur of Krelbe from the back of the room. Against the far wall lay seven tower shields.

They had been defaced, hacked at with longswords and used as target practice but were still intact — a testament to the ingenuity and craftsmanship of the Knights of Kriari.

Vohanen's face lit up when he saw the shields and he quickly distributed six of them among his men, keeping the last one for himself. He slipped his forearm into the leather straps, feeling the comforting weight of the shield on his arm. He had missed that feeling.

"Onwards," he said, and they took the stairs down to the next level, the galleries above the training hall. After the first few steps, Vohanen knew they had found the enemy. An echoing wall of sound spiralled up to meet them: shouting, clapping, and cursing, accompanied by bestial grunts and growls.

"What in the Pit is that?" he whispered to Krelbe. The other man didn't reply, only edged down the last few steps and pushed open the stairwell door with the tip of his short sword. They were on the edge of a wide gallery ten feet above the training room floor. Two sets of steps at either end led down to the lower level, a sand-covered indoor arena flanked by rows of benches. The benches were packed with Knights of Mithuna, close to forty in total, clad in mismatched pieces of plate armour. They were all similar in countenance: dark-haired and deathlike, their skin so thin it was almost translucent. Even at a distance, Vohanen could see pulsing purple veins writhing on their faces.

The crowd was enraptured, cheering and yelling, absorbed by the spectacle before it, a titanic struggle between man and beast. The man was huge, a colossus, well over eight feet high. He was wearing a pair of torn leggings, his bare chest and back covered in dark wiry hair. An unkempt mass of shoulder-length locks hung like a curtain across his face, obscuring his features. He was clearly a prisoner: two rusty manacles encircled each ankle, attached to chains bolted into the training room floor. Another chain wound up his back to a sturdy collar fixed to his neck.

Before him, four wolves loped back and forth, snarling. These were not the mangy animals Vohanen and his knights had met up in the mountains but well-fed, muscular beasts. The headless body of a fifth wolf lay on the ground nearby, its blood staining the sand red.

As they watched, two of the wolves leapt forwards in a simultaneous, coordinated attack. The first aimed low, fangs thudding into the man's calf. Its pack-mate pushed hard on its hind legs and sprang upwards, its claws aimed at the prisoner's neck.

The shaggy-haired giant batted the pouncing wolf out of the air with a hand the size of a spade. There was a dreadful cracking sound as the beast's neck broke. Its lifeless body hurtled across the room, landing among a group of watching Knights of Mithuna, who laughed gleefully. The man then reached down with his other hand and grabbed hold of the muzzle gripping his thigh. With a twist of his manacled wrist, he ripped the top half of the wolf's jaw from its body. Fresh blood spattered onto the hard-packed sand. The wolf gave a howl of pain and retreated, its lower snout a mess of mangled bone.

The colossus wiped his hand on his dirty tunic, and then something gave him pause. His head jerked round and he looked up towards the gallery. And now Vohanen could see what lay behind that curtain of long hair, a face he knew almost as well as his own. A beard matted with sweat and blood. Two great bushy eyebrows that ran into each other above a flat nose. And finally, instead of human eyes, two gaping chasms of pure blackness that pierced the very centre of his being, digging into his mind, assaulting his senses with a cascade of emotions: confusion, pain, loneliness and, above all, anger. A wave of visceral, relentless anger that buffeted him like the cold winds of the Spike.

It should not be possible, yet there was no denying who this was.

"Kriari," murmured Vohanen in a cracked whisper. "What have they done to you?"

He heard a cry of anger beside him and turned to see the normally stoic Krelbe quivering with rage, his teeth bared. "What have you done?" Krelbe said, echoing Vohanen. "WHAT HAVE YOU BASTARDS DONE?"

The knight pelted down the stairs, screaming. Vohanen ran after him, hoping the others would follow. The training room was in disarray; some of the Knights of Mithuna were scrabbling for their weapons, others sat unmoving, staring in shock, mouths agape. Kriari was watching them with furrowed brow, his head cocked to one side in confusion.

Krelbe ploughed through the two remaining wolves without stopping, his sword and bossed shield lashing out as he passed, scattering them. He reached the closest iron bolt and began hacking at the rusty chain, sparks flying.

The Knights of Mithuna had recovered from their initial surprise and were organising now, regrouping at the far end of the hall.

Vohanen reached Krelbe and caught his arm. "That won't work!" he said. "The chains are too strong!" Krelbe growled in frustration.

"KRIARI!" Vohanen yelled as more of his men arrived. "We are Knights of your Order, come to deliver you."

"Or ... der?" grunted the giant, his voice deep and guttural.

Pit!

The enemy were advancing, swords drawn. Forty armoured men against nineteen.

"Protect Kriari! Shieldwall!" ordered Vohanen, setting his tower shield down between his patron and their foes.

Krelbe appeared on his right, his shield slamming down next to Vohanen's. They had soon formed a rectangle seven men wide and three ranks deep. A throwing dagger ricocheted off the rim of his shield, spinning past his ear.

The Knights of Mithuna were charging.

"BRACE!" shouted Vohanen, setting his feet and lowering his shoulders.

"FOR MITHUNA!" came the answering cry, then two hundred pounds of armoured knight crashed into his shield. Vohanen bit back a curse as his weakened left arm absorbed the force of the blow. His opponent applied more pressure and he found himself being pushed back from the shieldwall. Then he felt an armoured gauntlet on his back, steadying him.

"We must not let them collapse the wall!" Caddox said from his place behind Vohanen. He nodded in reply, stabbing blindly over the top of his shield with his short sword. He was rewarded with a cry of pain and the crushing weight relented. He took a step forward, drawing level with Krelbe.

For a short moment, the two forces were locked in a stalemate, the Knights of Mithuna unable to push through the tower shields, Vohanen and his men not numerous enough to counter-attack. Kriari bellowed something unintelligible but made no move to come to their aid.

A scream from his left. They were being flanked. The shieldwall was not wide enough to cover the width of the training hall. This wasn't working.

"MEN!" shouted Vohanen over the clash of steel. "Remember your training! Folding leaf pattern on my mark!" He paused, praying they would remember the manoeuvre drilled into them time and time again by the temple masters back in Dirkvale. "MARK!"

He pulled his shield towards him and turned ninety degrees to the left, presenting his right side to the enemy. The other shield bearers followed suit, creating a series of gaps through which stumbled the surprised Knights of Mithuna, straight into the second defensive line.

Six short swords rose and fell, dispatching the fallen knights before they could recover. Vohanen saw Caddox punch his double-bladed axe forward like a spear, impaling an attacker on one of its curved tips.

Ten, no eleven Knights of Mithuna dead, and two of his own men down. The odds were not in their favour. The shieldwall was gone, the fighting now a chaotic melee as knight fought against knight.

The enemy were using their greater number to their advantage, attacking in pairs, using decoys, aiming for blind spots. Another two of his men fell, stabbed in the back. Krelbe, trying to marshal the remaining shield bearers into another wall, caught a pommel-strike to the forehead and collapsed, stunned.

Vohanen spotted Caddox a few feet away, keeping his two adversaries at bay with wide sweeps of his axe. A third was creeping up behind him, sword raised. Vohanen rushed forwards with an angry cry, his sword stabbing deep into the flesh of the fallen knight's thigh. He pulled his blade out as the man sagged to his knees and stabbed forwards again, this time entering through the cheekbone and up into the knight's brain.

Vohanen glanced round at the carnage. Three more Knights of Kriari lay unmoving on the sand. They were being overwhelmed. His heart sank as he saw the door at the rear of the training room bang open and five fully-armoured Knights of Mithuna enter, their visors closed.

He set his back against Caddox, protecting his rear. "You were wrong to come with us, Knight of Brachyura," he said. "I have led us to our doom."

"Brach ... y ... ura?" came a confused voice.

Kriari was staring at him through his mane of hair.

"Yes, Kriari! Remember! Brachyura! Your brother! You are one of the Twelve! Help us!"

"Twelve?"

"Yes, you Pit-spawned mammoth!" Vohanen cried in exasperation. A flicker of movement in the corner of his eye made him bring up his sword reflexively, deflecting an incoming blow. The blade caught on the strap of his ram's horn, and Vohanen drew his own sword across his assailant's neck before he could drag it free.

The ram's horn.

Vohanen threw down his shield and brought the horn to his lips. Taking a deep breath, he blew, deep and hard, sending the ringing call reverberating around the training hall, echoing off the walls until it was magnified a dozen times.

Kriari answered the horn with a roar of his own. He

wrapped a length of chain around his left forearm, gripped it hard with both hands and *pulled*.

The iron bolt was ripped from the floor with staggering force. The second one followed a moment later, then the third. And so, trailing his rusty chains behind him like broken wings, Kriari entered the fray.

Vohanen blinked, and two Knights of Mithuna were dead, their skulls crushed by a pair of gargantuan hands. Kriari jerked his left arm and eight feet of chain hurtled forwards, the iron bolt impaling another knight in the ribs and exiting his back in an explosion of gore. A fourth knight attacked with a clumsy overhead blow. Kriari caught the longsword in one hand and elbowed his startled opponent in the face, driving the cartilage of his nose up into his head.

Vohanen watched on in awe. Four dead in under a minute.

"FOR KRIARI!" he shouted exuberantly, feeling relief and hope invigorate his tired body.

"Kri ... ari," the giant concurred, and grinned.

CHAPTER 18

MANGONELS AND WILDFLOWERS

"The mangonel is one of the most potent weapons in our arsenal. They may not have the accuracy of trebuchets, but their low trajectory and high velocity make them perfect for destroying walls ... or caves. How do you think the greylings will be able to attack us if we fill their tunnels with rubble?"

GUANNA, SECOND OF THE TWELVE, 120 AT

❧

T HE FIELDS BEFORE the city of Talth reminded Jelaïa of Arelium. The greylings had set everything aflame. The woodlands. The villages. The crops. The people. A thin layer of ash covered every inch of the blackened earth like leaden snow. Small grey flakes of it became caught in her hair as she walked through the skeletal remains of burnt-out timber buildings. On the other side of the abandoned village, Sir Gaelin was assembling his catapults.

They were just under five hundred yards away from the town walls, camped on a natural slope reinforced with earthworks. Gaelin, stripped to the waist, was directing a group of sweltering Knights of Brachyura as they manoeuvred one of the supports into place. Jelaïa smiled as she saw Aldarin was among them.

"My Lady," Gaelin said. "What can we do for you?"

"I bring sustenance," she said, holding up a basket packed with dense, unleavened bread and strips of dried meat.

"By the Twelve, is it lunchtime already? Thank you." He called his fellow knights over and they helped themselves to the contents of the basket, Aldarin squeezing Jelaïa's hand as he passed.

They were making good time. One catapult was already built, and two others were well under construction, although both were missing their long wooden arms and metal buckets.

"Trebuchets would be better," said Gaelin, tearing into his chunk of bread. "But much more difficult to build, and I'm not an expert at setting the counterbalance." He patted one of the catapults. "These are called mangonels. A lot simpler to build and use. The lever on the side there ratchets the arm back, then when we release it, the arm will rocket forwards and send whatever we place in the bucket hurtling towards the enemy."

Jelaïa pointed at the twisted coils of rope wrapped around the axle-like pivot. "I've seen this sort of thing before, on the walls of Kessrin. The ballistae."

"Aye, you have a good eye, my Lady. Both work in the same way, by storing energy then releasing it. Ballistae are far more accurate though. I can get these mangonels to hit the wall, but that's about it. I won't be able to pinpoint the gatehouse or other structural weaknesses from this distance."

"How many will we have?"

"Probably just these three, four at the most. Wood's not a problem, but we're having to make the buckets. We've got a smithy set up in one of the ruined buildings, but it's a long process."

"Just four? I saw rows of cut trunks back at the lumber camp. What are the rest for?"

"The earthworks, arrow shields, and … that." Behind the catapults, Jelaïa could make out what looked like a wooden cabin without a roof, raised off the ground on four wheels.

"It doesn't look like much," said Gaelin. "But when completed, it could give us the edge we need. It's called a siege tower. Imagine three more levels on top of that one. Then we just roll it up to the base of the wall and use the ladders inside to climb to the top."

"Just roll it up to the wall," Jelaïa said with a dry chuckle. "Sounds easy enough."

"Yes, well … it will be difficult, but assaulting a fortified position always is. And I can promise you that we will lose fewer men this way. Now, if you'll excuse me, my Lady." He handed her the rest of his bread and returned to his men.

Pit, I think I vexed him, thought Jelaïa incredulously. *The Knights of Guanna obviously take their craft very, very seriously.* She turned to leave and nearly bowled over an out-of-breath messenger boy, his face flushed with effort.

"'Bin looking for you, M'Lady! Council meeting. Baron's

tent. Think they're gonna start the assault!" He beamed at her then sprinted away.

Jelaïa pocketed a piece of bread and left the basket for the others, climbing up the slope to the top of the hill where Derello had erected his command tent, with the allied flags of Arelium, Talth, and Kessrin flying from its roof.

She was the last to arrive. A hastily-drawn map covered in small coloured stones had been laid out; green for the siege engines of Talth, grey for the Knights of Brachyura, blue for Kessrin, and red for Arelium.

"Ah, Jelaïa," said Derello, looking up as she entered. "Thank you for joining us. We were waiting for you."

"The Baron appears to enjoy waiting," said Brachyura petulantly, his hairless scalp brushing against the ceiling of the tent.

"I didn't say that," the Baron replied. "I just said that I see no point in attacking Talth while the walls still stand. Let's use the catapults to create a breach, then send in the foot soldiers to assault the gap. Archers in support, protected by the shields."

"Doing so would surely be prudent and save more lives," agreed Kumbha, laying a restraining hand on her brother's arm.

"And take much, much longer, wasting valuable time. Time for the brood mother to escape. Or to call for reinforcements. Time we do not have."

"It is not for you to decide for them, Brother, remember? We are here now to guide, not to command."

Jelaïa looked down at the coloured stones. "I share your frustration, Lord, but Derello is right. We have no idea what is waiting for us beyond those walls. I propose a compromise.

We will give Sir Gaelin a day. If he is not successful, we will try a combined assault." She ran a finger along a narrow line on the map stretching from the gatehouse to the inner keep. "What's this?"

"Main road, my Lady," said Kayal in his shy voice. He looked lost and alone without Sir Gaelin. "Long and straight. My … father used it to take the fight to the greylings. It didn't work."

Jelaïa felt her heart go out to the orphan, who had suffered so much and yet was forced to carry such great responsibility on his frail shoulders.

"No," she said. "But the tactic was sound. Our cavalry is our greatest weapon. If we can force the main gate open, the Knights of Brachyura can ride unimpeded up to the keep."

"Unless the greylings have set traps," said Loré, thinking back to his own disastrous cavalry charge.

"Certainly. But it's a paved street, right? Much more difficult to dig through."

"It is a good plan," Brachyura admitted. "Once the wall is breached, the soldiers can open the gates from the inside. I will lead the charge."

"Really?" asked Jelaïa. "How? Has someone found a ten-foot horse?"

There was a muffled sound as Derello tried to cover his laughter with a cough.

"No." It was impossible to tell if Brachyura had found what she said amusing or not, his dark eyes showing no emotion. "You do know we have not always travelled everywhere on foot, my Lady? We used chariots. I requested Sir Gaelin

to make me one. It is a fairly simple thing; a wooden plat-
form and a couple of wheels. It will take me where I wish
to go."

"Of course, Lord."

"I knew the first Lord of Arelium, my Lady. He was
quite similar to you."

"Is that so, Lord?"

"Yes. Very disrespectful."

Jelaïa didn't flinch. "He sounds like a nice man."

The corners of Brachyura's mouth twitched. "He was."
His gaze spread to the other dignitaries huddled around the
map of Talth. "All of your ancestors were. Men and women
of courage; their hearts and minds filled with lofty ideals
that went beyond simply defeating the greylings. They
strived for unity and friendship. Mutual growth and protection. I believe they would be proud to see you standing here
together, allied for a common purpose. This is how we will
beat them. By working together."

"Thank you, Brachyura," said Derello. "And thank you
for standing with us. Now, let us go over the battle plan unit
by unit and make sure we are ready for the assault."

Pit, thought Jelaïa glumly. *It's going to be a long day.*

∽

"Why won't you do what I tell you?" fumed Jelaïa at her
unruly hair. A finger-length lock had sprung free from the
braid she had spent the last ten minutes making, hanging
impertinently across her forehead. Aldarin would be here
any minute. She grabbed a hairpin off the nightstand and

used it to shove the offending strands back behind her ear
with more force than she intended, pricking her scalp.

Cursing, she inspected the inside of her tent. The bed
was made, the sheets folded and tucked. Her riding clothes
were safely stored away in her wardrobe. She'd even cleared
everything off her little writing table, lit a candle and
arranged a pair of dinner plates and two chairs.

One last glance in the mirror, and she was ready. She
smoothed down the folds of her green dress and adjusted
her wolf's head brooch.

A knock on one of the wooden poles of her tent. "Jelaïa?"

She was about to tell him to come in when she suddenly
saw two pink toes poking out from under the hem of her
dress.

Pit! Shoes!

"Just a minute!" She swished over to her traveller's chest
and grabbed a pair of slippers. "Ready!"

The tent flap parted and Aldarin appeared, holding a
bouquet of wild flowers in one hand and his helm in the
other.

"Aldarin, how nice to see you. You are … fully armoured."

"Indeed, Jelaïa. We are in enemy territory. I must be
prepared for battle at all times."

"Right. My tent is enemy territory?"

"What? No, I mean … I meant …"

"I'm joking, Aldarin. Come and give me those flowers."

He moved closer, and she rose on tiptoes to kiss him.
"Thank you. I don't have a vase here, but I'm sure we can
find something to put them in."

"There are a few scant areas of grassland south of here
that were spared from the fire. I picked them this afternoon,

once we had finished with the catapults. All four are ready! Sir Gaelin is most precise with his instructions. We will begin the artillery barrage tomorrow morning."

"That's great news. Come, sit! I've sent one of the messenger boys to bring us two servings from the kitchens, he should be here soon."

"Thank you, Jelaïa. You look stunning. I especially admire your choice of shoes."

"What?" She looked down to discover that, in her haste, she had chosen two different slippers, one pink, one blue, both clashing with the green of her dress. "Um, yes. A stylistic choice. It's all the rage in Klief I'm told, mismatched shoes."

Aldarin just smiled and moved in to kiss her again, then stopped, his brow furrowed.

"What's that smell?" he said, sniffing the air.

"It's one of the perfumes Mava buys for me. It is rather exotic, but she seems to like it—"

"No, not that. Something else." He whirled and stalked out of the tent. Jelaïa ran after him and was hit by the smell of burning wood. "Oh no," she whispered. Further down the hill, near the earthworks, a great plume of dark grey smoke was billowing into the evening sky.

"The catapults!" said Aldarin in anguish, donning his helm. "TO ARMS! TO ARMS!" He unsheathed his axe and began to charge towards the smoke, yelling as he went. A dishevelled soldier poked his head out of one of the mess tents and Aldarin beckoned him over. "Get up to the command tent!" he ordered. "There's a bell set up right next to it. I need you to ring it as hard as you can." The man looked at him blankly. "Hurry, man!" said Aldarin, giving him a shake.

"We are under attack!" The soldier's eyes snapped open in shock and he set off at a jog.

"You should stay here, Jelaïa," Aldarin cautioned. "I don't know what we'll face down there."

"I can handle it."

"Very well. Then stay close." They plunged into the smoke. Jelaïa coughed as the hot air entered her lungs. Her eyes began to water. Then they were through and out the other side. A group of ten threshers wearing pieced together armour and carrying torches were standing among the broken bodies of the guardsmen assigned to protect the cata-pults. Three of the war engines had already gone up in flames and they were focussing on the fourth, holding the torches under the torsion ropes to set it alight.

"BACK!" shouted Aldarin, running towards them.

"WAIT!" Jelaïa screamed after him. There were too many for one man alone, even Aldarin. He was going to be torn apart. Her hand went to her chest to grasp her medallion.

It wasn't there.

She had taken it off while changing earlier and hadn't put it back on. Cold fear engulfed her. She was defenceless.

"ALDARIN!" she yelled. He couldn't hear her. She watched him career into the threshers, his axe slicing left and right. One of the beasts fell, its leg severed below the knee. Another stumbled backwards, clutching at its wounded throat.

Jelaïa stood rooted to the spot, unsure of what to do. Her medallion was back in her tent, lying on her bed. It was only a few minutes away, but it might as well be a mile. Her panicked eyes roamed the earthworks, looking for a solu-tion. A few feet away, a dead guardsman stared up at her with lifeless eyes, his hands still clasped around the haft of his spear. She ran over to him and wrenched the spear from his grasp.

I'm coming, Aldarin.

The Knight of Brachyura had his back pressed against one of the catapult's supports as flames lapped around his feet. A thresher lumbered towards him and took an axe blade to the face, cutting off the tip of its porcine nose and half its ear. The creature howled in pain, its return swipe denting Aldarin's plate and cracking a rib.

Somewhere in the distance, a bell began to ring.

Jelaïa started forwards, then nearly tripped over the hem of her dress. Shouting in frustration, she ripped off a wide strip of fabric and picked up the pace, her spear held out in front of her like a lance. She ran straight at one of the threshers and thrust the tip at its unarmoured back.

The spear broke.

The creature spun round with a roar. Its dirty yellow eyes looked down contemptuously at Jelaïa as it raised its fist, spittle dribbling from its jaw.

"No!" came the distant voice of Aldarin.

Then Gaelin was there, his round buckler catching the blow with a clang. His longsword arced upwards into the thresher's groin. The thing let out a bellow of surprise and collapsed. "Are you safe, my Lady?"

"Al … Aldarin," she replied fighting to catch her breath.

"I think he will be all right," Gaelin said. "Look."

Brachyura had thrown himself into the melee, his enormous axe moving so fast that it was nearly a blur. Everything he touched died. Ichor erupted in great gouts wherever he went, turning the ground black. In less than a minute it was over, leaving the dismembered remains of the threshers dispersed among the burning catapults.

The colossus walked calmly away from the desolation, one arm supporting a battered Aldarin. The Knight of the Twelve had lost his helmet and his left pauldron. Blood flowed freely from a gash in his scalp.

Jelaïa approached them on trembling legs, her hair and dress in disarray, her face covered in dirt and ash. She found that she still had enough strength in her to slap Aldarin hard across the cheek.

"You *idiot*," she said in a voice halfway between fear and anger. "What in the Pit were you doing, trying to take them on alone like that?"

"Jelaïa …"

"Quiet. Don't you *ever* do that to me again, do you hear me? Or I will finish what the threshers started."

Aldarin wiped the blood from his face and nodded tiredly. "Understood."

Gaelin was staring silently at the burning wrecks of the catapults, the flames reflected in his eyes. "They managed to torch them all," he said despondently. "Only the siege tower remains. I can try to build more, but we don't have enough metal to make more buckets. We'll have to melt down whatever iron we can find … it will take days."

"We do not have that luxury," said Brachyura. "There is only one thing left to do. Tomorrow, at first light, we will send every able-bodied man to assault the walls."

CHAPTER 19

CHOOSING A PATH

"Unity. A simple word, yet it means so many things. Brotherhood. Trust. Complicity. When you stand next to your fellow initiates in a shieldwall, your only weaknesses are the men to your left and right. If you stand united, you will be unstoppable. If you stand divided, you will fall."

KRIARI, FIRST OF THE TWELVE, 76 AT

VOHANEN SAT ON one of the wooden benches, watching his surviving knights as they worked their way across the floor, ending the suffering of the wounded and placing weapons in the hands of the dead so that they would not go unarmed to meet their ancestors. His left arm throbbed, from the top of his shoulder down to his palms. He would not be raising his shield again for a while.

He inhaled, recognising what his old temple master had called 'the aftermath smell'. Blood and sweat mixed with the pungent stench of urine; the dead and dying emptying their bladders as their muscles failed them. It was strange, in all the scrolls he had read, all the war stories he had heard, none mentioned the smell.

Krelbe joined him, a strip of fabric wrapped tightly around his forehead. His eyebrow was missing one of its silver rings.

"So … Is it really him?" he asked, jerking a thumb at Kriari. Their patron was crouched in the middle of the training room floor, tinkering with the manacles still attached to his wrists.

"I don't know," answered Vohanen honestly. "It looks like him, but he seems lost, like he has forgotten himself."

"Mind of a child."

"No, it's not that. There is understanding there. And he knows how to fight. Must have killed ten or twelve of the enemy with those chains. It's more like there is a piece of him missing."

"Great. So, now what?"

Vohanen sighed. He stretched and heard his joints crack. "We carry on. Clear the lower levels. Get to the Great Hall. Find and kill the usurper."

"And what about him?"

"He's one of the Twelve, Krelbe. I'm not going to tell him what to do. Are you?"

"No. But you could *ask* him."

There was a clanking sound as one of the manacles sprang open. Kriari gave a whoop of delight and started working on the second one. Vohanen approached cautiously.

The giant's hands were covered in blood, his naked torso smeared with white flecks of bone and gristle. "Kriari?" he said, trying to keep his voice neutral.

"Kri ... ari," the big man affirmed, twisting and tugging at the iron band around his wrist.

Vohanen squatted down beside him.

"We are going to leave here. We are going to look for Mithuna."

"Sister. Friend?"

"No. Kriari. I am afraid not. She means us harm. Will you help us?"

Kriari turned to him and once again Vohanen felt himself drawn into those eyes. It reminded him of stepping into the mouth of the Morlakian Pit. Leaving the light of the outside world behind. Descending into darkness.

"Yes," grunted Kriari, breaking the spell. Vohanen stood, and the room span. He closed his eyes.

"Vohanen?" called Caddox. "Are you all right?"

"Fine. Just stood up too fast. Are we ready?"

"As ready as we'll ever be."

"Then we should press on. Gather the men."

He had lost eight Knights of Kriari. Three more were in no state to continue. Only Krelbe and six able-bodied fighters left. Seven from the twenty-two who he had led up into the mountains. Fifteen families who had lost a husband, a father, or a son. It was by far the greatest loss the Order of Kriari had known in over fifty years, and it was all his fault.

His gaze swept over the survivors, their fur mantles ripped and torn, their expressions haggard but proud. All bore superficial injuries: an impressive collection of scrapes and bruises. All were looking to him for guidance. Caddox stood apart from the rest, bleeding from a cut above his left ear. He inclined his head respectfully. Strangely, this simple gesture gave Vohanen strength.

"Can't be many between us and Mithuna now," he said, as jovially as he could muster. "How about we go knock on her door, take back what's ours?"

"For Kriari," said the giant, nodding sagely.

"What he said," Krelbe agreed.

The living quarters were eerily empty, a succession of vacant beds and silent rooms. The group of men checked each one methodically, opening every cupboard, looking under every bed. Kriari ambled after them, humming under his breath.

"How many are normally stationed here?" asked Caddox, as they passed through another empty bedroom and out into a cramped corridor.

"About fifty of us at a time. Not enough space for more than that."

"And there were forty knights in the training hall …"

"Aye, if we're lucky there are only ten or so left to deal with."

"Maybe not even that many. You know of the Schism, of course. We drove them away, burnt their temple to the ground. We decimated them. Who is to say there are more than forty still alive?"

They reached the end of the corridor, with more stairs leading down.

"We are about to find out. Only one floor left."

A dozen stone steps opened out into a mess hall, its long, u-shaped dining table missing its plates and cutlery. To the right, a passageway leading to the kitchens. To the left, the meeting hall.

"Left," Vohanen said. "We're nearly out."

"Wait," warned Krelbe, pointing to the bottom of the door. Yellow torchlight filtered through the gap. "It's occupied," he said, drawing his short sword.

"Well, don't just stand there!" came a low-pitched female voice from the other side. "Come on in!" Vohanen raised an eyebrow at Krelbe, who shrugged as he pushed at the door with the tip of his blade. It swung open on well-oiled hinges.

On the other side, hands on her hips, stood a raven-haired woman in a dark purple dress. She may have been pretty once, but now deep bags hung under her bloodshot eyes. Her full lips were dry and cracked. Welts and bruises marked her bare arms.

"Greetings, gentlemen," she said. "My name is Verona. My mistress thought you might try to take back the garrison. I am here to stop you." Something or someone moved in the shadows behind her, down at the far end of the meeting hall, beyond the reach of the torchlight.

"Really?" Krelbe replied, his lip curling. "I mean, you are welcome to try, but there are more of us than there are of you." Kriari arrived, stooping slightly to pass under the doorframe. "Oh, and we have one of the Twelve with us, too."

Verona gave what could have been a seductive smile but, in her current state, it just made her look even more unhinged.

"What, you mean that thing? That's not one of the Twelve, Sir Knight. It's a bumbling simpleton. We used to take bets on who could cut through that tough skin first, poking and sawing with our blades." She tapped the hilt of the dagger in her belt. "He never even moved. You'll have to do better than that."

"We still outnumber you," Vohanen said.

"True. Let me show you my bargaining chip." She gave a low whistle and four figures detached themselves from the shadows at the end of the hall.

Two were Knights of Mithuna, their bodies encased in full suits of plate. The third was a young man dressed in fine clothes, with long blond hair and wild eyes. He was pulling a prisoner along behind him. The man's wrists were bound with rope, his mouth gagged.

As they came closer, Vohanen gave a bark of relieved laughter. The prisoner had lost some weight and gained some hair, but Vohanen would have recognised that salt-and-pepper beard anywhere.

"Reed!" he cried happily, grinning.

"Nidore!" Verona called. The blond man quickly drew his rapier and set the sharp point against Reed's neck.

"So, you know each other," the woman continued. "You must be one of the knights who were with Reed during the ambush. I was hoping as much. You can guess what happens now."

Vohanen glanced at Krelbe. He was very slowly moving to the right, angling himself closer to the Knight of Mithuna in front of him. Vohanen gauged the distance between himself and the other knight. Ten feet.

"I want to speak with him," he said.

Verona nodded and Nidore cut away the gag with a flick of his blade. Reed coughed and wet his chafed lips.

"You should not have come," he said, his voice raw.

"Nice to see you too, Reed," Vohanen replied. "Still telling others what to do, I see. What did I say to you when I left you?"

Reed gave a wry chuckle. "That you would find me, wherever I might be."

"Aye. I gave you my oath. The oath of a knight. What did you think I was going to do?"

"Still, you shouldn't have come. Mithuna, one of the Twelve, is here."

"We know. So is Kriari."

"Kri ... ari!"

"Well, here *physically*, at least."

"You need to get to the Great Hall," Reed said. "Mithuna has—"

"Enough, Reed. Enough," interrupted Verona. "You have already said too much."

"But—"

"*Enough*." Nidore hesitated, then pushed on his blade, breaking the skin and drawing blood.

"What do you want?" demanded Vohanen.

"Lay down your weapons and you will not be harmed. We will hold you for a couple of days, then set you free."

"I'm not leaving here without Reed."

"He will be released, too. We don't need him anymore. You will all be able to walk out of the front gate."

"What's the catch?"

"No catch," Verona said, smiling her unnerving smile. "I give you my oath as a Priestess of the Twelve. I know how important these things are."

"And Kriari?"

She paused. Her tongue darted across her lips. "You may take him with you."

Vohanen frowned. It sounded too good to be true. And when something sounded too good to be true, it probably was. He was about to open his mouth to reply when Reed did it for him.

"No," the guardsman said. "Mithuna is planning something. You have to stop her."

"*Quiet!*" Verona hissed.

"This is bigger than us, Vohanen. I relieve you of your oath. Stop Mithuna."

"Wrong choice, Reed," Verona said, shaking her head. "Nidore. *Kill him.*"

Nidore raised his rapier. Reed met his eyes. "You don't have to do this, Nidore," he said softly. "Do not be what Verona wants you to be. Or what your father wants you to be. Pit, do not even be what *I* want you to be. Look inside yourself. Choose your own path."

"It is too late," whispered Nidore. "Too late."

"No. The time is now. Choose *now.*"

Nidore smiled. A genuine smile of warmth and friendship. Reed felt a wave of pity for the young man, loved by few and derided by many; bullied, cajoled, and manipulated into doing things he didn't understand. Always trying to please those he loved, and always being pushed away.

"NIDORE!" shouted Verona, her face a mask of fury.

"I choose," Nidore murmured serenely and, still smiling, he pivoted smoothly and rammed his rapier through the eye of the knight standing next to him.

Time slowed to treacle.

The steel tip exploded from the back of the knight's skull.

Nidore withdrew his blade. Vohanen and Krelbe dashed forwards. Verona's arm flashed. Her dagger whistled through
the air and thunked into Nidore's stomach. Reed lowered his
shoulder and tackled the remaining knight to the ground.
Vohanen reached the pair as they were struggling to rise,
grabbed a handful of the knight's long hair, pulled his head
back and drew his blade across the exposed throat.

"Yonis!" Verona moaned as the knight pitched forwards
onto his face, his mouth opening and closing soundlessly.
Krelbe grabbed her arm.

Reed, his wrists still bound, crawled over to Nidore who
was on his knees, a strange expression on his face. One feeble
hand brushed against the dagger that protruded from his
abdomen.

"How did I do?" he said quietly to Reed. His white silk
shirt was drenched in blood. Again, a trembling hand pawed
at the knife.

"You did well, Nidore. You saved my life."

"It feels as if my entrails are on fire."

"You have a nasty gut wound. Try not to talk."

Nidore's skin had taken on a dull-grey pallor. He blinked
twice in quick succession and mumbled something too quietly for Reed to hear.

"What was that?" Reed asked, leaning closer.

"I said, why did you never love me, Father? I tried. I
tried so hard, but I could not make you see. I could not be
what you wanted."

Reed swallowed hard. He grasped Nidore's hand in his
own. "You were loved … Son. You were loved."

Nidore nodded. "Thank you, Father. I just wish you
would come home. Mother and I miss you. I—". He

coughed, gave a final, rattling breath and was still. Reed closed the dead man's eyes.

"Reed, your hands," said Vohanen. He severed the rope binding them with a quick, precise cut.

Reed rose to his feet, storm clouds brewing in his eyes. "You," he growled at Verona, his voice awash with a cold fury. "You *murderer*."

He advanced on the priestess like a hurricane, his hand raised, his cheeks red and blotchy. Krelbe released her and took a step back.

"Give me one reason why I should spare your life," Reed snarled.

Verona looked up at him defiantly. "There is none," she said fiercely. "I will not excuse or defend my actions to you, Reed. My Order has been struggling against men like you for hundreds of years. My family has been hunted and persecuted by those who thought they knew best, by those who believed they were doing the right thing, and to what end? It was all a lie. My father was killed defending our temple. Defending what he believed in. So, take your petty vengeance and be done with it. It doesn't matter, you have already lost."

Reed turned to Vohanen, his face expressionless. "Your sword."

"Are you sure?"

"She was the one who sent Syrella down into the Pit, Vohanen. Her Order is in league with the greylings. And she tried to murder Aldarin and Jelaïa. Why should I let her live?"

No one answered. Silence.

Kriari stepped forwards. The giant, bearded demi-god

laid a massive hand on Reed's shoulder and fixed him with his coal-black eyes.

"Be …" he said. He scrunched his face in concentration. "Be … bett … er."

Reed glowered. "Be better at what?"

Kriari shook his head in frustration. "Be … better … than … *her.*"

Reed tried to tear his gaze away, but Kriari held him fast.

"Let go of me," he said between clenched teeth. The anger boiling in his head began to drain away. He went after it, pulling at the flailing tendrils, ordering it to return, pleading with it to return, but it refused to obey. The red curtain obscuring his vision was pulled aside, and he saw Verona for what she was: an exhausted, defeated shell of a woman. Why break something that was already broken?

"Fine," he said. "She lives. We can take her with us to the Great Hall."

"Is that where we'll find Mithuna?" Vohanen asked.

Reed nodded. "I think so. Although she will not look like herself."

"What do you mean?"

"She will look … like me." Reed raised his right hand, and Vohanen could see a deep gash running lengthways across the palm from thumb to ring finger.

"She can change form," Reed went on. "Some sort of … magic. She needs spit, hair and—" he gestured to his cut hand, "—blood. That's why they couldn't kill Syrella. They needed her alive. Although I have no idea why she would want to impersonate *me.*"

Vohanen sighed as the pieces slotted into place. "I do.

We decided on two rescue attempts. One from above, one from below."

"Two ... who leads the second attempt?"

"Jeffson and Syrella," said Vohanen, already running for the door. "Pit! We have to hurry! They are heading straight into a trap!"

CHAPTER 20

THE ASSAULT

"I can build you great weapons of war. Trebuchets, mangonels, siege towers, and battering rams; but ideally you should never have to use them. The best way to take a castle is by attrition. Surround the place. Make sure nothing enters. Nothing leaves. Starvation, thirst, and disease will do more damage than my artillery. And if you do have to use them ... be prepared to pay a heavy price for every inch of disputed ground."

GUANNA, SECOND OF THE TWELVE, 121 AT

❧

THE FORCES OF Arelium and Kessrin stretched out before the walled city of Talth like a human forest of red and blue; thousands of archers and spearmen eager to face the enemy at last after weeks on the road.

Jelaïa sat on her palfrey near Derello's tent, her elevated position giving her an excellent view of the battlefield. Her

Arelians were dead centre, three squares of spearmen and a scattering of archers, the latter protected by a row of movable screens called mantlets that could be pushed forwards as the line advanced. Some of the spearmen carried ladders, others grappling hooks. More weapons of war designed by Sir Gaelin.

To the right of the Arelians, the Kessrin force was grouped into a single block of men wielding an assortment of scimitars, axes, and pikes. At the very forefront of the first rank, a flash of pink and purple stood out against the blue: Lord Bansworth, still looking to atone for his treachery. Aldarin had told Jelaïa that Bansworth had fought well during the skirmish to retake the port of Haeden, killing several greylings single-handed.

On the opposite flank stood the siege tower, all alone. Jelaïa knew that the four levels inside were packed with close to a hundred of Orkam's best men, led by Orkam himself. At the rear of the tower, twenty stalwart Knights of Brachyura were ready to push it up against the wall.

And lastly, behind the front lines, were Brachyura and his knights. They looked resplendent in their burnished silver armour and pronged helms. All save Aldarin. His helm had been knocked from his head during his altercation with the threshers and crushed underfoot. She remembered going to see him in the smithy deep in the temple of Brachyura. Remembered the smile on his face as he finished repairing his battered helm. It was important to him, and now that was gone.

"Ready, my Lady?" asked Loré, his warhorse stamping its hooves in anticipation. She nodded and glanced to her left where Derello was deep in conversation with Kumbha.

With an affirmation, the giantess left the command post and hurried down to the infirmary at the bottom of the hill.

"She won't be able to treat everyone," Baron del Kessrin said, watching as Kumbha organised teams of runners with stretchers. "She's advised me to let her use her gift at her discretion, and I've agreed. Only the most life-threatening cases. We'll have to find beds for the rest. Oh, and I almost forgot." He held out a bronze eyeglass. "You'll need one of these."

"Thank you, Derello," Jelaïa replied, smiling at him. "We've both changed quite a bit since our first meeting, wouldn't you say?"

"We have." There was a wistfulness in his eyes. "I sometimes wish we could go back to how things were before. The painted mask. Every decision made for me. All I had to do was show my face from time to time and entertain my suitors. No real responsibilities. No risk. A quiet life …"

"No real friends," Jelaïa continued. "No real purpose. No sense of adventure, of broadening one's horizons. I also lived a sheltered, carefree life, but it was stifling, Derello! Like a gilded cage. Think of all you have accomplished since you set yourself free! I remember how you hated having to wear that mask. Do not let a moment's nostalgia blind you to the truth."

"Maybe." He looked out over the massed ranks of Kessrin. "By the Twelve, if my parents could see me now … Shall we begin?"

"Sound the assault."

An Arelian hornblower stepped forwards and blew one long, loud clarion call. Jelaïa brought up her eyeglass and sighted it on the distant city walls. They appeared empty. The allied army began to move. Her position upwind allowed her to hear the cries of the officers as they fought to keep the men in formation, the jingling of chainmail, the pounding of booted feet, the creaking of the siege tower's wheels.

"Where are they?" muttered Loré, his own eyeglass trained on the ramparts. "What are they doing?"

The advance elements were only a hundred feet away now, still unchallenged. Ladders began to rise like flower stalks as they came within range.

An ear-piercing shriek exploded from somewhere inside Talth. It rolled over the battlefield, clamorous and deafening. Men dropped their weapons and clapped their hands over their ears. Horses bucked and shied in terror. Jelaïa's own horse rocked back and forth on its front legs, shaking its mane.

Threshers appeared on top of the wall. Each held boulder-sized chunks of broken masonry gathered from the nearby ruined buildings. As the strident cry of the brood mother faded away, the beasts launched their improvised missiles down onto the attackers, with deadly effect.

Half-raised ladders were shattered into splinters. Arelians and Kessrin were crushed. Some of the boulders bounced or rolled when they hit the ground. Jelaïa saw one plough through a row of five men, leaving a red-streaked trail of gore in its wake.

"Pit! We must pull them back!" she yelled.

"Not yet!" Loré shouted back. "This may be our only chance. Archers!" The hornblower belted out two short blasts and the bowmen stepped out from behind their mantlets to send volley after volley into the air.

The threshers, out of ammunition, retreated. The allies surged forwards with a ragged cheer.

Another reverberating screech.

On the far lateral edges of the battlefield, the earth collapsed in on itself, revealing two gaping holes that vomited forth a stream of chittering greylings, rushing in leaps and bounds towards the unprotected flanks.

Bansworth saw them first and screamed at his group of Kessrin to reposition. Further to the left, the siege tower continued its ponderous trek to the wall, oblivious to the danger it was in.

"There are too many of them!" Derello said, his face deathly pale. "We have to send in the knights or we'll be overrun! Two groups, one left, one right. Sound the horn."

Jelaïa gnawed at a stray lock of hair in frustration. They had fewer than a hundred riders whereas the greylings numbered in the thousands. There must be another way. Then it came to her.

"No! Wait!" she cried. "Send them all to the right. Save the Kessrin."

"My Lady?"

"DO IT! Loré, you have command." She tapped her horse's flanks and galloped away from the command post.

Twelve give me strength, she thought. The infirmary passed by in a blur, her palfrey kicking up clods of dirt as it accelerated. She heard the faint sound of the signal horn and saw the Knights of Brachyura peel away to the right.

It was all down to her now. She thought back to the temple, to her first meeting with Praedora. The First Priestess had demonstrated just how powerful their gift could be.

She was coming up fast on the siege tower. It looked like

she would reach it before the greylings, but it was going to be close. The tower itself was less than fifty feet from the wall now, it needed just a few more minutes.

She pulled hard on the reins and her horse skittered to a halt, nearly throwing her from the saddle. She leapt to the ground. The score of Knights of Brachyura who had been pushing the tower were staring at her in astonishment.

"KEEP IT MOVING!" she yelled, darting round the left side. The greylings were almost on top of them, a grey wave of snickering claws. She planted her feet. One solitary figure against thousands. But she didn't have to beat them.

She just had to break them.

I can do this.

She cracked open the vial of Aldarin's blood and emptied the entire contents into her mouth. Ever since her Awakening, she had always been taught the same things. Control. Focus. Accuracy. Restraint.

It was time to forget all she had learnt.

Her eyes snapped open. Her brain felt like it was being ripped apart. She was weeping from the pain. There was more power inside her than she had ever felt, almost more than she could handle.

Almost.

"ARELIUM!" she screamed, and the fires of Brachyura burst forth from her fingertips, a curtain of cerulean flame a hundred feet wide. The greylings squealed in panic. With a flick of her hand, Jelaïa sent the wall of flame crackling forwards.

The enemy were jabbering manically, the front lines pushing and prodding in an attempt to run away from the advancing firestorm. Grey skin began to pucker and blister.

Those closest were boxed in. They lashed out with their sharp claws, desperate to escape their fate, but there would be no salvation. The flames cascaded over them. Purifying. Cleansing.

Jelaïa could feel her vision blurring, just as it had done when she had used her gift to halt Brachyura himself. She would have to stop soon or risk going blind. She could see the greylings wavering, unsure whether they should fight or flee, searching for guidance. But there were no threshers here, no barbed whips, no harsh commands to force them on. They began to peel away in groups of two or three, then in dozens, then more and more until the stream of deserters became a flood, hundreds and hundreds of greylings fleeing back to the gaping hole that had spawned them.

The priestess of Brachyura let the wall of flame fade away and blinked to clear the bluish light from her eyes. She felt completely drained. A cramp spasmed up her left arm, causing her to grit her teeth.

She heard a crunch of sabatons on ash and turned to see Sir Gaelin, his eyes wide as he took in the heaps of smouldering bodies littering the charred earth. "My Lady, I ..." he stuttered. "I came to see if you needed some assistance, but it appears you do not."

"Lend me your arm, if you would, Sir Knight. I fear that if I try to move, I will collapse."

"Of course! Orkam can handle the deployment of the siege tower. Let me escort you to the infirmary. We will have Kumbha check you haven't damaged anything."

Above them, the tower had reached the battlements, and the Knights of Brachyura pushing it had disappeared inside. They would be first onto the ramparts, hopefully establishing a foothold for Orkam and his spearmen. Threshers were throwing great slabs of stone at the raised drawbridge, but Gaelin had done his job well and the reinforced wood was holding.

"I'm not going back," Jelaïa said, her hands gripping Sir Gaelin's arm tightly. "I won't be lying in some infirmary cot or watching through a spyglass while my people give their sweat and blood to take back this city. Where's my horse?"

"I think your firework display may have spooked it, my Lady."

"Hmm. Then I'll need to borrow your arm for a while longer, Sir Gaelin. Would you mind taking me up to the wall?"

The drawbridge slammed down, spewing forth a host of knights in their magnificent pincer-shaped helms, their raised axes shining in the sun. The threshers barely had time to drop their boulders before the knights were among them, cutting and slashing. Aldarin and Brachyura had spent several hours describing the enemy's weaknesses and how to exploit them: the face, neck, armpits, and backs of the knees were targeted with unerring accuracy by a score of blades.

Sir Gaelin led Jelaïa inside the siege tower and the tired Baroness let out a groan. A series of ladders enabled soldiers to climb from one floor of the tower to the next. The second and third levels appeared empty, and she could hear the muffled voice of Orkam barking orders from the fourth.

"Pit-spawned ladders," she muttered. She dragged her feet onto the lowest rung and began to haul herself upwards, ignoring the aches in her arms and legs.

"We can still go back," said Gaelin tentatively, watching as she arrived breathless on the second level.

"Shut up." She gritted her teeth and attacked the next ladder. Distant cheering filtered through the wooden planks. All being well that meant that the other greyling ambush had been repelled. She kept her eyes fixed on the rung in front of her and concentrated on slowly putting one hand above the other. After an age, she reached the third level of the tower and lay there on her back, winded.

Gaelin joined her, making it seem easy despite his heavy plate. He ran a hand through his spiky hair. "One more to go. Um, would you perhaps like a boost?"

"What? No! I …" she looked at the rungs stretching up to the top and sighed. "Fine. But no telling Aldarin."

She allowed herself to be manoeuvred onto his back, then his shoulders, before finally being raised even higher as he grasped her heels and extended his arms above his head. She managed the last few feet without difficulty and emerged, blinking, on the edge of the drawbridge.

The ramparts were covered in the dead and the dying. The plaintive whimpering of Arelian soldiers mixed with the mewling of injured greylings. The enemy had suffered the worst: a group of threshers had been cut to pieces, their dismembered arms and legs scattered over the battlements like a gruesome jigsaw puzzle. Here and there, Jelaïa could see the crimson red of Arelium or the silver plate of a Knight of Brachyura, but the greyling dead outnumbered them by four or five to one.

Peering over the top of the wall, she saw that her allies had indeed repelled the flanking assault and that Derello and Loré had pulled them back out of range of the threshers, trusting Orkam to do his job without support.

"My Lady." One of the wounded Arelians, his face a

mass of flayed skin, had found her boot with his hand. She crouched down beside him. "Yes, soldier?"

"Are we winning, my Lady? I can't see clearly. There's something in my eyes …"

Jelaïa took his hand. "Yes. We are winning. Now stay still, help is on its way."

She stood up and turned to Sir Gaelin. "I need you to get some stretcher-bearers up here. Some of these men can still be saved."

"But—"

"Please, Gaelin. I no longer need an escort. I can handle myself."

"Yes, my Lady." The Knight of Guanna bowed hastily and ran back to the siege tower.

Right, Jelaïa thought. *On to the gatehouse.*

She picked her way along the ramparts, ignoring the pleas for help, stepping over broken spears, going around piles of rubble. The roof of the gatehouse came into view and, below it, a portcullis protecting a huge pair of barred wooden doors, reinforced by strips of metal. Orkam's spearmen and the remaining knights were fighting to reach the portcullis, held in check by several hundred greylings. As Jelaïa watched, an Arelian was pulled to the ground and set upon by two of the creatures, a darker red staining his uniform.

Her hand went to her necklace before she remembered that the vial of blood was empty. Pit! She couldn't just stand there and do nothing. She hesitated. If she couldn't be a priestess, maybe she could be a Baroness. She moved closer, close enough to be heard, took a deep breath and shouted as loud as she could, "MEN OF ARELIUM!"

Orkam looked up at her, a grim smile on his face.

"Men of Arelium! Remember who you are! You are here because you are the best of us. The bravest. The strongest. It is you who have been chosen for this essential task. On you lies the heavy responsibility of bringing an end to this siege. You have already stopped the greylings from taking our city. Let us stop them from taking another! We are the tip of the spear. The fangs of the wolf! My father is gone, but Arelium remains! The Lady of the White Wolf remains! Show us your strength! Show us your courage! Arelium! ARELIUM!"

"ARELIUM!" came the reply, and a crimson tide surged forwards with a roar, pushing the enemy back.

"SPEARWALL!" yelled Orkam. Before the greylings could react, his men adopted the formation, spears pointing outwards.

Orkam cleared his throat. He appeared to be almost embarrassed. Then he began to sing in an off-key tenor.

"*I saw a girl at the country fair, pretty as I could see.*"

The spearwall took a step forwards, an unstoppable barrier of steel. Greylings died.

"*I saw a girl at the country fair, her name was Marjorie.*"

The greylings were pushed back again. They were being hemmed in, their backs to the portcullis that they had been trying to defend.

Orkam kept on singing, and the spearwall kept on advancing.

Jelaïa could hear the shrieks of pain as the greylings were impaled, stabbed, pummelled, and crushed. She had heard rumours of how Reed had used the song during the siege of Arelium but could never have imagined just how effective it was.

The spearmen had reached the gate. "Knights!" ordered Orkam. The Arelians parted to let the Knights of Brachyura through, and three of them began tugging on the chain that would raise the portcullis.

Jelaïa left her vantage point and met up with Orkam, who was turning his spearwall around. The main road up to the keep stretched out behind the gatehouse, straight and wide. Perfect for horses. Burnt-out houses lined the street, their windows shattered, their roofs caved in. Shadowy forms moved in the darkness of the ruined buildings.

"My Lady," Orkam said with a scowl. "It is not safe for you here."

"It is good to see you too, Orkam."

"This is no laughing matter. The enemy are out there, preparing to attack. You are the last of the bloodline of del Arelium. If you fall, it is the end."

If only you knew, Jelaïa thought. "I will be fine," she said out loud. With a creak, the portcullis was raised a few feet off the ground. Immediately, a group of knights ducked underneath and began chopping at the barred wooden doors with their axes.

"They won't let us in without a fight, my Lady," Orkam said. His wall of spears was now pointing the other way, tips aimed at the dilapidated townhouses. He called over a young recruit and pressed a square of blue fabric into his hands. "Get up to the roof and wave that about, lad. Tell them we're ready."

The shadows coalesced. Not greylings, but threshers. Ironclad, holding a mixture of swords, clubs, and barbed whips. Twenty of them. Thirty. More arriving by the minute. They would rip the spearwall apart.

"Come on, you arrogant bastards," muttered Orkam, eyes fixed on the frantic swings of the Knights of Brachyura.

Jelaïa heard a faint sound, a deep rumble, like thunder before the storm. The threshers heard it too. The first wooden bar split with a crack and the knights started hacking at the second.

"COME ON."

The threshers lumbered forwards, growling and grunting in their alien tongue. The rumbling grew louder.

"Here, my Lady." Orkam ripped a dagger from his belt and held it out to Jelaïa. She took it with one shaking hand.

The ground was vibrating beneath their feet. The knights were nearly through the second bar. The threshers, sensing danger, increased their pace.

"CLEAR!" yelled one of the knights as the second bar gave way in a hail of splinters.

"MOVE!" screamed Orkam, grabbing Jelaïa by the hand and pulling her to the side. The noise was deafening.

With an explosion of shattered metal, the doors burst open and Brachyura, Fourth of the Twelve, his face an expression of righteous fury, descended on the threshers with the force of an angry god. In his wake came row after row of mounted knights, trampling the greyling corpses underfoot.

They had made it into the city of Talth.

CHAPTER 21

ONE TOO MANY

"Why do you continue to defend them? We have saved them from the greylings. We have taught them all we know. We have even helped them create nine great Baronies, which will stand the test of time. And yet, still they come to us. Whining. Complaining. I, for one, am tired of it. The next ungrateful human who looks at me the wrong way will taste my blade."

MITHUNA, THIRD OF THE TWELVE 121 AT

JEFFSON WATCHED AS the squad of six town guard entered the latrines. A shout of surprise told him they had found the unconscious servant. He retreated slowly and crept back to Syrella and Reed, who were hiding in one of the storerooms nearby.

"I'm afraid they've reached our entry point," he said. "We won't be leaving the same way we came in."

"Can I not just order them away?" Syrella asked. She had found what looked like an old tablecloth and was tearing off a piece to replace the grimy bandage wound around the stump at the end of Reed's right arm.

"I don't think that would work. Since when does the Baroness use the ground floor latrines? You saw what happened when we tried to get into the prison."

"How many men did you see?"

"Six, my Lady. I could probably incapacitate them, but not silently, and assuredly not without the risk of one of them raising the alarm."

"Then we will have to go through the Great Hall," Reed said, grimacing as Syrella unwrapped his dressing. The ragged remains of his lower arm were red and raw, weeping a foul-smelling mixture of pus and blood.

"Oh, Reed," said Syrella. "We need to get you to a healer. Why did they do this to you?"

"I was trying to escape. I think they thought this would make it more difficult."

"And your beard is even scratchier than before," she said teasingly, placing a hand on his cheek. "I thought I told you to do something about that!"

"What?"

"After you helped us escape from the Pit. I told you to shave, remember?"

"I ... yes, of course. I forgot. It's been a difficult few weeks, and my mind is a bit muddled. So, out through the Great Hall?"

"That does appear to be the best option in our current predicament, my Lord," Jeffson agreed. "Vohanen suggested we meet there if something went awry. We will just have to pray to the Twelve that we do not run into Mithuna on our way out."

"I need a weapon."

"Sorry, my Lord?"

"I need a weapon. I'm not going out there unarmed."

Jeffson drew a dagger from his belt and passed it over. "That's all I have, I'm afraid, my Lord. I hope it will suffice."

Reed nodded, holding the weapon clumsily in his left hand.

They met a couple of guards on their way to the Great Hall, patrolling down the corridor in the opposite direction. Syrella set a haughty look on her face and swept past them without stopping, her eyes riveted in front of her. Jeffson saw one of the guards open his mouth as if to say something, then they turned a corner and were lost from sight.

A non-descript side door led them from the dingy corridor into the Great Hall itself, with its vandalised banners and wrought-iron throne.

"By the Twelve, where did they find *that* thing?" said Syrella, eyeing the throne with disgust. "It was my great-grandfather's; a sadistic and violent man by all accounts. I thought Father had ordered it to be melted down."

"Maybe he changed his mind and kept it, just in case," Reed said, a glint of steel in his voice. "Sometimes violence is the only option."

Syrella turned on him. "No, it isn't. Violence is never the only option. Certain people just think it is. There is *always* another way."

Reed shrugged and looked away.

"Mithuna is not here. But neither is Vohanen," Jeffson said, visibly disappointed. "That does not bode well. Either he has failed, or he has been delayed. We should not risk waiting for him." He began to walk towards the double doors at the end of the hall. Once out of the keep, they would only need to cross the inner courtyard and pass through the gatehouse. They were almost there.

Suddenly, the doors were thrown open and a crowd of people charged into the room in a whirlwind of sound. Jeffson saw Vohanen at their head, yelling and pointing. Krelbe and an axe-wielding warrior were two steps behind, leading a half-dozen Knights of Kriari and a huge, bear-like monstrosity with obsidian eyes. And to the rear, a dark-haired woman who looked vaguely familiar, her hands bound. Holding her tightly by the arm was a slim, middle-aged man with greying hair.

Reed.

No.

But that means …

He wheeled round, fear coursing through his veins.

The creature he had believed to be Reed was advancing on Syrella. It was laughing, a high-pitched female sound, eerie and alien. The thing's face was melting, changing, bits of hair falling from its head in chunks. The right arm writhed, the bandage tearing as rosy-pink flesh pushed its way through. The other arm held a knife. *His knife.*

"Syrella, RUN!" he shouted, sprinting towards her as fast as his tired legs would carry him.

The Baroness was rooted to the spot, shaking with fear. She gave no indication of having heard him.

"SYRELLA!" He shoved her aside. She careened into one of the fallen banners.

The knife came down.

Jeffson felt a sharp pain in his torso and knew without looking that he would find his own knife embedded there. The creature grinned, its lips stretching far wider than should be possible. The right arm swung round, the pulsating mass of flesh at its extremity crashing into his skull with the force of a hammer.

He sank to his knees. A kick to the chest sent him sprawling onto his back.

Hundreds of small black spots appeared in his vision; twisting, expanding, and merging, draining the light from his eyes.

A child laughed, somewhere nearby. It was joined by the sound of another voice; a woman speaking softly. He could almost see her. Hair so blond it was nearly white, shimmering like a wall of ice.

"Cerra," he said. The woman smiled.

Jeffson smiled back.

The last of the light flickered and died.

᠙

"JEFFSON!" Vohanen yelled as his friend's body hit the ground. The thing that had once been Reed was growing in stature, now reaching well over seven feet.

Mithuna.

"Caddox, check on Syrella!" The knight nodded, veering right.

Attacking one of the Twelve with no shield and no armour, Vohanen thought. *I must be mad.*

Mithuna's features were beginning to take shape from the doughy mound of flesh. Stubbly grey hair sprouted along her scalp. Her face was all hard lines and sharp angles, her square jawline almost masculine. With a soft sucking sound, four fingers and a thumb slithered out from the stump of her right arm.

The pinkness faded from her skin. It became pallid, criss-crossed with veins, much like that of her knights. Empty eye sockets were filled with a gurgle of black liquid.

Vohanen aimed low with a lunging stab. His sword hit her leg just above the knee and bounced off without breaking the skin.

Pit! What is she made of? Iron?

Two Knights of Kriari joined the attack, shields raised. Mithuna took a blade to the arm and another to the thigh, both failing to penetrate. She lashed out with a bare foot, denting a shield. Vohanen saw a newly-formed fist coming his way and dodged sideways, but he was not quite fast enough and caught a stinging blow to the shoulder.

Mithuna was now fully transformed. An eight-foot colossus, her gargantuan form barely clothed by the remains of the dirty tunic she had worn when impersonating Reed. Her soulless eyes landed on one of the attackers and she bounded forwards, ripping the tower shield from the knight's hand and cracking it down on his head. The force of the blow was enough to fracture the man's skull.

Where in the Pit was Kriari? Vohanen saw that his patron had not moved since the battle had begun, sitting on the floor with his hands over his ears.

"KRIARI, WE NEED YOU!" Vohanen cried. "HELP US!"

"Sis ... ter. Sis ... ter," the giant was saying over and over again. He started to rock back and forth. "Sis ... ter."

Vohanen cursed. Another knight was down, his arm twisted at an unnatural angle. Mithuna now held a short sword, the weapon looking tiny in her oversized hand. As Vohanen watched, she stepped around the shield of an attacker and stabbed him in the side.

There must be a weakness, he thought. They just had to adapt. He had fought armoured enemies many times before, and this was no different. The joints: back of the knee, under the arm, top of the neck.

Mithuna had her back to him, walking unhurriedly towards Krelbe and a group of three knights who had formed a shieldwall. Vohanen darted in, his sights set on the skin behind her right knee. He roared in elation as he felt dark blood splash onto his hand. The monstrosity stumbled.

He thrust upwards as she fell, opening a second cut in the back of her neck. Then an enormous hand grabbed hold of his belt and he was sailing through the air. He hit the shieldwall like a boulder, and the pain was tremendous. One of the shields split in half. The Knights of Kriari were scattered. His ram's horn broke with a crack.

Vohanen pulled a finger-length sliver of wood from his shoulder.

"So, you must be this Vohanen I have heard so much about," said Mithuna conversationally. "It was surprisingly difficult to find out who you are. It didn't help that Verona stupidly killed that traitor Quinne instead of bringing him back here for questioning. My Order has suffered from the lack of a guiding hand."

A Knight of Kriari rushed her from the left, hoping to take her by surprise. She batted his sword away with one hand and wrapped the other around his neck.

"At least they are not so drab and predictable as your own men," she continued, examining the knight caught in her grip like he was some kind of bug. She shrugged and broke his neck with a twist of her wrist, discarding his still twitching body. "I *did* find out that you had a son. Avor, wasn't it? Died in the Pit, poor thing."

"Shut up," Vohanen hissed, willing his broken body to move. "You are not worthy even to speak his name."

"Hmm. I wonder what he would say if he could see you now; a tired, defeated old man?"

"I don't know. I hope he would say that he was proud of me. And that he loved me. It's all that matters."

Only two Knights of Kriari remained upright. They began to advance, but Vohanen waved them back with a flick of his hand.

"And so, we speak of love," Mithuna said with a sigh of frustration. "No matter how many times it is explained to me, I still do not completely understand what it is. What makes—"

She coughed. The left part of her face *drooped*, the skin distorting.

"What makes—"

Another wracking cough. Blood ejected from her mouth and spattered onto Vohanen's face like droplets of red rain.

She fell to one knee and, behind her, Vohanen saw a ghost.

"Jeffson?" he whispered.

The stooped manservant, his face ashen, his leather jerkin stained crimson, drove his dagger for the third time into the open wound on the back of Mithuna's neck.

"Stop!" Mithuna spluttered.

Jeffson, impassive, calmly withdrew his dagger and stabbed again.

"STOP!" she screeched. With a moan, she turned slowly to face him. "You think I don't know you, *Nissus*? You think I don't know who you are? What you have done?"

She flailed at him wildly.

Jeffson's next thrust opened a hole in her cheek.

"A conjurer of lies," she slurred. Spittle dribbled down her chin. "A master of deceit." Her body began to change, shrinking, collapsing in on itself. Her hair lengthened, changing colour. The hole in her cheek closed with a popping sound.

"A loving husband."

Vohanen gasped. In Mithuna's place knelt a vision of beauty, with ivory hair and sky-blue eyes. Blood spilled from a deep wound in her neck, running through her hair and down her back.

"Look what I can give you," the woman said to Jeffson in a voice that was as refreshing as a cool breeze on a hot summer's day. "I can take away the pain."

Jeffson stared at her, emotions waging war across his face. A solitary tear slipped from one eye, tracing a clean line through the grime and blood on his cheek.

"Take away the pain?" he said, his voice low. "By showing me the face of Cerra, my dead wife? By reminding me of my guilt? All you have done is make it worse. Much, much worse."

Vohanen caught a flash of steel as Jeffson moved, burying the dagger in Mithuna's eye socket up to the hilt. She screamed and tried to change again, but she had pushed herself too far. A third eye opened in the middle of her forehead, the iris a swirling mix of green and blue. A streak of black and grey hair lined her chin. One leg lengthened, toned and muscular; the other remained thin and pale.

"Help me!" mewed a chorus of voices, Reed's strong tenor intertwining with the softer lilt of Cerra and Syrella.

Jeffson crossed his arms and watched.

The skin of Mithuna's stomach bulged outwards, swelling and distending as if she were in the last stages of pregnancy. With a sickening tear, the flesh was ripped open. A hairless, eyeless head appeared, covered in gore.

"Sis ... ter," Kriari murmured sadly.

Mithuna's mouth opened wide one last time. Her scream was long and piercing, then with a crack her spine broke and she toppled over, the mismatched legs spasming.

Dead silence filled the room. Verona started to sob.

"Jeff ... Jeffson," Vohanen rasped. He pulled himself into a sitting position, wincing as the movement sent a tremor of pain through his body. "How ... are you—"

"Alive?" Jeffson removed something from his pocket and tossed it into Vohanen's lap. Something small and red. A book. It was badly damaged, a dagger-sized hole running through it from cover to cover. Vohanen read the title slowly.

"'*Morlak, a political conundrum*'. What is this?"

"Open it."

On the first page was the pencil-drawing of a newborn child. It was astonishingly lifelike, each individual hair on its head lovingly rendered. The entire bottom half of the drawing was missing, torn away by the passage of Mithuna's knife.

"My daughter," Jeffson said in a choked voice.

Vohanen turned the pages. More sketches. He recognised

Cerra, sitting on the grass by a lake. The infant, older now, smiling, chasing a chicken. There were other images; drawings of a thatched house in the countryside, an oak tree covered in snow. A burning fire. The last half of the book was empty, scores of blank pages that would never be filled.

"'*As long as the memory of those we loved and lost remains, then they are never truly gone*'," quoted Vohanen, running his hand over the cover.

Jeffson nodded sadly, taking the book back. "These are my memories. I look at them every day. This is how I will never forget. I will remember them. Always."

"Hey!" Reed was fast approaching, grinning like a madman. He caught hold of the startled manservant and hugged him close. "Don't you ever scare me like that again, you stupid man! I thought we had lost you!"

A perturbed Jeffson tried to disentangle himself. "My Lord, it is not proper for a noble of your pedigree to show such displays of affection—"

"Jeffson?"

"Yes, my Lord?"

"Be quiet and enjoy it." Reed held on for a moment longer, then released him. He glanced at the bloody pile of mutated flesh that had once been Mithuna, suppressing a shudder. "By the Twelve, looks like she went one too far. What prompted her to change into that woman?"

"Did you not hear, my Lord? That was Cerra, my deceased wife. I think she thought the sight of her would make me stay my blade."

Reed was shaking his head. "What do you mean? She died? That's not possible."

"I watched our house burn, my Lord. I held her burnt

and charred body in my arms. I buried her and my child. My wife is dead."

"No, no, you don't understand. That's not how it works. Mithuna needs three things to take on the appearance of another: spit, hair ..." he held up his wounded hand, "... and fresh blood."

Jeffson began to tremble, his eyes brimming with tears. "I don't ... I don't ..."

"She's not dead, Jeffson. I don't know who you buried in that grave, but your wife is still alive."

CHAPTER 22

BROOD MOTHER

"You keep asking me to explain how my gift works, but it's so extraordinarily difficult to put into words. It's like shouting from the top of the tallest mountain, except that instead of hearing my own voice echoed back to me, I hear yours. The closer I am to you, the more distinct the echo becomes. And once I am within a few feet, I can perceive not only your spoken thoughts, but your unspoken ones, too. The secrets you would rather keep to yourself..."

MAKARA, TENTH OF THE TWELVE, I AT

∽

AFTER THE INITIAL group of threshers, Brachyura and his knights encountered no further resistance between the curtain wall and the inner keep. The greylings had torn down the doors during their assault and had not bothered to repair them, allowing the cavalry to ride unimpeded into the courtyard. Jelaïa arrived to find Brachyura and Aldarin discussing what to do next.

"The brood mother must be inside," Brachyura was saying. "Let us attack now and subdue it."

"Where are the rest of the threshers?" Aldarin countered, shaking his head. "Why is the courtyard not defended? It shouldn't have been this easy."

"A fair point," the giant replied, looking up at the empty walls. "Maybe they committed their entire strength to the first line of defence? Maybe they have fled?"

"It is certainly possible … something just doesn't feel right. We should make a full sweep of the city and post some men up on the walls in case the enemy decide to reveal themselves."

"Agreed. I will do so immediately." Brachyura inclined his head and strode off.

"Giving orders to one of the Twelve, now?" Jelaïa teased Aldarin with a smile.

"Jelaïa! You are safe! I saw the wall of blue flame, most impressive."

"Thank you," she said with a mock curtsy. "Though it is not an experience I would like to repeat. My body feels like Brachyura has run me over with his chariot."

"Hmm. And your eyes?"

"Still a bit blurry. And I emptied the vial. I will need you to give me some more of your blood."

"I don't think that's a good idea."

"Aldarin, I—"

"No, Jelaïa. You have become incredibly strong, possibly even as strong as Praedora, but you still have limits. You were not there when Praedora lost her sight. She was tired, just as tired as you are now. Her irises were tinged with blue, as are yours. She knew she was on the brink of self-destruction and yet made the choice to carry on as she believed it was the only way to avenge Sir Manfeld and stop Mina."

"Aldarin, I'm fine. A little more won't hurt."

"But it will. It hurts you every time. And it pains me to see you suffer. You have helped us come this far, let us finish what you have started."

The sun blazed in a cloudless sky. A group of knights jogged past, heading for the sprawling maze of burnt-out buildings. Archers were arriving, splitting left and right to take the stairs up to the battlements. Jelaïa's gaze fell on one of the younger soldiers, barely old enough to hold a longbow, struggling with his cumbersome quiver.

"I came through a nightmare to get here," she said softly. "I walked over the bodies of injured Arelians, ignoring their cries for help. I passed men with shattered legs, broken shards of bone piercing their skin. I saw crushed skulls, ripped flesh, and twisted limbs. These are my people, my responsibility. And I left them to suffer."

Aldarin leant forwards and wiped a tear from her cheek with a gauntleted finger.

"You did. But you are not thinking straight. You are responsible for their *lives*, not for their deaths. You did not force these men to come here, they chose to do so. The men in the siege tower volunteered. You cannot try to carry the entire population of Arelium on your back, Jelaïa."

"I think … I think I just need some time."

"We never did finish that meal, did we? Never really started it, even. How about we try again this evening? I will come without my armour."

Jelaïa took his hand. "Sounds wonderful. Bring some fresh flowers. And no running off this time. Promise?"

"I promise."

"Good. In return, I will attempt to wear two shoes of the same colour."

"Are you sure? I quite liked—"

"Aldarin," boomed Brachyura, stalking towards them, Sir Gaelin and a dozen knights traipsing behind him. "We are ready."

The tall knight nodded and gave Jelaïa's hand one last squeeze before unsheathing his axe. The doors to the inner keep had been shoddily repaired with bits of half-burnt timber. Brachyura eyed the patchwork construction. "It does not seem particularly resistant," he said. "If you would please give me some room."

He walked back a good distance, then charged at the door, slamming into it shoulder first. It buckled but held. Brachyura frowned, rolled his shoulders and tried again. This time the door exploded inwards; the armoured colossus carried through by his own momentum.

"FOR BRACHYURA!" Aldarin cried, running after him. The Great Hall was teeming with threshers. At the far end, lounging under the leaping-stag banner of Talth, the brood mother chittered a warning.

Brachyura came to his feet and lay around him with his enormous axe, carving through the tough flesh and bone of the threshers. Aldarin and Gaelin were the first to reach him, and they positioned themselves protectively on either flank. More knights poured through the door to enter the fray.

The brood mother became agitated, sniffing the air with its wrinkled snout. A thresher jumped at Brachyura, but he caught it in mid-air with the tip of his curved axe blade, opening its chest from sternum to belly. Coiled ropes of intestines burst from the creature's midriff. Neither Gaelin nor Aldarin was wearing his helm, and both were doused with sticky black ichor.

"PUSH FORWARDS", the demigod ordered, elbowing a thresher in the face and breaking its nose with a crunch. Another beast tried to dodge under the titan's reach, but Gaelin was waiting for it. He hit it hard with his buckler, knocking it off balance, before plunging his sword into its neck.

We cannot lose, Jelaïa thought, watching Brachyura rampage through the hall like a force of nature. Before him was a score of threshers, each one the size of Aldarin, with skin as hard as bark and muscles the size of logs, and yet they could barely dent his armour.

Maybe this was why the weaver conceived the Pact. She knew they were losing. Maybe it had been a last-pitch gamble, risking everything in the hope that they would concede rather than let the land be torn apart.

Only one thresher remained now, interposing itself between the knights and the brood mother. A gigantic, hulking monster almost as tall as Brachyura himself. Its torso was covered in weeping sores, and a necklace of what looked like human hands dangled from its neck. It pointed its saw-toothed blade at Aldarin.

"Uuuu … mann," it growled.

Aldarin almost dropped his axe in astonishment. "So, it's true! You speak!"

"Ourrr … land."

"Silence," Brachyura ordered, lifting his own axe

menacingly. "We will not give in. What my brothers and sisters did was wrong. We should never have stopped fighting. Now stand aside."

The thresher tilted its head to one side, then raised its free hand and beckoned.

"A challenge? So be it. I will … Wait. What is that sound?"

The brood mother was humming, its eyes closed, its head swaying rhythmically from side to side.

Brachyura took a step forwards, then stopped, confused. The humming grew louder.

"Lord!" Aldarin said. "Your eyes."

The twin ebony globes were bulging in their sockets, the surface pulsing and rippling as if there was something inside trying to escape. They began to leak a thick, tarry substance, dribbling down Brachyura's face like tears.

The giant opened his mouth to speak, and more of the black goo spilled over his lips. He quickly shut it again.

There was a sound akin to a barking dog. The thresher was laughing.

"I don't know what the brood mother is doing," Aldarin said, "but we need to stop it! Knights! Protect your Lord! Gaelin, with me!"

The surviving knights formed a circle around Brachyura as he jerked and spasmed, no longer in control of his own body.

Aldarin charged at the thresher, his axe held low, the tip making sparks as it was dragged across the stone. He sent it arcing upwards in a powerful two-handed swing, barely deflected by the thresher's sword. He felt Gaelin coming up behind him and ducked. The knight's sword sliced over his head and gouged a bloody furrow along the thresher's stomach.

The creature retaliated, grabbing Gaelin's buckler and using it to yank him close enough for a bone-crunching headbutt. Gaelin managed to twist his neck and took the blow on the cheek, cracking the bone.

"PIT!" he yelled, slashing at the straps that held the buckler attached to his vambrace. He staggered backwards, leaving the thresher with the metal disc. The thing turned and threw the buckler like a discus at Aldarin, catching him below the knee and knocking him off his feet.

Gaelin tried again, flaps of skin hanging from his broken cheek. His sword whisked under the thresher's guard and nicked an inch-deep hole in the thing's hide. The return strike tore off Gaelin's ear. He howled in pain, his hand going reflexively to the side of his head. The thresher used the moment of inattention to kick the knight in the stomach. Gaelin dropped to the ground, moaning.

Aldarin stood alone. A duo of knights stepped out of the protective circle, but Aldarin waved them back. "No, protect our Lord. I will deal with this … filth."

He brought up his axe and kissed the silver 'Brachyura' inscribed on the haft.

"This is not your land," he said, walking calmly forwards. A rusty blade came whistling towards his unprotected face. He batted it away. "It is ours." He turned to the side, narrowly avoiding an overhead chop that hit the stone floor, kicking up a flurry of stone chips.

"And we do not fear you." He feinted low, and the thresher lowered its sword to block. At the last moment, Aldarin changed direction, driving his axe into the thing's chest with all his strength. The blade bit deep, stuck fast in the thresher's ribcage. The beast howled and dropped its weapon.

"Yes!" cried Jelaïa, punching the air ecstatically.

The dying thresher's hand clamped down on Aldarin's skull. "Uuuu … mann," it muttered, ichor cascading down its chest. It began to squeeze. Aldarin cried out and grabbed its fingers, but it was like trying to prise open a vice. Muscles rippled in the thresher's arm as it sought to tighten its grip. The Knights of Brachyura saw the danger and began to move, leaving their patron to charge at the mortally wounded beast.

Jelaïa was still by the entrance of the Great Hall, but she heard with perfect clarity the sonorous crack as the thresher broke Aldarin's skull.

"NO!" she screamed in panic, as seven axes buried themselves in the thresher's body, silencing its mocking laugh forever. The thresher released Aldarin's inanimate form as it fell. Almost simultaneously, the brood mother shivered and the humming faded away. Brachyura hauled himself to his feet, blinking as if awakening from a long slumber. Jelaïa ran past him, falling to her knees before Aldarin and taking his head onto her lap.

His hair was drenched in blood, and she could see the flash of white bone protruding through his scalp. "Aldarin," she called. "Aldarin, can you hear me?" The knight's eyes were rolled into the back of his head. Drool dribbled from his half-open mouth.

"Stretcher!" she called desperately to one of the Knights of Brachyura.

"My Lady …"

"Do it," came the exhausted baritone of Brachyura

himself. He was wiping the black tarry sludge from his nose. "Send a team, and tell Kumbha to prepare. There are many wounded." The knight nodded smartly.

"Don't do this to me, Aldarin," Jelaïa sobbed, stroking his cheek. "Don't leave me to do this all alone. I can't do this alone."

There was a great commotion as teams of stretcher-bearers arrived and went to work on the wounded.

"Over here," Brachyura said. "Take this one first."

Jelaïa bent close to Aldarin's ear. "We still haven't had that meal together, you hear me? You promised. You promised me you would be there. I will be waiting for you."

She felt a hand on her shoulder.

"They need to take him now," Brachyura said quietly. She let herself be pulled away from Aldarin. A stretcher was slid under his unresponsive body and, with a heave, four Arelians lifted him into the air. Jelaïa made to follow them.

"Hello," said the brood mother.

Jelaïa stopped in mid-stride, frozen to the spot. She turned around slowly, every fibre of her being screaming that what she had heard was impossible.

The brood mother hadn't moved, its eyes were still closed, its slug-like tail quivering. Then the mouth of the creature opened wide and a strange sound burst forth from its maw.

"Hello, Jelaïa." The gelatinous blob sprawled in front of her should not be capable of such comprehensible speech. Even the threshers could only manage to grunt a few words. How was this happening?

"Who … who are you?" she asked, hearing the fear in her own voice.

"Why, I'm the one you came to find. Brachyura knows."

The Fourth of the Twelve was furious. "Weaver. How are you doing this?"

"More or less the same way as Makara spoke to you. But better. No shared minds. Complete control. You have betrayed me, Brachyura. You were to relinquish these lands to my children."

"The Pact was wrong."

"Perhaps. And yet you signed it and are bound by it. As am I." The brood mother whimpered. Cracks were appearing along its tail, splitting the skin.

"I disagree," Brachyura said. "Pacts can be broken. And remade. Let us work together to stop this."

"No, I must uphold the Pact. The wyrm will be released."

"Why? In doing so, you doom both our species."

The brood mother let out a shrill cry. One of its eyes popped from its socket and hung there. Three teeth fell from its mouth and clattered onto the floor. "You do not understand. The caverns and tunnels are full. There is no more room. The surface is our only solution. Our only way out. You will give it to us."

Brachyura shook his head sadly. "I cannot. It is not for me to decide such a thing."

"So be it." The voice grew hard. "Then this is what I will do. I will turn your nine Baronies into a molten wasteland, one by one. There will be no escape. I have already chosen the first. Once it is gone, you will have one month to surrender the surviving Baronies to me. If you do not, I will send the wyrm to another one. And again. And again. Until there are none left."

"Wait! Please!" Jelaïa pleaded. "Let me convene a

Council of the Baronies. Give me a few more months. We can help each other."

"Too late. I have already started. The wyrm is gone. I sent it to the Barony closest to its lair. I sent it to Morlak."

And with an agonising shriek, the brood mother's head burst, showering them with blood and bone.

CHAPTER 23

THE BURNING TEARS OF MORLAK

"You talk of pity? What hypocrisy! You slaughtered my children for a hundred years, without ever trying to understand what we were fighting for. You drowned them, buried them, massacred them. This final solution is of your own making. It is time to reap what you have sown."

'WEAVER', 123 AT

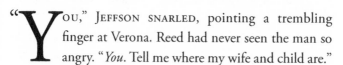

"YOU," JEFFSON SNARLED, pointing a trembling finger at Verona. Reed had never seen the man so angry. "*You.* Tell me where my wife and child are."

The priestess of Mithuna drew herself up proudly. "Why should I?"

He came close, his eyes pools of liquid fire. "You know who I am, do you not?"

"Yes. You're the strange man who follows Merad Reed everywhere and tells him what to do."

"I am not in the mood for games, Verona. Who am I?"

"Nissus." It came out as a hiss.

"Correct. Your Order specialises in the gathering and trading of information. I would surmise that you are familiar with my work. You have reports, perhaps?"

"We do."

"Good." He put his hand behind her neck and pulled her near, bending to whisper in her ear. "Then you know what I am capable of doing for money. Just *imagine* what I would be prepared to do for my family."

Verona was close enough to see the specks of blood — the blood of her former patron — on Jeffson's face. She could see how he trembled with restraint, fighting to keep his fury in check. She swallowed. "They are not here."

"Where?"

"Promise me you will spare my life."

"WHERE?"

"Lostthorn. We are keeping them in Lostthorn. They are safe. It's just like Reed said; Mithuna needed them alive if we were to use them as leverage." Her eyes flickered to the lump of mutated flesh. "A backup plan that appears to have failed."

"Let her go, Jeffson," Vohanen said. "You've got what you need."

The manservant said nothing for a moment, weighing the decision in his mind, then released the priestess with a disgusted shake of his head. "I do not understand how you can live with yourself, Verona. I have done some bad things in my time, to bad people. But even I have not kept women and children locked up for years against their will in the eventuality they might someday be useful as a bargaining chip."

Verona shot him a perplexed glance. "What are you talking about? How long do you think we have been holding them captive?" She gave a short, sardonic laugh. "We are good at being a few steps ahead but not hundreds of steps! We had no idea of your involvement until I saw you in Arelium and, even then, I wasn't sure it was you. It was only when I saw you again during the ambush near the Morlakian Pit that I finally put a name to the face. Mithuna ordered the capture of your family a month ago."

"But then ... Lostthorn ..."

"Oh, your confusion really is quite delectable. We put the word out through our usual channels; beggars, taverns, brothels, and the like. The same name kept cropping up. Ner'alla, I think it was? Big Da'arran? Man with a chain on his cheek? Supposedly, it was this Ner'alla fellow who helped them fake their deaths and set up their new lives in Lostthorn, far away from prying eyes."

"Careful, Jeffson," Syrella murmured gently. "She may be lying. Remember who you are speaking to."

"What would be the point of that?" Verona retorted. "I'd have nothing to gain from doing so. Ask Ner'alla yourself."

"I intend to," said Jeffson in a tight voice. "Right away."

Syrella laid a hand on his arm. "You should. And return here when you are done, Jeffson, or Nissus, or whoever you are. I do not know much about your past but, since meeting you, you have saved me from the Pit, helped me return to my Barony, and killed the usurper responsible for my capture. I and Morlak owe you a great debt, a debt I intend to see repaid."

She turned to Vohanen, Caddox, and the surviving Knights of Kriari, curtsying eloquently. "And you, Sir Knights. Nothing forced you to come to the aid of Morlak, and yet you did so, at great peril. Your Order has never known a more difficult time … I cannot bring back those who were lost, but I will do all I can to keep our alliance strong and mutually beneficial; starting, of course, by reopening the garrison here."

"Thank you, my Lady," Vohanen replied.

"Kriari," the befuddled member of the Twelve agreed, his mouth twitching.

"What about … him?" Syrella continued.

"Pit. I don't know," Vohanen answered with a sigh. "Take him back with us to the temple, I suppose, see what the temple master thinks we should do with him. Either we manage to reverse whatever's muddling his brain, or … we find a remote location where he can live out the rest of his life undisturbed."

"The rest of his life? Aren't the Twelve quasi-immortal?"

"What about one of his brothers or sisters?" Reed asked. "We know so little about the Twelve, but if they are all returning, surely one of his siblings may be able to help."

"Maybe." Vohanen stroked his braided beard. "It'll be up to Bjornvor to decide, not me. The only thing that's waiting for me when I get back to Dirkvale is having to explain to everyone how I managed to lose over half the men under my command."

The Great Hall doors creaked open and Krelbe reappeared with a couple of knights. "Had a good look round," he said gruffly. "No more Knights of Mithuna. We did find two of our initiates who missed the garrison roof. Dead, I'm afraid. Oh, and there's something else. If you'd come with me?"

They followed him outside. The moon was still obscured by thick clouds, adding to the dark, foreboding atmosphere.

"What do you want to show us?" asked Caddox.

"Not show you, exactly. Now quiet. Listen."

They were silent. Reed strained his ears but could only hear the wind sweeping over the battlements. *Ah, to breathe some fresh air again!*

"I can't hear anything," Syrella complained.

"Wait a minute."

There. A faint rumble. Reed crouched down and put his hand flat against the dirt of the courtyard. It felt like the ground was vibrating.

"What is it?"

"I don't know," Krelbe hissed. "But it's getting louder."

The ground was now shaking hard enough to make small shards of loose stone and gravel bounce up and down like rubber balls.

"I think maybe we should—" Reed began, before the earth was split asunder. The entire courtyard was rent in two by an enormous tear, as if it had been grasped at both ends and pulled apart. A Knight of Kriari fell screaming into the chasm that had opened under his feet.

"GET BACK!" Reed yelled. The fissure started to widen. Syrella shrieked in surprise as the ground she was standing on crumbled. A sudden jolt sent her tumbling towards the abyss.

Reed cursed and threw himself after her, grazing his knees and thighs as he slid through the gravel. He flailed frantically with his uninjured hand as Syrella toppled over the edge, miraculously catching her boot by the heel.

"Hold on!"

He pulled hard. But weeks of imprisonment and mal-nourishment had weakened his bicep and it was all he could do just to hold her in place.

"Reed, I can feel my boot slipping. I'm going to lose it!"

Pit. Pit. Pit.

He pulled again, to no effect. The sweat from his arm was dripping down onto his fingers, loosening his grip. Despite his best efforts, his hand started to slither from the heel of the boot towards the toe.

"HELP!" he yelled. "ANYONE?"

An enormous hairy forearm, a rusty manacle attached to its wrist, shot past him and wrapped around Syrella's ankle.

"Kriari," the giant said seriously and heaved the Baroness out of the chasm, depositing her carefully on the dirt of the courtyard. Reed held out his hand and pulled her to her feet.

"Thank you, Lord," Syrella stammered, visibly shaken. "That was very unpleasant." Kriari smiled and nodded, before motioning to the rapidly expanding tear in the earth. "Wyrm."

"Wyrm? What's a wyrm?"

"No idea," said Reed. "But I don't think we should wait around to find out. Let's run."

"REED!" Vohanen shouted from the other side of the chasm. "We'll find our own way out! We have a camp outside the city. Syrella knows where! We'll rendezvous there!"

Reed nodded as a great cloud of steam rocketed up from the crack. A drop hit one of his bare feet, making him yelp. It burned. The steam brought with it a sickening smell, one he was very familiar with, one he was used to smelling through a mask. Rotten eggs. Sulphur.

"Syrella. Kriari. I think worse things are coming. We have to go, now."

Kriari was shaking his head. "Bell."

"What in the Pit ... Look, just follow us, all right?"

"Bell," Kriari repeated adamantly, pointing at the roof of Morlak keep.

"The signal bell!" Syrella realised. "He wants to sound the alarm."

"It's on the roof, Syrella," Reed replied in frustration. "The ROOF. There's no time."

"Reed, that bell could save thousands. Every Morlakian will know to evacuate. It will even reach the slums down in the lower city. They deserve a chance."

Reed ground his teeth. "Fine. Kriari, escort Syrella out of Morlak, I'll go ring the bell and — wait, what are you doing?"

Kriari had taken a few paces back and was staring at the gaping chasm and the keep beyond through his curtain of greasy hair. He was grinning. "Kriari," he said, with a wave of his hand, and began to run.

The chasm must be forty feet wide, Reed thought. *And growing wider by the minute. No one can jump that far, not even a demi-god.*

Kriari whooshed past him, gathering speed. Faster than a man, faster than a horse. He seemed to be carried by the wind itself, his feet barely touching the ground. One foot pushed down hard on the lip of the chasm and he sailed into the air like the release of a coiled spring, catapulted through the scalding steam. To Reed, it looked like he was flying.

Then the colossus landed hard on the far side of the gap, his legs tucked under him, rolling like a tumbleweed before coming to a stop. Reed was about to call out when the demi-god stood up and gave him another wave. Reed waved back, smiling weakly.

The fissure had reached the inner wall now, and a large portion of it collapsed, bits of fallen masonry vanishing into the deep. Syrella was still waiting patiently for him to move. There was no sign of the others.

"I'll follow your lead," he said to her. "The only part of Morlak I'm familiar with is the inside of my cell."

"It's easy enough," Syrella replied. Her hair had come loose and she was tying it back into a ponytail. "Straight down the main road and out of the gate in the curtain wall."

A deep, guttural roar burst forth from the chasm, a terrible mixture of sadness, anger, and hate.

"GO!" Reed yelled and they set off at a jog. They'd barely covered a hundred feet when the first peals of the signal bell echoed out over Morlak, loud enough to wake the dead. Doors and shutters were thrown open as the Morlakians were roused from their slumber. Reed and Syrella were soon overtaken by fleeing citizens, some dragging crying children, others helping the aged and the infirm. More and more filled the street, until the trickle became a flood. There was another angry roar and people screamed in terror.

"Keep calm!" Syrella shouted above the cries of panic. "Keep calm and keep moving!" Reed wasn't sure whether she was heard or not, but if she was, it didn't work. Fear is like a disease, spreading unchecked from one person to another unless it is stopped. The escaping crowd became a stampede, altruism abandoned for self-preservation.

Reed saw an elderly woman trip and fall on the cobbles, only to be trampled to death by a throng of booted feet. A portly man, bent under the weight of his travelling chest, was not moving fast enough and was pushed aside. He hit the wall of a house with a crack and collapsed, twitching.

"Stop it!" Syrella was pleading helplessly. "Stop it!" Reed grasped her hand and pulled her along. "We have to keep moving, my Lady!"

The gatehouse was in sight, surrounded by crowds of frightened Morlakians, pushing and shoving to get through. The bell had fallen silent. Reed felt Syrella stop again. He turned round in annoyance. The Baroness was looking at a little girl, standing alone, clutching a soot-stained stuffed rabbit and sucking her thumb.

"Where are your parents?" Syrella asked. The girl just shrugged.

"Reed, we have to take her with us."

"Are you sure?"

"I've failed my people in so many things, Reed, I'm not letting this child be crushed or eaten … or whatever else is going to happen when that wyrm appears. Help me."

Reed pressed a hand to his ribs. There was a slight twinge of pain but nothing too bad, and his breathing was good. He sighed and lifted the girl onto his back. The crowd in front of them was thinning as people were funnelled through the bottleneck and out onto the plains on the other side.

"Come on," muttered Reed. "Come on. Come on."

There was a gigantic booming noise from up near the inner keep. A bright yellow fountain of lava, thirty feet high, erupted into the night sky, spewing deadly droplets of super-heated magma in all directions.

The wyrm had arrived.

It was immense in size. Only its head and the very top

of its snake-like body were visible over the crumbling wall of the inner keep. It was covered in a carapace made up of thousands upon thousands of glimmering ruby red scales, each one the size of a man. Two rows of overlapping, triangular teeth lined its powerful jaw, and a chain of spikes ran from its forehead to the tip of its snout. Its eyes were boiling globes of golden flame as bright as the morning sun. Magma trickled from their edges, giving the impression that the beast was weeping.

Its jaw snapped open and the wyrm roared loudly enough to make the ground tremble. The glass in the window of a nearby shopfront shattered, peppering Reed with shiny, stinging pellets. With an almost leisurely turn of its head, the wyrm demolished the top two levels of Morlak keep, pulverising the hundred-year-old fortress as if it was made of sand. *Kriari!* Reed thought as the wyrm moved again, reducing another level to rubble.

The beast inhaled, its scaly cheeks expanding, then spat forth a cone of incandescent flame, its centre so bright that Reed had to look away. The fiery torrent splashed over the garrison building, hot enough to turn stone into slag and wood into charcoal. Magma ran sluggishly down the melting walls. The roof sagged, then caved in, disappearing in a great cloud of steam.

The wyrm tipped its head back and screamed its defiance at the snowy-white peak of the Spike.

"My Barony ..." Syrella whispered, aghast, her face wet with tears. "My legacy. My people ... How is this possible? What can we do against such a thing?"

Reed felt the weight of the child on his back, her frail hands around his neck, the furry tickle of her stuffed toy.

"We start by saving those we can," he said softly. "Then we find a way to fight back."

CHAPTER 24

AFTERMATH

"Do you know where the nickname of White Rose came from? My father. Always my father. I think he became frustrated with my refusal to find a suitable husband and paid a few men to start spreading it around the local taverns. I'm sure he hoped it would shame me into capitulation. But he forgot, as he often did, that I am his daughter, and just as stubborn as him. I embraced it, and became stronger because of it."

BARONESS SYRELLA DEL MORLAK, 417 AT

I T TOOK THE wyrm less than two hours to destroy the town of Morlak. Reed and Syrella watched from a safe distance as it rampaged through the lower city, flattening whole blocks of housing with its body, setting fire to shops and warehouses with every boiling breath until there was nothing left but a burning pile of wreckage. Clouds of ash and smoke rose from hundreds of fires, further darkening the moonless night.

The little girl they had rescued watched with them for a while, chewing on the ragged ear of her stuffed rabbit, before curling up like a cat on Syrella's lap and falling asleep. Reed felt something soft brush against his palm and looked down to see that Syrella had interlaced her fingers with his.

The gatehouse was the last building to fall, resisting the tremendous heat of the wyrm's breath for a few short minutes until the creature, with a snort of its slitted nostrils, rammed the portcullis with its head. It was enough to make the structure crumble under its own weight. The wyrm weaved back and forth as if surveying the destruction it had wrought, then disappeared back the way it had come.

"Let's get back to the others," said Syrella, removing her hand and dislodging the sleeping girl. "See who else has survived."

The camp had become an unofficial rallying point for thousands of Morlakian survivors, now homeless. They gathered miserably in small groups around crackling bonfires, tired and hopeless. Knights of Kriari and the pitiful remains of the town guard were coordinating the distribution of food and blankets. Reed was pleased to see Jeffson and Vohanen among them.

"Where are we?" came a drowsy voice close to his ear.

"Safe," he replied, bending his knees so that the girl could slide down off his back.

"All right. Where's my mummy?"

"I don't know, but I'm sure someone here will help you find her." He tapped the arm of a passing guard, nearly making him drop his pile of blankets.

"What?" the man snapped angrily.

"I need you to help this girl—"

"Mila," the child piped up. "And bunny."

"I need you to help Mila find her parents."

"Now look, *friend*. I don't know who you are, but I've already got my hands full with these blankets, and these are the last ones we managed to bring with us so the rest of this sorry lot are gonna freeze to death. And we've got no food. So probably starve to death, too. Anyway, I hope you understand when I tell you that you and your Pit-spawned brat can go—"

"Guardsman!" Syrella had wiped her face clean of dirt and restyled her hair. "This man is with me. Please do as he asks."

"Y … Yes, my Lady," the man stuttered, abashed. "Apologies. I did not recognise your Ladyship. Follow me, Mila." Reed watched her trot along complacently after the haggard guard before they were both swallowed by the crowd. The altercation had turned some heads, and low-key murmurs spread out from around Syrella like ripples in a pond. Reed heard whispers.

The White Rose.

She betrayed us.

This is all her fault.

"You must say something," he said urgently to her. "These people have been living under the corrupt rule of Mithuna for a long time. They need an explanation. They need to see your strength."

Syrella nodded, her visage resolute. "Help me up onto that cart."

Reed lifted her onto the back of an empty wagon. She

took a deep breath and cleared her throat. "Men and women of Morlak," she began. Her voice was immediately lost in the noise of the crowd.

"YOUR BARONESS SPEAKS!" Reed yelled as loud as he dared. The hubbub died down, replaced by an expectant silence.

"Men and women of Morlak," Syrella tried again. "You are cold. You are hungry. And you are angry. I know this, for I am angry too. Over the last few months, I have been imprisoned against my will, held captive while another took my place. I have been betrayed by those close to me. I have lost much. But I have gained much also. I have made new friends; new allies to help us through these dark times. My eyes have been opened to things that I was too stubborn or too stupid to see for myself: poverty, inequality, crime, and corruption. The town of Morlak is gone, but the Barony of Morlak remains. The Baroness of Morlak remains. And we will build a new capital, stronger and more prosperous than before!"

"And what of the beast?" A voice from the back of the crowd cried. "What's to stop it coming back again?"

"That is an easy question to answer. The Twelve have returned."

The news crackled among the Morlakians like lightning. Men and women sank to their knees, raising their hands skywards. A few murmured fervent prayers. Mothers hugged their children close, crying out in thanks.

"The Twelve have returned," Syrella continued confidently. "And they will be our salvation. I vow to you now, here before the ruins of my city, that I will find them, and together we will discover where this creature — this wyrm — has made its lair, and we will destroy it."

"FOR MORLAK!" Vohanen shouted, echoed by his fellow knights. "FOR MORLAK! FOR THE BARONESS!" came the answering cries, and Syrella leapt off the wagon to thunderous applause.

Reed was waiting for her, a peculiar look on his face. "I hope you know what you're doing. Preaching about the return of the Twelve. We have only seen two of them in the flesh: an insane shapeshifter and an unwashed half-wit. Oh, and Mithuna spoke to me of another, Mina, who is also dead … do you see where I am going with this?"

"Don't be so negative, Reed," Syrella replied, patting his cheek. "Let me have this one moment of hope. For the first time in ages, I feel like myself again."

"Glad to hear it, my Lady," said Jeffson dryly, navigating his way through a gang of cheering Morlakians to join them. "I hope your time spent mingling with the common folk hasn't tarnished your noble demeanour in any way."

"Nice try, but even you can't break my good mood. Did you all manage to escape unharmed?"

"Yes, we—". He stopped, looking at something over her left shoulder. His face took on a pained expression "If you would excuse me, my Lady?"

A horse and cart were coming up the road from Morlak, two silhouettes sharing the driver's seat. One was missing a leg, the other was heavy-set and dark-skinned. The sky was beginning to brighten, and the first of the sun's rays glinted off a golden chain.

"Ner'alla," Jeffson said.

The cart rolled to a halt and the big Da'arran climbed

down from his perch, clapping his hands together for warmth. "I come bearing gifts!" he said with a smile. "Wine from my cellars! Sheets and quilts from my guest rooms!"

"I told you if you lied to me again, I would kill you, Ner'alla."

The man's smile faltered. "What are you talking about, Nissus?"

Jeffson drew his dagger. "My family."

The colour drained from Ner'alla's face. "Wait, Nissus, I can explain. Put down your blade."

"The time for talking is over. I thought them dead for years. *Years.* I grieved. I still grieve. I think about them every hour of every day. And they are alive. And you didn't tell me. You lied to me, Ner'alla. I am going to cut you into pieces."

"Jeffson …" cautioned Reed.

The manservant had a dangerous glint in his eye. "Stay out of this, my Lord. I have nothing but respect for you. However, if you stand in my way, I will strike you down."

Stick limped over to interpose himself between Ner'alla and Jeffson. "Sounds like you're angry, Nissus. People don't think straight when they're angry. How about you listen to what your friend has to say?"

"Ner'alla is no friend of mine."

Stick spat and drew his own set of well-worn daggers. "Well, he pays me, so I need him to stay alive."

Jeffson didn't answer, his right hand already moving. Stick caught the dagger with his own and pushed the blade aside. The manservant attacked again, a quick flurry of blows alternating left and right, high and low. Stick dodged them all, swivelling on his peg-leg, his uninjured foot scarcely touching the ground.

"It wasn't a wolf that took your leg, was it … Stick?"

"No, it wasn't." Stick lashed out with his peg-leg, hitting Jeffson's shin with a crack. The follow-up dagger thrust knocked the preacher's hat from his head and left a trail of blood across his balding scalp.

The fight had gathered quite a crowd of onlookers, including Syrella, who was staring at them in dismay. "Stop it!" she shouted. "Has there not been enough death for one day?"

"Just one more," Jeffson said ominously, squaring one foot behind him and raising his dagger to his cheek in an offensive stance. He thrust once, twice, left. Stick parried, his return thrust taking Jeffson in the shoulder. The manservant smiled thinly and grabbed Stick's wrist before he could withdraw the blade, holding him in place. A well-placed kick to his peg-leg and both men fell to the ground. Jeffson ended up on top, his dagger hovering over Stick's eye.

"Well fought," he said. "In another life, you would have made an excellent Red Sparrow." He lifted his knife to strike.

Vohanen punched him hard in the jaw.

Jeffson tumbled over backwards, his dagger flying from his grasp. He tried to rise, but Vohanen hit him again, sending him back into the dirt.

"Know that I do this because I am your friend," the knight said, rubbing his knuckles. "And that I understand your pain. I would give anything to see my son again, and if I found out his death was a lie … Well, I would be angry too. But you are an intelligent man, Jeffson, far more so than I. Think for a moment. There are only two possible explanations. The first is that Ner'alla is a traitor." He looked over at the Da'arran who was helping Stick to his feet.

"Which is possible. But he got us into Morlak keep. He kept your identity safe. Does that sound like the actions of a traitor?"

"No," admitted Jeffson. He tore Stick's dagger from his shoulder and cast it aside.

"Then that leads us to the second possibility. He didn't tell you because …"

"… He was asked not to," Jeffson finished, his voice filled with anguish. "Is that true, Ner'alla? Did my wife ask you to fake her death? The death of my child?"

The Da'arran was struggling to reply. "She … she didn't know what else to do, Nissus. You wouldn't stop. You would go a few months without taking a contract, then something or someone would draw you back in, like a moth to the flame. She tried so hard to get through to you, she tried everything. You were addicted to the life you had before, and she couldn't drag you away."

"I … No …"

"She came to me while you were off on a job, a robbery I believe it was for some minister up in Klief. She begged me to help. And I agreed."

"By the Twelve, what have I done?" Jeffson murmured. "I have single-handedly destroyed the only thing that was good in my life. How can I have been so stupid?" He took the leather book of drawings out of his pocket and leafed despondently through the pages.

Reed looked on helplessly. He didn't know what to say. Syrella pushed her way through the crowd of onlookers and took Jeffson's bloody hand in her own.

"Do you believe you have changed?" she asked him.

"Of course. That life is long gone. Gone and buried."

"And you still love your family?"

Jeffson traced a drawing of his daughter with his finger. "More than I can say."

"Then it is not too late. Vohanen! Get this man a horse!"

"He can take my own, my Lady. It's already saddled. I'll ride back to Dirkvale in a wagon if I have to." He whistled, and a young Knight of Kriari brought over Vohanen's stallion.

"Go on, then!" Syrella said, giving Jeffson a nudge. "Go find your family."

Jeffson pocketed his book and vaulted onto the horse, his face full of purpose, his balding pate shining in the light of dawn. "Thank you, my friends, for all you have done."

"What about this?" Reed said, holding out the battered wide-brimmed preacher's hat.

Jeffson laughed. Not the dry, sarcastic chuckle Reed was used to hearing but a full-on guffaw that stretched the corners of his mouth and deepened the lines around his eyes.

"Hold on to it for me, my Lord. You can give it back to me when we meet again." And with a touch of his boot, he sent the stallion bounding forwards in a cloud of dust. The crowd parted to let him through and he galloped away, heading south towards Lostthorn.

"Nice fella," said Stick, rubbing his shoulder. The crowd of Morlakians, sensing there would be no further entertainment, began to disperse. "Anyone got a bit of tobacco?"

"So now what?" asked Reed. "I suppose I should report back to Praxis, although Mithuna said something about Aldarin and Jelaïa heading to Talth …"

"Or you could stay here for a while," Syrella said in a low voice.

He felt her blue and green eyes studying him. *Surely, she*

can't be interested in me, can she? he thought, feeling his cheeks redden. *I'm nobody! A watchman! And a bad one at that! What in the Pit does she see in me?*

Vohanen spoke before Reed could reply. "Perhaps he'll know," he said, pointing back down the road to the ruins of Morlak. A figure was approaching slowly, dragging one leg behind it, its naked torso covered in painful-looking burns.

Kriari.

The giant had lost most of his hair, the scalp underneath puckered and red. The entire right side of his body had been subjected to the wyrm's flames. Half his beard was gone, his cheek covered in angry welts. The manacle on his right forearm had melted and fused itself to his wrist.

He limped closer; the bone of his right knee a visible flash of white each time he pulled his injured leg forwards.

He looked up at them and smiled.

All around him Morlakians were staring in wonder.

"By the Pit, man, you look terrible!" Vohanen exclaimed. "I mean, you look terrible, *Lord*."

Kriari shrugged. "Kriari."

Vohanen laughed. "Kriari, indeed. We are all glad to see you are still alive. It does not seem to be an easy thing, killing one of the Twelve. We were just discussing what to do next. Once those wounds have been treated, you are welcome to join us."

Kriari waved him away and lowered himself to the ground, careful to avoid bending his knee. He began drawing in the dirt with his left index finger.

"What is it?" Reed asked, squinting at the strange shape. "A horse?"

"It's a map," Syrella answered. "I've seen enough of them to recognise the nine Baronies."

The First of the Twelve continued sketching. The plains and deserts of the south. The Sea of Sorrow. The Redenfell Mountains. And, further north, Talth. Kriari finished and stuck his finger in one precise spot.

"Here," he said. "Go. Here."

"Where?" Reed asked, craning his neck to see. "What's he pointing to?"

"It's Klief," Syrella said, frowning. "He wants us to go to Klief."

CHAPTER 25

SEVENTH OF THE TWELVE

"I despise card games or any other activity where chance plays a predominant role. They are for the weak and stupid. They allow a beggar to win against a king or even one of the Twelve! On the other hand, give me a challenge that can only be won by the application of logic, and I will never, ever lose."

ZYGOS, SEVENTH OF THE TWELVE, 39 AT

❧

I<small>T DID NOT</small> take long for Praxis to realise that he had exchanged one prison for another. He was no longer chained to a post, but he might as well have been for all the freedom the Knights of Zygos allowed him. All of his time was spent in a tiny underground cave barely bigger than the goat pen back in Arelium. His life's possessions had been reduced to a writing desk, a quill, paper, ink, candles, and a straw mattress that appeared to have a life of its own; infested with mice or beetles … or whatever else made its home down here in the damp and gloom.

At first, he had feared that Zygos or, more likely, Aldos would want to punish him for failing to carry out his orders, but instead they had applauded his ingenuity. Aldos had gone on to demand a detailed written report containing everything of interest that had happened in his ten-year tenure as steward. *Everything.*

Both his superiors had impressed on him the urgency of the matter. Praxis was to be confined to quarters until the task was finished and forbidden any contact with his fellow initiates. Meals and a … slop bucket would be brought directly to his room so that he could work uninterrupted.

After five excruciatingly monotonous days, Praxis was beginning to wonder if a bit of torture might have been better. His wrist ached from hour upon hour of continuous writing. His hands were stained with blotches of black ink. The scratchy sound of the quill as it worked its way across the page was etched into his brain. And he hadn't even reached the end of his first year.

Several rolls of parchment were filled with how he had slowly poisoned the previous steward, and how he had subsequently managed to worm his way into the Baron's good graces by revealing the extent of his predecessor's financial ineptitude, arguments that had been validated by the Baroness herself.

It was on the sixth day, as he was halfway through describing the unfortunate demise of one of Lord del Conte's mistresses, that he was disturbed by the sound of raised voices and running feet coming from somewhere outside. He poked his head around the hanging curtain that served as a door and saw six Knights of Zygos, kitted out in close-fitting black leather armour. Aldos was among them, tightening the straps of his vambraces.

"You were followed," he said disapprovingly. "It took them a few days of searching, but they appear to have picked up your trail."

"I don't know why you're blaming me … my Lord," Praxis retorted. "I had my hands tied for half the journey and had no idea of our destination. I couldn't have led them here. I didn't even know where 'here' was!"

"Hmm. The initiate responsible for your escape has already been punished for his failure to mask his tracks efficiently—"

"Well, to be fair, he could only use one arm."

"Do NOT interrupt me, initiate. He has been punished, and now we will deal with this rabble."

"Let me help you, my Lord," said Praxis, almost instinctively. Anything to get out of that claustrophobic room.

"And what advantage would you give us?"

"They may be people I have spent time with," Praxis replied, thinking fast. "And if there are Arelians and Kessrin among them, I am familiar with their tactics and training. That makes me an asset."

Aldos sucked in his cheeks, something he always did when contemplating an important decision.

"Very well. You may assist us. You there, Helios! Remove your armour and weapons and give them to Praxis. Hurry now! The intruders were sighted less than a mile away."

The initiate named Helios scowled from beneath his overhanging brow and began stripping off his gear. Praxis felt his confidence return, each segment of leather reminding him who he was. A Knight of Zygos, and one who had achieved more than any other, save perhaps Zygos himself.

"My thanks, initiate," he said blandly to Helios. He followed the others up to the surface.

"We only have three working crossbows," Aldos was saying. "The rest have damaged strings from spending too long in these Pit-spawned caves. I want the crossbowmen up above the entrance. Hold your fire as long as possible. Wait until they get close. Then loose. Praxis, you're with me." He led the way to a secluded space behind the pile of rocks obscuring the mouth of the cave.

It was not long before the men who had been tracking Praxis came into view.

Hirkuin!

The ginger-haired Kessrin was in the lead, his crossbow held confidently in his hands. More blue-uniformed soldiers followed, then a rearguard of armoured knights.

"Knights of Brachyura," Aldos said in a voice full of disgust. "The Order responsible for the destruction of our temple and the maiming of our patron."

The men fanned out. One of the Kessrin, his scimitar drawn, crept closer to their hiding place.

Ready yourself, Aldos signed with a flicker of his fingers. An instant later, a crossbow bolt hummed through the air and punched the Kessrin clean off his feet.

"AMBUSH!" shouted Hirkuin, throwing himself onto the scrubby grass. Two more bolts whisked overhead and dropped one of the Knights of Brachyura who had been foolish enough to forego his helm. The survivors unsheathed their battle-axes.

Hirkuin, still lying flat, closed one eye and sighted down the length of his crossbow. His shot winged a Knight of Zygos in the leg, enough to make him lose his balance and lurch off his rocky perch. He hit the ground hard and did not get up.

"FOR ZYGOS!" Aldos cried, revealing himself and charging the Kessrin flank. Praxis took a deep breath and followed. The soldier closest to him yelled out in panic, bringing his crossbow to bear, but Praxis was faster, lunging forwards with his stiletto dagger. The blade sliced through his opponent's windpipe and out through the back of his neck.

Aldos had rather unwisely thrown himself at a pair of knights and was having a hard time holding his own. The clumsy swings of the enemy were easy enough to avoid, but the knights were well-trained and protected the weaker joints of their plate armour with skill, making it difficult for Aldos to find an opening.

Hmmm. Should I help him or not? wondered Praxis, putting his own opponent out of his misery with a well-placed thrust. He still wasn't one hundred per cent sure that the temple master had Praxis's best interests at heart.

His decision was made for him as four more Knights of Zygos emerged from the mouth of the tunnel and joined the fray.

"Praxis."

He knew that voice.

Hirkuin clambered to his feet and tossed his crossbow aside. "I've come to take you back to Derello."

Praxis favoured him with a half-smile. "I like you, Hirkuin. You always seemed to be the one Kessrin with an ounce of sense. Apart from Lady Arkile, of course. You were right not to trust the Knights of Mina. And you were right not to trust me."

Hirkuin drew his curved blade. "Been doing this long enough to know that if something doesn't feel right, then it probably ain't. Now are you coming along nicely, or do I have to beat that stupid smile off your face and throw you over the back of my horse?"

The skirmish was slowly turning in favour of the Knights of Zygos. The last Kessrin soldier fell, his back peppered with bolts. Only two Knights of Brachyura remained, standing back-to-back as the black-clad forms closed in. Aldos signed a quick message. *Help?*

No, Praxis signed back. "You're welcome to try," he said to Hirkuin.

The captain powered forwards, hoping to catch Praxis off guard. The scimitar came dangerously close to removing his ear.

"I fought against a Kessrin like yourself not too long ago," Praxis said conversationally, avoiding another cut to the face. "A man named Diacrosa. An unfortunate consequence of an assassination attempt gone wrong."

"Quiet," Hirkuin growled, attempting a low swipe to the leg, which Praxis evaded easily.

"A small part of my plan to have Listus del Arelium killed. Just like I tried to have Derello killed. It's true, you see, everything I've been accused of. I'm guilty. I'm guilty of it all."

"QUIET!" Hirkuin charged him, overcome with rage. Praxis swayed to the side and cracked the pommel of his dagger into the other man's skull, knocking him out cold.

Another perfect demonstration of the fallacy of emotion, he thought. *A few goading words and even the most proficient fighter is reduced to a lumbering buffoon.*

"He's still alive?" Aldos asked, wiping speckles of blood from his face.

Praxis nodded.

"Then bring him. Zygos will want to find out what he knows."

⤷

Hirkuin's screams echoed along the natural tunnels of dirt and stone, finding their way to Praxis's ears. He jumped at the sound, spilling his pot of ink all over a half-written sheet of parchment.

Pit! he cursed, dabbing at the rapidly spreading stain with a corner of his tunic.

Aldos had been interrogating the Kessrin captain for hours and apparently had still not managed to extract the information he needed. Praxis had always despised physical torture. Not because he was especially squeamish but because it was incredibly inefficient. A good torturer could, with time, make his prisoner say more or less anything, and therein lay the problem: there was no way to be sure he was telling the truth. A man in pain would confess to crimes he did not commit or give false information in the hope that it would be enough to satisfy his captors.

Praxis preferred a different kind of torture: that of the mind. Every man had his secrets, be it a hidden mistress, a bastard child, a gambling debt, or any one of a thousand other vices. The major advantage was that the threat of exposure not only elicited a truthful confession but could be used again and again.

His curtain was drawn back by the surly-looking initiate who had lent Praxis his weapons and armour. *What was his name again? Ah yes, Helios.*

"You are summoned, initiate," said the man, a trifle smugly. "You are to attend Lord Zygos in his quarters ... immediately."

"Thank you, *initiate*. And sorry about all the blood on your dagger. I'm sure it will be fine after a good cleaning." Praxis pushed past Helios and followed the sound of Hirkuin's screams to the large carpeted cave where he had first met Zygos.

Three people were waiting for him when he arrived. Hirkuin was strapped into a high-backed chair, his torso covered in razor-thin cuts and what looked like burn marks. The man's hands were a bloody mess and Praxis realised that most of his fingernails had been removed. A mirror had been placed nearby, carefully orientated so that Hirkuin could see perfectly everything that was being done to him.

Opposite the Kessrin captain sat Zygos, his horrendous visage void of all emotion. He was speaking to Hirkuin in a low monotone. Aldos stood off to one side, bent over a table upon which lay a gruesome assortment of devices, some of them already wet with Hirkuin's blood.

"Ah, Praxis," Zygos said as he came in. "I must apologise for disturbing your writing, but the prisoner refuses to talk to anyone else but you. Tedious."

"It is no trouble, Lord."

"Excellent. Prisoner? The initiate you asked for is here. You may proceed."

Hirkuin focussed with difficulty on Praxis. "There you are, you two-faced son of a whore." Aldos cuffed him round the back of the head. "Show some respect."

"Why? He never showed me any."

The temple master sighed, picked up a sharp knife from the table and stabbed it down into Hirkuin's hand, pinning it to the armrest of the chair. The Kessrin howled in pain.

"Talk to me again in that way and I will remove a finger," Aldos said calmly. "Now, tell this initiate what we need to know."

Hirkuin spat a mouthful of blood. "Remember what I told you, Praxis. Trust your instincts. You betrayed Kessrin, but you also betrayed Mina, Zygos's sister. Do you not find it strange that there have been no consequences of that?"

Aldos moved forwards with his knife, but Praxis raised a hand to stop him. "He does have a point. Why are you having me compile everything I know?"

"I told you," the temple master replied, frowning. "It will be an invaluable source of information. We may even learn something we can use to hasten the greylings' return."

"Yes," said Praxis, taking a step closer. He could feel Zygos's gaze boring into his back. "You did say that. But it seems superfluous to do so when you could simply consult with me directly. Unless …"

It was then that Praxis saw it. The flicker of fear on Aldos's face. There and gone in an instant. If Praxis hadn't been looking for it, he would have missed it entirely. The temple master shot a furtive glance at Zygos. "Well …" he began.

Praxis elbowed him in the stomach, then brought his knee up as Aldos doubled over, smashing into the man's jaw with a solid crunch. He fell against the table, sending the torture instruments flying. Praxis stamped down with his foot, but Aldos was faster, rolling out of the way. He came up on the other side of the table and smiled, showing a mouthful of blood-stained teeth.

"You were always one of my most promising initiates, Praxis," Aldos said. "So astute. I taught you well. A little *too* well, apparently."

"Then why?"

There was a creak from the wheelchair as Zygos turned to face him. "Because you are everything I despise," he said coldly. "You are a mockery of all I wish my descendants to be. You have no respect for authority. You are incapable of following simple instructions. You have allowed your personal lust for power to take precedence over upholding the Pact. And, worst of all, you have let your decisions be ruled by emotion, eschewing all sense of logic and reason. The only value you have to us now is the knowledge you have gained, knowledge that either you can give to us freely … or you can take this Kessrin's place in the chair and we will extract it from you piece by painful piece."

"Tantalising choice," Praxis replied sardonically. "But I have another proposal." He kicked the table as hard as he could. Aldos yelled as the length of wood hit him in the thighs, pushing him back against the wall of the cave. Praxis was already moving, angling low, his hand grasping one of the many glittering objects that lay strewn on the floor around him. The blade of the scalpel was so sharp it cut through three of Aldos's fingers before embedding itself in his shoulder. Praxis wrenched the instrument free in a spray of blood and cut the temple master's throat.

Aldos's eyes widened as he realised what his former student had done. He put his injured hand to the crimson waterfall pouring from the wound in his neck and then held it up to his face, surprised at what he saw. He pushed feebly against the table, trying to dislodge himself, but by then it was too late. With a final gurgle, he fell forwards onto the table's surface, his head hitting the wood with a thunk.

"Aptly done."

Praxis, breathing hard, turned to see Hirkuin watching him.

"I did not do it for you. I did it for me."

"Let me go."

"Why would I do that?"

Zygos sat up straight in his chair. "Praxis! Don't listen to him."

Praxis frowned, grabbed the arms of the wheelchair and swung Zygos around so that he faced the wall.

"Two reasons," Hirkuin said slowly. Although he looked more alert, he was obviously still in considerable pain. "The first is that you still need to escape from here, and you'll have a better chance of doing so with me. The second is that I can maybe persuade Derello and the others to wait a while before hunting you down, give you a bit of a head start."

Praxis thought for a moment. The Kessrin had a point; releasing him would increase his chances of success. He stepped round to the back of the chair and cut through the man's bound wrists with the scalpel. "Where will you go?"

Hirkuin rubbed his chafed skin. "After Talth, our plan was to carry on north to Klief. I would suggest you head in the opposite direction."

"I will find you first, you know," said Zygos from his

place in the corner. "More and more of my descendants are joining us every day. They have contacts in every city of the nine Baronies. You will never be safe. You will live with the constant fear of death until the very end of your short existence."

Praxis looked pensively at the scalpel in his hand. "You may be right, Lord. I should probably kill you now to stop any further retribution."

Zygos snorted. "I am your progenitor. Your creator. You wouldn't dare."

"I murdered Listus del Arelium, I think I can manage to dispatch a decrepit hundred-year-old cripple."

"Then do it to my face. Or were you thinking of stabbing me in the back?"

"It would only be fitting, wouldn't it? But whatever you think of me, I am still a Knight of Zygos. I am still of your bloodline. I will grant you this final favour."

Praxis spun the wheelchair back around, half-imagining his patron would have one last trick: a final ace he had been holding back. Instead, all he saw were the sorry remains of a relic, a vestige of another age, a living legend reduced to a brittle shell, his mutilated stumps wiggling in frustration, his scarred lips moving as he muttered something inaudible.

"Ah, some famous last words, perhaps?" Praxis sneered, bending closer to hear.

Zygos opened his mouth and vomited a thick stream of black, tarry liquid all over Praxis's face.

The gooey substance filled his nostrils, his ears, his eyes. He opened his mouth to scream and more of the liquid rushed inside and down into his lungs. Zygos, his breathing slowing, vomited again, spewing forth even more of the foul-smelling darkness. Praxis could feel it soaking into the pores of his skin, seeping into his body through every orifice until he was drowning in it.

A terrible memory resurfaced of his frantic escape from Kingfisher Isle, of being dragged underwater by the swell, pushed and pulled in all directions, losing all sense of above and below as the air was squeezed from his lungs.

He was feeling a similar sensation now, a burning in his chest, black spots on the edge of his vision. He opened his mouth again to draw in some air but only swallowed more of the black liquid.

His head was pounding, a rhythmic knocking resonating inside his skull. Two pinpricks of agony formed behind each eye, growing steadily wider.

A hand landed on his shoulder. Hirkuin. Praxis's arm jerked around of its own accord and the metal scalpel embedded itself in the centre of the Kessrin's forehead with inhuman force, ripping through the hard bone with ease.

It's not me! Praxis wanted to scream, but he could no longer open his mouth. *It's not me!*

With a sickening, squelching sound, both his eyes popped. Black liquid flowed into the empty sockets. Praxis fought to move his arm, his leg, his head … anything. It was useless. He had lost control.

The body on the wheelchair had been transformed into a withered husk the colour of ancient dust. Whatever had been inhabiting it was gone.

No.

Yes. A cavernous voice filled his mind. He could hear the power behind that voice, and he cursed himself for his foolishness.

I told you Praxis. You are weak. And, above all, you are arrogant. I have walked these lands for one hundred years. I have studied everything. Seen everything. Thought of every possible complication. And every possible solution. You thought to measure yourself against me? You have done exactly as I thought you would. And now you are MINE.

And Zygos, Seventh of the Twelve, flexed the fingers of his new body, caught sight of himself in the mirror, and favoured his reflection with a perfect half-smile.

EPILOGUE
THE UNBROKEN CIRCLE

"It is better to have loved and lost than never to have loved at all."

UNKNOWN, 189 AT

❧

J ELAÏA HOVERED NEAR the entrance of the infirmary, summoning her courage. She had come straight from the Great Hall of Talth, where Kayal and Sir Gaelin were in the process of reclaiming their lost Barony. Squads of knights were trawling the inner city, routing out any surviving greylings. Kessrin and Arelian soldiers had been sent further afield to check farmsteads and manor houses.

They had already discovered how the threshers had managed to sabotage the catapults. Ironically, it was the same tunnel that Sir Gaelin had used to lead Kayal to safety all those weeks ago. It was now permanently sealed: Brachyura had done the deed himself, dropping several enormous boulders over the opening.

The infirmary was almost full, but it was a very different atmosphere from the nightmare Jelaïa had been subjected to during the siege of Arelium. No amputations, no grievous wounds, only superficial cuts and lacerations. All thanks to Kumbha.

The Eleventh of the Twelve had been invaluable in treating the wounded. She could immediately discern those who were beyond her help, those who would survive without it, and those in between, the soldiers who needed just a small jolt to pull them back from the brink of death.

She was walking slowly to greet Jelaïa now, her large frame brushing against the ends of the cots on either side of the aisle. Jelaïa could see that she was tired. No, tired was not the right word. She looked utterly exhausted. Deep bags hung under her obsidian eyes, and the skin of her face was saggy and wrinkled. She half-tripped against one of the cots and nearly fell before righting herself.

"Kumbha. I mean, Lady. Are you well?"

The giantess nodded. Her beautiful hair was stringy and unwashed. "I am fine. The last few hours have been … complicated. Let me take you to him."

Aldarin lay on a cot at the far end of the tent, his head wrapped in bandages, his eyes closed. His face looked peaceful, as if he was lost in a deep slumber.

"I have healed his skull," Kumbha said wearily, pinching the bridge of her nose. "There appear to be no other physical injuries. However, as I have already explained countless times, I can do nothing for the troubles of the mind. The blow he suffered did not simply break his skull, it rattled his brain. I cannot lie to you, Jelaïa. He is badly hurt. I do not know if he will wake."

"But ... he promised," Jelaïa said, fighting back tears. "We are to meet this evening for dinner. He *promised* he would be there."

"I am sorry," Kumbha replied quietly. "You should get some rest. I will send someone for you if there is any change."

"I ... Yes, thank you." Jelaïa spun on her heel and hurried away, almost colliding with Brachyura and Praedora on her way out. The Fourth of the Twelve looked physically drained, his face still covered in black streaks.

"My Lady," he said, his voice hoarse. "Have you seen Aldarin? Is he well?"

Jelaïa felt her lower lip begin to tremble. "He is not, Lord. Kumbha tells me that his condition may be permanent."

"I see." He furrowed his prodigious brow. "I am sorry. I know you were close. I do not pretend to understand these ... emotions that are such an important part of your psyche and guide so many of your actions, but it is apparent he was ... *is* ... important to you."

"He is. It took me some time to realise it, but he is."

"Then you will have to decide what you wish to do. We have met with Derello and Loré. Despite not having been able to capture the brood mother, I impressed upon them my desire to travel to Klief in search of Makara. I have tried sending my thoughts to him several times since I returned to these lands, and he has not replied, which is most troubling. They not only agreed but wish to accompany me. Our forces will consequently be split into three. Those who wish it may journey north with us to Klief. Others will need to stay here to consolidate Talth. And the wounded will travel back to their homes in the wagons."

"Aldarin …"

"Will return to Kessrin. He will be well looked after, my Lady."

What should I do? Jelaïa thought. Tears welled in her eyes and she blinked them away. *I cannot leave him again!*

"Would you please give us a moment, Lord?" Praedora asked. Brachyura nodded and disappeared into the infirmary tent. "Jelaïa, could you help a frail old blind lady find a place to rest her aching feet?" The First Priestess linked her arm in Jelaïa's and let herself be led to a flat, moss-covered rock on the edge of the allied camp.

"I have an idea," she said as she sat. "But I don't want you to become all worked up about it. I've been think-ing about the Scrying and how two beings can be linked together through their blood. My predecessor called it the '*Unbroken Circle*'."

"Hmm," said Jelaïa distractedly, looking out over the blackened fields of Talth.

"Well, if I understand correctly, when you share your blood with Aldarin, you establish a link to his mind; a sort of gateway into his memories. I believe this conduit could work both ways."

"So, I could use it to help him?"

"Maybe … As I said, it's only an idea, I—"

"Oh, thank you, Prae," said Jelaïa excitedly, throwing her arms around her aunt and kissing her on the cheek.

"Keep your expectations in check, Jeli."

"Yes, yes," Jelaïa replied, springing to her feet. "I'm

heading back there now. Will you be able to return to your tent unaided?"

"Oh, I'm sure someone will come along eventually. I am quite happy to sit here for a while. Off you go."

Jelaïa was almost running by the time she reached Aldarin's cot. The Knight of Brachyura was unchanged, his eyes closed. She drew a dagger from her belt and opened an inch-wide cut in her palm, then took one of his warm, calloused hands and did the same.

"Come on. Come on. Come on," she whispered, chanting the words like some kind of mantra, pressing their hands together.

Immediately, she was assailed by a swarm of angry memories. Aldarin was hiding so much pain and sadness: his abusive father, his sickly mother, his constant oppression and segregation at the temple. Terrible things that he never shared, weathering the storm alone, as unyielding as the cliffs of Kessrin.

Let me in, Jelaïa thought, pushing back.

She felt the fires of Brachyura begin to stir inside her, and she forced them away, concentrating instead on her own memories.

A tiny boat, caught in the current of the River Stahl. Aldarin singing her to sleep.

A bedchamber in Kessrin, Jelaïa weeping. Aldarin encircling her in his strong arms.

On the road to the temple, lying together by the fire, looking up at the stars.

Her head began to throb with the effort. She braced herself and carried on.

Jelaïa, standing over Aldarin, shouting those three words that changed everything.

Aldarin, in a forest clearing, brushing back a lock of her hair.

A pair of mismatched shoes.

Her hand was burning. With a final cry, she let go, breaking the link. Her palm was raw and sensitive like when she used the fires of Brachyura. Ignoring the pain, she bent over Aldarin's unconscious form, searching his face for some sort of change. A flicker of the eyelids, a twitch of the mouth. Anything.

A minute passed. Two minutes.

"Please, Aldarin," she murmured, stroking his cheek. "Please come back to me."

An hour later, she felt a hand on her shoulder.

"The sun is setting, my Lady," Kumbha said. "Why don't you get yourself a hot meal and some rest? He will still be here tomorrow."

"I ... I really thought it would work," Jelaïa said sadly. "It's so unjust. Our story had barely begun."

"It has not ended yet, child. You are tired, and you are not yourself. Things will feel better tomorrow."

Jelaïa kissed Aldarin on the forehead and returned to her tent. The writing table was where she had left it, complete with two plates and chairs.

She began to change, pulling off her riding boots and hooded cloak, taking a clean green dress from the dresser. Finding a pair of mismatched slippers. One pink. One blue.

She struggled to put them on, her hands trembling.

"PIT!" she shouted and flung the pink slipper away.

Tears came now, hot and angry. Why was this happening to her? It wasn't fair.

Then she heard something.

A knock on the pole of the tent.

A shadow blocking out the setting sun.

The smell of freshly picked wildflowers.

"Jelaïa," a familiar voice said softly.

And the worries of the world faded away.

End of Book Three

APPENDIX

A BRIEF TIMELINE OF EVENTS

The calendar used throughout the nine Baronies is intrinsically linked to the Twelve, with the year of their first appearance among the scattered tribes termed 'The Arrival of the Twelve' (AT). The events described here take place in the year 426 AT.

❦

-58 AT	A series of natural disasters, later known as the Calamity, wreaks havoc on the land and its inhabitants
00 AT	The first appearance of the Twelve among the human tribes
13 AT	An innumerable host of greylings is defeated in the Battle of the Northern Plains
14 AT	The Twelve separate, dispersing to aid the

surviving tribes and eliminate the remaining greylings

33 AT   The Old Guard is established, sworn to defend the Pits

35 AT   The Council of Baronies is created by the Twelve, who gradually concede rulership of the nine provinces to the tribal leaders

41 AT   The first founding of the great temples of the Twelve and their Orders

122 AT   The battle of Hellin Pass

123 AT   The building of the wooden dam at Terris Lake

123 AT   The last recorded appearance of one of the Twelve

313 AT   The battle of Torc

365 AT   Birth of Listus del Arelium

366 AT   The Schism divides the Knights of the Twelve into two factions, those who wish to aid the return of the greylings are cast out and named 'fallen'

370 AT   Birth of Loré del Conte

386 AT   Birth of Merad Reed

394 AT   Birth of Aldarin

404 AT   Merad Reed joins the Old Guard

404 AT   Birth of Nidore del Conte

405 AT   Birth of Jelaïa del Arelium

407 AT   The Scrying. Aldarin is accepted as an initiate at the temple of Brachyura

416 AT   Praxis begins his tenure as steward to Baron Listus

418 AT   Auguste Fernshaw is elected Mayor of Jaelem

421 AT   Derello del Kessrin becomes Baron after the
          death of his parents, lost at sea

426 AT   Greylings appear in great numbers at the
          Southern Pit and attack the town of Arelium.
          Listus del Arelium is killed. The greylings are
          finally routed by the Knights of Brachyura

Autumn   Mina, Last of the Twelve, is found on Kingfisher
          Isle. Kessrin is attacked by a group of kraken.
          Mina is defeated by the combined efforts of
          Brachyura, Manfeld, and the priestess Praedora,
          who loses her sight
          Mithuna, Third of the Twelve, imprisons Merad
          Reed in the cells under Morlak keep
          Kumbha awakens

THE TWELVE ORDERS

MINA
Last of the Twelve

KRIARI
First of the Twelve

KUMBHA
Eleventh of the Twelve

GUANNA
Second of the Twelve

MAKARA
Tenth of the Twelve

MITHUNA
Third of the Twelve

DHANUSA
Ninth of the Twelve

BRACHYURA
Fourth of the Twelve

LURIDAE
Eighth of the Twelve

SIMHA
Fifth of the Twelve

ZYGOS
Seventh of the Twelve

SHALA
Sixth of the Twelve

Made in United States
North Haven, CT
07 May 2022

18974511R00211